P9-CFG-154

WITHDRAWN

Baldwinsville Public Library
33 East Genesee Street
Baldwinsville, NY 13027-2575

JUN 0 4 2013

JOSH WHOEVER

WITHDRAWN
Baldwinsville Public Library
33 East Genesee Street
Baldwinsville, NY 13027-2575

JOSH WHOEVER

MICHAEL GUILLEBEAU

FIVE STAR
A part of Gale, Cengage Learning

 GALE
CENGAGE Learning·

Detroit • New York • San Francisco • New Haven, Conn • Waterville, Maine • London

GALE
CENGAGE Learning

JUN 0 4 2013

Copyright © 2013 by Michael Guillebeau.
Five Star™ Publishing, a part of Gale, Cengage Learning.

ALL RIGHTS RESERVED.
This novel is a work of fiction. Names, characters, places, and incidents are either the product of the author's imagination, or, if real, used fictitiously.

No part of this work covered by the copyright herein may be reproduced, transmitted, stored, or used in any form or by any means graphic, electronic, or mechanical, including but not limited to photocopying, recording, scanning, digitizing, taping, Web distribution, information networks, or information storage and retrieval systems, except as permitted under Section 107 or 108 of the 1976 United States Copyright Act, without the prior written permission of the publisher.

The publisher bears no responsibility for the quality of information provided through author or third-party Web sites and does not have any control over, nor assume any responsibility for, information contained in these sites. Providing these sites should not be construed as an endorsement or approval by the publisher of these organizations or of the positions they may take on various issues.

LIBRARY OF CONGRESS CATALOGING-IN-PUBLICATION DATA

Guillebeau, Michael.
    Josh whoever / Michael Guillebeau. — First edition.
       pages cm
    ISBN-13: 978-1-4328-2684-0 (hardcover)
    ISBN-10: 1-4328-2684-0 (hardcover)
    1. Bank tellers—Fiction. 2. Bank robberies—Fiction. I. Title.
PS3607.U4853J67 2013
813'.6—dc23   2012043410

First Edition. First Printing: March 2013
Find us on Facebook– https://www.facebook.com/FiveStarCengage
Visit our website– http://www.gale.cengage.com/fivestar/
Contact Five Star™ Publishing at FiveStar@cengage.com

Printed in Mexico
1 2 3 4 5 6 7 17 16 15 14 13

More thanks than I can express to the three girls and one boy who shout love at the heart of my world. Without their love, I would be just another derelict in the back of just another bar.

ACKNOWLEDGMENTS

First there was a great song.

The song was "Here at the Western World," by Steely Dan. The image of a guy spending all his time in a broken-down bar was too good not to expand on.

So I wrote a story from the song. The story was "Fired Up," published in the webzine *short-story.me* by Dixon Palmer in March of 2010.

"Fired Up" became the first three chapters of JOSH WHO-EVER, which was a mess until Pat Guillebeau, Jeremy Bronaugh, Bob Spears, and Marion and John Conover read it and suggested changes. Thanks to the talented Deni Dietz, who reviewed my submission and passionately believed in it. Gordon Aalborg fixed what needed fixing. Tiffany Schofield guided a newbie writer through the publishing process with charm and grace.

Stephen King says that you don't write stories, you discover them. Without every one of these people to point the way and keep me on track, JOSH WHOEVER would never have been discovered. I thank you all for the privilege of putting my name on your book.

CHAPTER 1

I only took this job to get fired, but now I stood here raising my hands in the air like any good citizen being robbed.

Two robbers had popped into the bank from nowhere. From inside my little bank teller window, I had no real view of them walking in the door but now they strutted around in white paper lab suits, looking like big bunny rabbits waving guns at random around the bank lobby.

The tall one did all the talking. "Open your cash drawers, put your hands in the air, and shut up."

His eyes darted from teller to teller looking for a challenge. The young girl in front of him just stood there frozen. He waved his gun at the ceiling and let off a burst and the girl screamed and opened her drawer.

"This. Is. A. Robbery." He shouted each word loud and important, like he was hyping a band at a rock concert.

Like we needed a program to tell us what's going on here. Like I needed a program to tell me that my own future was over if they got away with this robbery.

The short one reached up with the barrel of his AK-47 and pushed away the video camera over the door so that it saw only the ceiling. They started at the far end and worked their way down the long row of tellers toward me.

I stood motionless and watched, curious about how they did this. I knew plenty about small-time scams, but I'd never seen a big-time bank robbery like this before.

The tall guy did all the talking but looked at the silent one for something. There: that was it. Silent shook his head, and Tall skipped a teller. Silent knew something; he skipped the tellers with dye packs.

I admired them for pulling this off, admired the details: the paper lab suits were a good touch. No one would remember anything about the robbers except the white suits with hoods. Probably buy them cheap at some med supply place; add a white ski mask, and you can wear anything you like underneath.

Except for the shoes. Tall had flashy basketball kicks that demanded respect on the street, what you'd expect from a robber. But Silent had a pair of black Ferragamos, rich businessman shoes that cost three hundred dollars new, except his weren't new. The kind of guy who would buy these shoes wouldn't keep his shoes this long; he either had money or worked for guys with money and had to keep up. Either way, it stood out and it offended me. I was a pro in my own way. I respected pros. You've got to get the details right.

The two guys moved the same way: pro, but with a flaw. They looked casual, even random, but I could tell it was rehearsed. No one but me would remember that later, and that was good.

But the body language had a flaw. Tall moved like a bank robber in a movie, all swagger and attitude, waving the gun around and yelling at anything. Silent faded into the background and that was good, too, but the pose was wrong. He hunched over and shuffled like a kicked dog. This wasn't a man used to demanding other people's money. Silent begged people for money every day and hated doing it but had to pay the rent.

There, in a flash I had it. Silent's walk and Silent's shoes belonged to Robert, the assistant manager of the bank. I watched him get pushed around every day by the manager. Now Robert was getting his payback.

See, that was the tell, the one detail that betrayed all your hard work because it was too much a part of who you were for you to even know it was there. I knew how to stay in character and keep the game going until I got to the payoff. Even now, when I wanted to grab the guys and tell them to start over, to come through the doors this way or that, even now I just stood there impassively with my hands in the air.

I wanted to tell them: be a pro. Be a pro, or be burned.

I reached over quick and took the dye pack from Kelly's open drawer, one of the old-style packs with a timer. Kelly smiled weakly back at me, chewed her gum faster and looked away. I pressed the timer button and put it in my own drawer.

Tall came to me and waved his gun. I smiled and scooped up the cash and dye pack and shoveled them on top of the money in the bag. I felt like saying "sorry" to the big bunny rabbit, but the best I could do was apologize in my head.

Sorry, I thought, but I can't let San Francisco's finest look at the personnel records and ask me questions, the kind of questions these giant companies *should* ask before they hire someone but never do. Big dogs can't be bothered checking on the little guys who really make up their companies.

And that's why I hated these companies, hated so much of the world: be a pro, treat people and your job with respect, or get out.

Me? I got out.

CHAPTER 2

I stood in the bank and wondered what my next scam would be, hoping it would be easy again like the last one. Remembered sitting in the conference room of the big environmental company: just me, the company lawyer, and the boss, all in jeans and shirts from all-natural materials to show how much they respected the earth. But they didn't respect the earth, didn't respect anything else either, including me, so there we were.

"So, do you prefer to be called Mr. Smooth Water, or Joshua?" said the lawyer, smiling, trying to be my friend so it would cost the company less.

"It's pronounced 'Ya-wa.' " I folded my arms across my chest, trying hard to swell up with pride. "Joshua is just the white spelling. And Smooth Water is my formal Chippewa name from my mother's tribe. It should not be used by whites."

There. Let the lawyer know there's no friend of his here, and this would cost the company more. I could see him wondering, maybe this guy's Native American, maybe not. I've got the kind of light-dark look that could be Hispanic, Middle Eastern, white, black, whatever I need. In any case, the lawyer couldn't challenge me on it. I also knew that this company had too much to hide for them to risk a big fight out in public.

"Thank you, Joshua," the lawyer said, pronouncing it "Ya-wa" like I asked, and smiling while he did it. I gave him no smile back, just sat there with my arms crossed like the picture of Sitting Bull, offended but impassive. "It's my understanding that Mr. Johnson here, acting in his position as your supervisor, has terminated you from your position here at California Green Industries. He believes he had cause, you believe he did not. Is that a fair statement of the situation?"

I glared at the lawyer and played out the part of a proud, offended man forced to describe a painful insult.

"I came to this company because it said it would help protect the land of my fathers, clean up the streams, and take the white man's poisons out of the air. In the week I have been here, I have been insulted and shamed, despite doing my best."

"The jerk hasn't done a lick of work since the day he came in," said Johnson. He was having trouble sitting still. "He just sits on that cheap blanket drinking company coffee, explaining that each day is a sacred day of some kind or the other that won't let him do this job or that."

The lawyer held up his hand to Johnson, but they had given me an opening.

"Coffee is a sacred drink to my people. It is the water of life for me, the source of all movement. We have proudly shared it with the white man."

"I thought you people preferred something stronger," said Johnson, and the lawyer shook his head furiously but too late. The price had gone up.

"And now this racism," I said, "the true source of our problem here."

Johnson stood up. "The problem is you won't work. The problem is I've got a boatload of jobs that need to get done, and you're just dragging us down—" The lawyer held up his hand and interrupted.

"None of which you've documented, Mr. Johnson." He turned to me, his buddy, and smiled again. Amazing the problems that can be solved if we all just smile. Smile, and offer money. "Joshua, I think we all have the same interests here. We all want to see that the values shared by this company and your forefathers are not damaged by a pointless, bitter, public struggle. Clearly, we no longer have a position available for you at this company, but we want to treat you fairly. Would two thousand dollars help you find a position more suited to your talents?"

We settled on five thousand dollars. Johnson was taken out of the room still screaming. Sometimes I got more, sometimes less, for a week or so's half-assed work at a company that would rather pay me off than fight publicly.

The scam worked best at companies that had something to hide, like this one that was taking money to clean up the environment but doing little more than generating publicity for itself. Mostly, I find companies already ripping off the public before I rip them off. Of course, sometimes just the fact that a company has money goes a long way to prove to me that the company is corrupt and needs to return some money to the community. And me.

So I strutted out the door with a check in hand, threw the sacred blanket in the trash by the big Fred Meyer store, dealt with the check, ran a few errands, and headed back to the Western World bar.

Mayor was behind the bar by himself. Three in the afternoon was too early to have a hired bartender, not to mention that Mayor was way too cheap to pay somebody to just sit behind his own bar and watch sports reruns, which is all Mayor ever does anyway. He looked up at me like I was just another channel on the old RCA.

"Thought I might not see you this time," he said. "Make a score, keep going someplace better. Become a citizen."

I looked at him and tried to smile. I hated seeing the disappointment rise in Mayor's eyes, knowing that I put it there.

Mayor and the skinny girl who danced here were my only real links to the world. And, truth be told, this was the only world I could stand anymore.

"Hey, you know you'd miss me." But Mayor just stared, not willing to keep it light and make it easier on me.

"I've got twenty-five hundred." I pulled out a stack of bills without explaining the errands that had eaten up the other half. "How long will that carry me?"

Mayor stared a long time, and I thought for a minute that he might say no this time. But the money clock ran slow here; most drinks were paid for with wadded-up dollar bills and change counted slow from dirty pockets. A pile of crisp fifty-dollar bills was rare, except from me. Mayor looked at the calendar, studied it like the football coach on the TV studying his playbook.

"Let's say the end of October. Same deal as always: sleep in the back room, sweep up at night, and drink only the cheap stuff, only enough to stay drunk. Eat from the lunch buffet, though you never eat much anyway. Don't cause trouble, though you never cause trouble. You can be everybody's buddy, but you can't buy them drinks 'cause you got no money and I ain't fronting you any.

"End of October, skinny girl and I will wake you up. Last two weeks, no booze, nothing but coffee and the buffet, sober up and go back, jack, do it again. Wheels turning round and round, find some scam or an actual job until you show up here again. Or not. Cash aside, won't break my heart if someday you get stuck in the real world and don't make it back here."

"Deal," I said, and shoved the bills across the bar. "Let's get started." Mayor reached under the bar and pulled out the plastic tumbler that was my cup and the gallon jug of the cheap stuff he used to top off the expensive-looking bottles behind the bar. No need for the pretense of a nice bottle. He filled the tumbler half full. No need for the pretense of dishing this out one shot at a time either. I looked at him and wished that I was one of those who got the good glasses with the tiny drinks. One of those that came in, had a couple of drinks, and toddled home to a happy wife and kids.

What bullshit. I picked up the glass and emptied it. I picked up my crushed and sad paper sack and headed to the back.

"Think I'll take my luggage to the Presidential Suite. I'll join you in the Main Ballroom for happy hour after I've freshened up."

"What do you do back there, anyway?" Mayor turned back to the TV.

"I'm a writer."

"Need any paper?"

"I don't write anything down."

The next thing I remembered clearly was Mayor and the skinny girl shaking me awake at the end of October. The coffee cup in front of me looked like a swimming pool I was supposed to drink. Mayor just looked at me like I was another mess at the bar that Mayor had to clean up, but the skinny girl said to Mayor: "You don't know. I talked to a guy who knew him on the outside. He's somebody. Used to be somebody, anyway." I looked at her sweet, wasted face and wanted to thank her. Thank her, and tell her how wrong she was.

"He's a cork in a bottle," said Mayor. "And you're a professional heartbreak. Don't waste it on this one."

In a flash I remembered something else less clear: the skinny girl, sometime in the middle, holding my head, saying, "Oh Josh baby, oh Josh baby. You could do it for me, Josh baby." I couldn't remember if the words came during one of the times she had shown me a kindness, or just one of the times when I was too drunk to get to my room without help. But she said it, I was sure, and now I wondered what to do with it.

CHAPTER 3

I shook the memory of the Western World away and snatched my head back to the here and now in the bank. The robbers finished and told us all to lie down and face away from the door. Then they were gone and the bank was silent until the police crashed in like heroes here to save the day now that the day had walked out the door.

The detectives gave us all numbers, like we were in a deli waiting for a corned-beef sandwich, but instead we waited our turn to be brought into the conference room to have our formal police interview. My number was nine; they were on five. I was sweating and hoping the sweat wouldn't dissolve the little bits of glue that held my eyelids up to make me look more Chinese. Once they saw I was phony, or once they pulled my record and checked me out, then everything would all be over.

I shuffled humbly over to a detective standing around drinking free bank coffee and texting on a cell phone. Tried to tell him about the silent robber, nudge the detective into solving the crime before they pulled my record and talked to me. But no, the detective waved me back. Take your turn, sir, follow procedure, sir; we're not really interested in solving the crime, sir, just doing our jobs, sir.

I spotted the manager leaning on one of the desks in the middle of it all. He could have been watching guys mow his lawn for all the interest he showed.

"Mister—ah, sir?" I said to him.

"Romanov."

Christ, I thought. All I said to him was, "Romanov?"

The manager smiled at my surprise.

"Yeah, that Romanov. I run the bank for my father. He owns a lot of stuff."

Yeah, I thought, some of it's even legal. I hadn't known the Romanovs owned the bank. Now I wished I'd picked a different one.

Romanov looked up, squinted a minute, then it came to him.

"Joe Chan?" he said.

"Yes, sir." I answered to the name I'd put down on the application at the bank. "Though it's pronounced 'yow.' It's a traditional Chinese name, taken from my honorable grandfather who first came to this country seeking freedom. I'm honored that you know my name, sir."

Romanov shrugged. "Yeah. Dad believes I should know the employees. So I memorize names of new hires to impress him."

"Sir," I said, polite and deferential. "I've tried to talk to the detectives, but they seem to be busy. I believe I have information that might be helpful."

"So? What do you want me to do? Haul my ass over there; tell them Charlie Chan here has solved the case and saved the day? The bank's got insurance, son. Let it go."

"Sir, did you notice the way the silent robber walked? Now look at the assistant manager."

Romanov tried to look bored, but he looked at Robert at the other end of the bank and smiled.

"You weasel," he said, watching Robert. "Good for you. Finally grew a pair and stopped begging for it."

He turned back to me.

"Yeah, maybe," he said. "Cops already said they got one witness outside the bank. The witness saw a tall guy come out alone. Not wearing a white suit. Not carrying a bag. So they're looking inside already. Probably got him in their sights right now. I'll go tell them for you; you get the credit. You got good eyes."

A detective came out of the interview room and called out for number eight and I knew my time below the radar was running out. Romanov waved the detective over, snapping his fingers like he wanted another glass of water. I grabbed Romanov's sleeve but Romanov shook me off.

"Sir, it might be better to tell them you thought of this yourself," I said, "and leave me out."

The detective walked over and stood waiting for orders, knew he couldn't offend the manager. Didn't like being ordered around either, so he stood there, refusing to be the first to talk.

Romanov talked to the detective, not taking his eyes off me while he did. "Just wanted to know how the investigation's going."

The detective tried to smile politely but his mouth tightened into a narrow line. This rich jerk called him over for a personal status report?

"You'll know as soon as we do, sir." He drew "sir" out to about five syllables, and left.

"So." Romanov turned back to me. "You work in a bank where there's just been a robbery, but you want to stay below the cop's radar?"

I saw the detective looking for another witness, skipping number eight and coming for me. I saw Romanov looking at me and needed a story and needed it right now.

"Yes, sir. I'm really a private investigator, sir, and don't need to attract the attention of the police. I only took this job because I need the money."

"Got a license you can show me?"

"No, sir, I'm kind of unofficial. That's why I'd prefer to stay anonymous."

"Yeah, I bet. Unlicensed private detective who can't pay the bills, and is afraid of the cops. Good luck with that. I think we'll just let the police do their job." He turned away and said back over his shoulder, "Good eye, just the same."

Nervous, screwed, no help anywhere. The detective was looking for me; somebody else in another room was pulling my application. I thought about running, a calculated risk sure to draw attention. Maybe if I could get through the door, maybe even get to another city, find another bar, maybe I could start over. It was more than I could handle just thinking about it.

Bang. There was an explosion in the assistant manager's office. The texting detective leaning in the office door looked in and saw red dye everywhere and a hole in the ceiling. He pulled his gun but there's no threat there, no one in the office, just an answer or the start of an answer anyway. The dye pack has gone off finally, stashed in the ceiling with the money and clothes and guns. Robert made a break for the door but everyone was on edge now, and they wrestled him to the ground. Maybe running wasn't such a good idea.

They stopped bringing in witnesses. The detectives had an easy job now, and I had an easy out. Stay quiet and they'll send people home. Call in tomorrow too traumatized to come back to work. May even make some money here. I eased toward the door.

"Charlie Chan?" Romanov came up behind me. I thought about correcting him but decided, no, get this over with fast.

"Thinking about what you said."

I stared at him with a polite look on my face and my eyelids starting to sag and my feet already pointed to the door.

"You did pretty good back there. My family could use a detective, an unlicensed detective, do jobs other people can't."

The door looked good now. I needed to fail this job interview.

"What you charge?" asked Romanov.

21

"Five hundred dollars a day, plus expenses." There, that ought to do it. I had seen that on Mayor's TV, thought it was absurd. It sounded even more like a joke when it came out of my mouth. No straight citizen would pay that. But Romanov just looked back like I'd told him the price of a hamburger.

"Sounds about right. Look, my brother's got a twenty-three-year-old daughter who disappeared three days ago. Cops aren't interested, say she probably just ran off. Plus they don't like my brother too much. Or the rest of us Romanovs, for that matter. So my brother's got a couple of his guys looking into it, but they're bozos, plus they're not going to tell him anything he doesn't want to hear because they're afraid they'll get hurt 'cause that's what my brother does for my dad, hurts people.

"Come up with an address for her by the end of the week, and I'll pay your five hundred a day. Actually get my niece back home, and I'll double it."

He poked a business card at me.

"Deal with my brother's wife; it'll be better for you." He started to walk away and then came back. He smiled at me, a big Chamber of Commerce smile between partners.

"Enjoy your new job. Do a good job and there'll be more," he said.

Romanov stepped into me, nose to nose, and lowered his voice to a growl.

"Course, you don't do a good job for us, know this: we don't forget, and we don't forgive. My brother will come for you."

Romanov stepped away, laughed, and said over his shoulder, "Welcome to the real world."

CHAPTER 4

The next morning I put on a grubby gray service uniform with an old straw hat and picked up a rusty pair of pruning shears. As I got on the bus, the driver looked at the shears and maybe wondered if this was the start of one of those bizarre crime sprees. Then he looked at the bus token in my other hand, and money and routine trumped any desire to be a hero. He shrugged as I put the token in and walked down the aisle.

I sat down next to a frail-looking old woman knitting in one corner of the seat. She looked at me out of the corner of her eye and looked at the shears. She pulled a sharpened and shining landscape spike out of the pink blanket she was knitting and pushed it into my crotch until I, literally, got the point.

"Irving," she said, "You may be the one hundred and forty-second fastest draw in the West with that thing." She jerked her chin at the shears. "But you just met number one hundred and forty-one. Keep your distance."

I dropped the shears and pointed at them. "Must to work carry," I flashed the biggest, friendliest smile I had.

"Goddamn foreigners," said Grandma, going back to her knitting. But the spike stayed close and one eye stayed on me.

I got off the bus on the edge of a rich neighborhood and headed for the address for the Romanov estate. The plan was to get there unnoticed and bargain before Romanov went to work. I needed to explain why I wouldn't be any help in looking for the manager's niece, then ease back to the Western World and forget about all this. I could have tried a phone call or just going back to the bank, but I wanted to catch Romanov on his home turf, and catch him unexpected. Besides, I just like dressing up. So right now I was just another neighborhood gardener in a rich neighborhood, shuffling along with my head down in deference to the rich people who deserved to be here.

I found the city block that the Romanov compound occupied. I followed the trucks around to the service entrance and slipped inside, idly clipping at a stray twig here and there, heading toward what looked like the main house. "Main house" was kind of an understatement here. There were three houses arranged around a central pool area. The smaller two houses were at least ten thousand square feet and could have been used in a remake of *Gone with the Wind*. The big house looked like somebody had taken Notre Dame Cathedral, upscaled it, and dropped the spires from the Kremlin on top for decoration. Must be Daddy's house. That would mean the two smaller—relatively speaking—houses belonged to the two brothers. Both brothers probably each spent their days stewing there in their relative poverty, waiting for Daddy to die so they could kill their brother and get everything they deserved.

A beautiful young woman, six feet tall, blonde, and topless, climbed out of the waterfall at the end of the pool and picked up a quart-sized drink. She walked over to a set of chaise lounges where three other young women lay sunning and listening to Mick Jagger complain about a lack of satisfaction.

There was a shot, and I hit the ground at the base of a holly shrub. Stuck my head up when I heard someone laugh at the end of the lawn downhill from the pool. The someone was a tall blond man dressed in black holding a shotgun, breaking it down to put in another shell. There were two other young guys with shotguns. They were tough-looking and speaking Russian. A servant set up another clay target in the target thrower beside them. The pellets from the last shot clattered down on the roof of a house beyond the wall, a voice from that house cursed, and the young Russians laughed some more. One of them yelled something to the servant, and the clay target took off. Two of the men, laughing and drunk, fired at the same time in no particular direction. The clay target appeared to be the only thing safe.

I stood up and clipped and worked my way to the house on the right, hoping to find the bank manager. The other yard workers noticed the man in the wrong-colored uniform and moved away. Anything out of place here was dangerous and they wanted nothing to do with it.

I was busy watching the men with too many shotguns and the women with not so many clothes and didn't realize how close I had gotten to the house.

"The knife you will put down," a woman's voice said. I looked up and saw a woman with a gun standing ten feet away on the patio of the house on the right. Not an angry woman, just a woman bored with small boys and their small toys.

"So, has Sergei sent you to kill my husband? Or maybe my father-in-law? It does not matter." She waved the young men in from the skeet range. They reloaded as they walked toward us.

She looked like a woman who would make a hell of a good grandmother in a few years if her kids would just cooperate. Fiftyish, enough weight to have some authority, and warm brown eyes. She held the Glock in her hand like a nun would hold a ruler.

"No." I put down the clippers. "No, ma'am." I stood up, hands out, and pointed to my chest pocket. "Can I show you? Not a gun."

She shrugged. I reached into my pocket and pulled out the card the bank manager had given me with the name of the bank manager's sister-in-law written on it.

"Is you, miss?" I said, beginning to acquire a Russian accent. She took the card and read the name.

"Detective from the bank?"

I nodded and smiled as big as I could.

"Sergei—my husband's brother—he tell me you come. You find my Kiev." She shooed the young men and they went away, disappointed at having to satisfy themselves shooting at clay targets.

"Kiev is my baby." She dropped the gun in a pocket of her apron. "You no look like no detective I heard of. Why you dress in this way?"

"I've learned to keep a low profile," I said. "It helps in my job. Plus, when my family came here from Russia, we learned to blend in. You may not believe it, but Russians are discriminated against in this country."

"You are Russian?"

"Proud Cossack." I drew myself up proudly, trying to look like Yul Brynner in *Taras Bulba*.

"Us too."

"No." I opened my eyes wide in what I hoped was amazement. "I thought you were German."

"I spit on Germans." She turned her head and did just that. I spat too, twice as hard.

"It is true how hard we must work here. My father-in-law and his sons work like dogs, harder than Americans, and this is all we have."

I nodded. She headed into the house. I followed.

"So I know you will bring my baby back to me."

"Well, I sort of need to talk to you about that. I may not be able—"

"Yes, yes." She waved the Glock in the air like a theatrical gesture and sat it down on the counter next to a long butcher knife. "You can't do your job without help from me. I have. You follow."

We went through the kitchen to a dining room that would have made a good auditorium. The table was covered with old photographs, school records, even a small clear plastic box full of baby teeth.

"Here is everything you need for my baby. You need to know her third grade teacher, is in here. We start at beginning."

She picked up a baby picture, and I gave up on telling her I couldn't take the case. Better to talk to the bank manager when he got here.

"Mother, let's start the other way—do you mind if I call you 'mother'? You remind me so much of my own mother, bless her soul."

"I would rather you would call me grandmother, but my boys are only interested in guns and not babies. And the girls." She made a motion toward the pool and screamed, "Put some clothes on you sluts," but her voice just echoed back from the window at the far end of the room.

I picked up a picture of a young woman at the end of the table. She was pretty, with bright blue eyes and blonde hair like the girls by the pool. But she had an intensity to her they didn't: hair spiked up on the top, eyes that warned the photographer this was his last shot at a picture of her.

"No, not that one. This one." Mother held up a glamour shot of the same woman posing on a red carpet wearing a look-at-me dress and flashing a big smile for the cameras.

"Didn't she used to be—I mean isn't she . . ." I said.

"Yes. She was in all the papers, all the time. Never enough for that one. She spoiled, but in her own way. All the tabloids have her picture. Then she no want to be the hot girl no more. 'Sick of being famous for being famous. Want to do something,' she say. All the time saying, 'Feel like my skin cracking.' You know expression, from American South, she pick up from bums at coffee shop she hang out at? It means, 'I feel like a snake who's about to shed his skin, ready for new skin.' Something like that. She'd walk around, mad like a loaded pistol. Spend all her time down at coffee shop by university, never home. Turned into what you see in picture you have in hand. Look like boy."

Even with her hair in a Mohawk, she didn't look like any boy I had ever seen. I looked out the window. The bank manager was marching across the lawn from the house on the other side. Behind him was a thug dragging a little guy. The woman saw what I was looking at.

"Ah, Sergei come. We talk to him." She went back to the kitchen and I followed.

Sergei Romanov and the thug and the little guy walked over to the boys with the skeet guns. Sergei said something to one of the boys, and the thug threw the little guy at the boy's feet. Sergei and the thug kept coming toward Mother and me without looking back. One of the boys picked up the little guy. Another one hit him in the stomach. The third one, a guy dressed all in black, laughed.

Sergei walked into the kitchen, and Mother gave him a big hug.

"Yeah, yeah," he said.

"Thank you so much for this fine young detective. He will find Kiev, I know. He is Russian himself, you know this?"

"Russian?" Sergei eyed me, and then smiled. "Course I knew." He looked at me. He snapped his fingers, and the thug handed him a roll of bills. Sergei pushed the roll into my hand. "No way for a detective to dress. Get yourself some decent threads."

I tried to hand back the money.

"I wanted to tell you that I've got good news for you, sir. I won't be able to take your case, but I've found you a much better detective, a licensed one, to handle this case." Actually, I had found him in the Yellow Pages, but there was no point in dwelling on details. "I'm sure he'll find Kiev in no time."

A dark cloud came over the woman's face, and her hand hesitated between the gun and the knife, as casually as if she were deciding whether to wear the red earrings or the green. Sergei was calm.

"This is important to us. Makes it really important to you. What's the problem?"

"I've got a commitment I made to another client some time ago. I'm sure you understand."

"I do. Give me the name of the client, and Mook here will talk to him and straighten this out." The giant thug pulled out a ridiculously small notebook and pen and stood waiting to write down the name, looking like a cartoon character but a cartoon character that killed people.

I hesitated as long as I could. "Maybe I could work with the other detective I mentioned, stay in touch, and see that the job is done right."

"No. This is an important case. This is your only case until Kiev is home."

Behind Sergei, the boys finished roughing up the little guy. They stood him up, and one of them gave him a loud warning. I thought they were going to let him go. Then the laughing boy in black shoved the barrel of a shotgun in the little guy's gut and pulled the trigger. The sound was muffled, but when the other boys turned loose of the little guy, he collapsed into a pile of red meat on the grass. One of the other boys muttered something to the laughing boy, switched to English, and said, "You didn't need to do that." Laughing boy laughed and waved for one of the yard workers to clean up the mess.

"I can see that this is an important case," I said, pocketing the money.

CHAPTER 5

I was running errands just before dawn with the money from Sergei Romanov. The street light on the corner was the only working light still shining on a broken-down Toyota that had sat here on flat tires for weeks. I peeled one of Romanov's bills and shoved it through a crack in the window onto the woman sleeping on the seat, wrapped around her two children.

The woman sprang to life like a spring had been coiled inside her. She bounced up with a long knife and jabbed at the opening in the window while I tried to yank my hand back without damage.

"Leave my babies alone!" she yelled. This wasn't the same Terri I'd seen on the street before. Cleaned up as much as you could clean up when you lived in a car, she dragged her young son and baby with her up one hopeless block and another, looking for any work that would let her keep her family together in their current home in the back of the Toyota.

But now that her babies were threatened she was a beast from hell: screaming with crazy eyes and one fearsome butcher-knife claw stabbing out at whatever demon the uncaring world had sent at her this time. I backed away and put my hands up, and Terri calmed down a little now that her babies weren't threatened. I still had a handful of bills in one hand. I waved them and hoped she could see them in the pale light in the hour before dawn.

The boy woke up and picked up the bills from the neat pile

of folded clothes on the floor of the car. He looked at his mother and saw that she was watching the stranger and not him. He shoved one of the bills down the front of his shorts and waved the rest at his mother.

"Ma," he said. "Ma, it's like money but it says 'fifty' instead of 'one' or 'five.' Leave him alone, Ma. It's money."

The knife stopped chewing up the air for a second. She turned her head a little so she could see the boy without taking her eye off me. I smiled and waved the hand with the bills to say, look, there's no threat here. Her look said that she knew that the world always held a threat, even when it smiled. Particularly when it smiled.

She took the money from the boy. She reached into his waistband and pulled out the remaining bill. She gave him a look, opened the car door, and came out knife first. I backed away with my hands up.

"We don't take charity, Mister. And I don't do the only kind of work around that pays fifty-dollar bills. Them kids ain't got much but we got pride, and we're holding on to it, thank you. They've seen their ma work every beat-down job this city has, but they ain't never seen her beg."

"Not charity," I said. "This money doesn't belong to me." I wanted to say that money never belongs to you, you belong to it—it eats you up like acid and turns you into something you're not, and you need to get rid of it as soon as you can before it owns you. But I knew that kind of thinking came from a luxury that would only insult her now.

She looked at me and tried to figure out what this game was. Fear won out over hope. She shoved the bills back at me.

"Ain't mine neither," she said. "I'm going to keep working. Get me enough money to fix up this old car and drive it home to my parents in Georgia. Stay with them and get back on my feet somewhere in a small-town world that still makes some sense to me. But I'll do it on my own. I do thank you. But no."

I lowered my hands. "I thought the money was yours. It was sitting there by your car, wadded up. I thought about taking it, but I know what you mean. I don't want to hold onto something that's not mine. I was shoving it back in your window when I woke you."

"Really ain't your own?"

"Really ain't. Ain't charity neither. It's yours. The world put it there for you, whether it knows it or not. The world owes you more than it's giving right now, whether it knows it or not."

"The world don't owe me nothing, and I don't owe the world," she said. She sighed and put out her hand and took the rest of the money from me. "But I'll pay the world back someday, just the same."

I nodded and walked around the corner. The cold wind off the bay was blowing hard this morning. I reached in my pocket and took out some more bills and threw them up in the air as high as I could. In this neighborhood, they would find homes that needed them. I stood there with arms outstretched as the bills swirled around me like a cleansing rain. It was the only thing that felt better than being drunk.

CHAPTER 6

"So you got yourself a real job?" Mayor grinned that grin that a poppa gets when his son finally gives up on being a rock star and takes the job down at the Jiffy Lube that'll let him support his pregnant girlfriend and live the same miserable life his poppa did. He poured a dirty glass of the cheap stuff and shoved it across the Western World bar. I just stared at it.

Finally, I shoved the glass back at Mayor.

"I can't do this screwed up."

Mayor laughed. "Gone from screwed up to screwed over."

The skinny girl walked over. "Told you," she said to Mayor. She looked up at me. "I told him you used to be somebody, be somebody again someday. Now you got a job and everything."

Mayor and I both looked at her.

I said, "So you think this is like a good career move, hump it for the Russian boss till they get tired of me and the boys throw me up in the air for a skeet target?"

"Just saying," she said. "Got money." She pointed at the wadded-up bills on the bar, a few fifties I had held back.

"How long?" I said to Mayor.

Mayor shrugged. "Tell you what. When you don't drink you don't cost me nothing. Good to have somebody in the back room when the bar's closed. Kind of like a pit bull, except with no bark or bite. You keep half. The other half reserves the back room for you anytime you're sober. Start drinking, I'll start charging. Till then, we declare that eight-by-five closet to be the

Josh Whoever Memorial Suite."

I stared at the bar, overwhelmed at the high honor I had achieved in my life.

"You know," said Mayor, "we need a name to go over the room. You never did tell me your last name."

"No. Never did."

Mayor glared. The prodigal son who had showed signs of turning his life around was now showing signs of slipping back into teen rebellion.

"So what now?" said the skinny girl. She was so excited she couldn't keep still. Either that, or she was still high from the night before. Hard to tell.

"Are you going to get like an office and a trench coat and talk funny?" she said. "Oh—am I going to be your sidekick? Let me be your sidekick. You can call me doll and I can lean on your desk and everything."

Mayor shook his head and poured the drink back into the bottle.

I said, "Look, I got no place to look for this Kiev girl. If I get lucky, she comes home on her own and I'm off the hook. If not, one day the Russians get tired of me stringing them along and they feed me to that pack of hyenas they call their sons. It's not like a cute detective movie. More like this: Hemingway had a story, one of his better ones, called 'The Killers.' Guy has pissed off somebody in the mob, they never say how in the story. Whole story is about him waiting, knowing they're coming to kill him. That's what this feels like."

"So that's the whole story," said Mayor. "Guy in a room, waiting to get shot? No guts, no action?"

"There's a couple of guys telling him what he should do," I said. "But yeah, that's about it. Hemingway made it work."

Mayor leaned over. "John Woo—that's a guy would have made it work. Killers come into the bar, hero's behind the bar, like me, waiting. Killers start blasting away. Hero's cool, ducks under the bar, comes up with an Uzi, starts blasting back. Kills a couple of guys. Now it's just the hero and the main killer, blasting away, air filled with slow-motion bullets, brass casings ejected from the guns falling in slow rainbow arcs. Hero runs out of bullets and the killer sneers, knows he's got him now. But the hero pulls a grenade launcher from behind his back and fires, one time, quick. You see the grenade fly across the room as the killer's face turns to panic. Boom! The killer's a bloody mess on the wall. Hero picks up a rag, starts wiping the counter, looks into the camera, and says, 'So much for'—and now he pauses for what they call dramatic effect. The camera zooms in as he says, 'the killers.' "

"Yeah," I said. "Think I saw that on TV last night. And the night before."

"Probably get Bruce Willis to play the bar owner."

"Probably."

The skinny girl was having none of this. "You can't just give up on this like you give up on everything else. This girl has a mother who loves her. She had dreams before she wound up in a broken-down bar."

"She wound up in a broken-down bar?" I said.

"My bar's broken-down?" said Mayor.

"You know what I mean. You gotta try."

I sighed. "So Mayor thinks we're in a bullet-porn movie. You think we're in the cute *Sunday Night Mystery*. You think the door's going to open any second now. A colorful character will stumble in and say, 'Girl's at the corner of Fifth and Main. Tell them Maxie sent you.' I'll rush off to follow that clue and save the day."

The door opened and bright light flooded the dark bar. For a moment a shadow loomed across the floor larger than life. The door closed. When our eyes adjusted back to the darkness, it was just a homeless guy in an old brown corduroy sport coat and a purple beret, coming in to stay warm.

Mayor laughed, "There's a colorful character for you. Guns, Josh, you need guns."

The skinny girl looked down. "Maybe the next guy can help." It seemed to be a line she knew well.

"No," I said. "He'll do."

CHAPTER 7

I was on my fourth cup of coffee and getting jittery. It was bad coffee but at five bucks a cup I figured I needed to get at least four refills to make the coffee shop lose money. Let them find some other sucker to pay for the kitschy unmatched furniture and the tuneless New Age music that came from somewhere in the ceiling.

Still, the coffee was giving me a headache. Either the coffee, or sitting in the dark corner of the university street coffeehouse, squinting at Mayor's old laptop while wearing a scratched pair of reading glasses I'd borrowed from the skinny girl.

I glanced at the reflection in the window and thought I had the look right: brown corduroy jacket and purple beret I bought off the guy in the Western World, then added a pair of turquoise reading glasses from the skinny girl. If the look didn't say weird professor nothing would.

A girl leaned over my shoulder. "You a writer?" She read the screen on Mayor's laptop.

"No."

"Well, you're writing. By the way, 'university street coffee' isn't capitalized. They make a big deal out of that here to show how cool they are."

"It's nothing."

She shoved me and my chair out of the way without much effort and took over. "Actually, it's a good lead. Written in a solid AP-style format. Nice hook. You're either a reporter or a journalism professor."

I slammed the laptop closed, almost on her fingers.

"Actually, I'm a professor of Buddhist literature. I'm not a reporter and I've never been one."

She held up her hands and backed off. "One of those." She took in the beret and glasses. "Should have guessed. I'll leave you to your meditation. Say hello to the Godhead for me."

She walked to the back, and I couldn't help following her with my eyes. More good-looking than cute, looked thirtyish but probably more like forty if you studied her eyes, which looked like they had done some living and still had some life left in them. She walked with a no-nonsense, in-charge walk back to a table in the corner by herself and opened her own laptop.

I looked around the coffee shop. Most of the tables had young twenty-somethings trying to be something they weren't; more piercings and tattoos than bodies at most tables, the F-word used as casually as good morning. But when you looked close, they were all just scared, middle-class kids who had outgrown their soccer uniforms and were looking for what uniform to put on next. My look fit in and confirmed to them that looking weird was something real grownups did.

I fit in; she didn't and that was the key. By sitting alone at the high table in the corner, she ruled. She was who she was, and the energy of the place flowed from her confidence.

I opened Mayor's laptop. The little bar in the corner of the screen said I'd written seventeen hundred words since I'd sat down. Funny how easy things come to you when it doesn't matter. I moused over to the save button, hesitated, then hit the delete key and closed the laptop.

I went to the counter and ordered an expensive coffee drink, something with about seven names. I dropped the beret and glasses next to Mayor's laptop and carried the drink over to the woman.

"An apology for my rudeness."

She looked at it and laughed. "So you think a woman with a large cup of coffee needs more caffeine?" She looked at me carefully, locking up our eyes for a long time. It was hard not to look away. "You either haven't done this in a long time, or you're not very good at it."

I wondered what the "it" was I was doing.

"Besides." She read the side of the cup. The barista had written the name of the drink in flowing script, in case the person drinking it forgot what the drink was and had to be told so they'd know if they liked it or not. "Do I look like a double-Peruvian-cappuccino-with-soy-whipped-and-cinnamon-sprinkles sort of girl? Really?"

I was uncomfortable. Uncomfortable, but I liked it.

"Doesn't matter," she said. "I'm not big on fake apologies, but I love honest rudeness. Marci Harris." She put out her hand and I took it.

"Marci Harris? Didn't you used to be a reporter? Did crime pieces for the *Chronicle*?"

She laughed. "Oh yeah. I'd do a crime piece on my own. The paper would print it and send me back to the society page where they thought I belonged. After the third time, I told them what I thought of that, using some of the best language I'd ever created. They took the suggestions literally. Got offended at language like that from their society editor, and fired me, also literally."

"Shame. You had a style." I corrected myself. "Have a style." Now I needed another correction. "Your writing, I mean."

She laughed. "God, you're a smooth one, aren't you?"

"This is as good as it gets for me."

She smiled. "Never know."

"Never do. So what now? For Marci Harris, I mean. Where do I go to read her next exciting story?"

39

"Mostly the unemployment line. Or here. I'd like to write a book, but I need a job for little things like rent. So I come in here to write, in between going on pointless interviews. Not much demand for a society editor. Particularly if you've been fired from the only paper in town that actually has a society editor. I don't want to leave San Francisco, but I may not have a choice." She paused. "May have to take a job as a professor of Buddhist literature. What do you actually do for that, anyway?"

"Sometimes just look weird and pontificate. Sometimes actually read. Sometimes, you just hang around coffee shops and wait for students who don't show up."

"You've been stood up. Shame."

"I've been stood up. The department admin told me there was a girl who wanted to be my assistant. Gave me her picture, said she'd meet me here at two. It's two cups past three now, and no girl. I'm about to hang it up."

"Show me the picture."

I pulled out the picture of Kiev, the recent one with the spiked hair. Marci laughed.

"Oh yeah. Sweet Georgia Brown."

"Georgia Brown?" I took the napkin from under her coffee to write that down.

"Not her name. I called her that. Always putting on a fake Southern accent, except that her pronunciations were Russian. 'Georgia' covered it all for me. Here, these kids know her." She motioned to a table of kids.

The kids were all in black, with chains around their waists and bits of metal shining at random places on their faces. They sulked at a table in the corner, too bored and cool for the world. When Marci waved to them, they smiled and came bouncing over like puppies called to play.

"Hey, Marci," said a tough girl who seemed to be the leader.

"Hey, Bea. Want you to meet somebody, new professor of

Buddhist literature." She motioned for me to give my name.

"Lo-Mein Burroughs," I said. Bea raised an eyebrow, too cool to grin.

"Lo-Mein? Like Chinese junk food?"

"Dad hung out at a Chinese takeout. Said everyone should be named after something good in the universe. Got a brother named John Coltrane Burroughs."

"Cool," said one of the boys, a small, bookish kid lost inside a motorcycle jacket two sizes too big. "The Burroughs part, that is. There was a cool writer, William Burroughs, wrote a lot of dirty stuff."

"An uncle. Not popular in the family, but, of course, a pretty good writer."

A girl giggled, "Is it true that Steely Dan actually got their name from something in *Naked Lunch*? It was a—" She hesitated.

"Yes," I cut her off.

"And you're his nephew?"

"Yes. Well, of William Burroughs. Not of Steely Dan. Not either Steely Dan."

"Wow."

Marci leaned forward. "Lo-Mein here," she looked over at me like, *I know that's a fake name.* "Lo-Mein needs to find that crazy girl that hangs out with you." She pushed the picture across the table.

"Leo-nard Ski-o-nard," said the bookish boy. Marci looked at him.

He shrugged. "That's what I call her, account of her accent. I tell her, the band's name is 'Lynn-nerd Skin-nerd,' she says 'Leo-nard Ski-o-nard,' can't see the difference because of her Russian accent. She's trying hard, though, just wants to be something real and good and true."

I looked at the boy and wondered if anyone real and good

and true could actually say the phrase "real and good and true."
Kids.

"She's famous, you know," said the girl. "Used to be on TV
all the time, fast cars, partying, get a DUI and Daddy would
pay it off."

"Then she got real spiritual," said the boy. "Spent time hanging out with the monks from the monastery up around Placer-
ville. She ought to be in one of your classes; I can see why she'd
be looking for you. Why you looking for her, though?"

"She's supposed to be my assistant. If I can interview her. If I
can find her."

"I can do that job," a girl with white hair said. "I've read a lot
of Alan Watts, that sort of thing."

Bea cut her off. "Kiev needs something like this. Poor kid's
being torn about twenty different directions: Daddy wants her
to stay a pampered rich girl; tabloids want her to be a bad girl
for their stories. Ass and Hole leaning on her all the time."

I looked at Marci.

Marci said to Bea, "Ass and Hole? That like a rock group or
something?"

"No, two guys, always coming around, acting tough, trying to
push Kiev about her father. Big black guy, always wears a rebel
flag t-shirt, little white guy still wears a mullet, tries to dress like
Don Johnson from *Miami Vice*."

"I think they're narcs," said the boy.

"Narcs, thugs," said the girl. "Not much difference. They just
seem to hang around her to make her uncomfortable. Seems to
work. Something's been bugging her lately.

"You try to find her, though. She could use a gig like yours,
something to hang on to. She hangs out with them most nights
down at General Lee's, redneck rock club a couple of blocks off
campus."

"General Lee's?" I said.

Marci leaned over, and I smelled fresh soap and healthy girl hair. "Pick me up here about nine. I'll get you in there."

"I haven't decided if I'm going," I said. "Now *we're* going?"

"It's a date." She turned back to her laptop.

I was going to tell her that I hadn't asked. But then again, she wasn't asking either.

CHAPTER 8

"That hat's not going to work in there," said Marci. It was a quarter to ten at night and Marci and I were walking over from the coffee shop to the bar. Marci had on a straw cowboy hat, painted white and rolled up on the sides, shit-kicker boots and a tight NRA t-shirt.

"Be surprised what people will tell you when you wear one of these to a redneck place," she had said when I met her at the coffee shop and commented on the shirt.

Now I was walking down the street with her, looking at the way the shirt fit and thinking people probably told her a lot of things. Part of me wanted to tell her those same things. Part of me wondered if I could pull off the same look with a good bra and tissues. It would open up a whole new line of possibilities. I shook my head at myself, and Marci thought it was directed at her.

"Hey, don't laugh at me when you're walking around with a purple gumdrop on your head."

"So you think the beret's not going to work."

"No," she said. "Here." She reached up and snatched the beret and walked over to a couple of homeless guys. She came back a couple of minutes later with a beat-up John Deere ball cap.

She put the hat on my head and pulled it down low. I thought about pulling it up just so she'd have to touch my head again to pull it back low. "Now, Joe Street-person over there's got better style, and you've got a Dixie Rock union card," she said. "The jacket's OK, long as you keep the hat on. Jacket'll make people think you're trying to impress me. Which they'll be thinking anyway, with your looks and mine. And which." She looked me in the eye, cocked her head, and walked away fast. "You should be."

I had to run to catch up. I was breathing hard and had to grab her elbow to slow her down. She looked back and smiled, proud that she had won a race of her own making.

"Look," I said, "there's something I need to tell you. Probably nothing, could be something. Anyway, you ought to know about it. She's probably not, but she might be. In trouble, that is. You just should know."

Marci folded her arms. "Can you say that again? In English this time?"

"Look," I sighed. I was still huffing some and needed a pause to catch my breath. "Some people have hired me to find her. She probably just ran off, but there's a chance that there's something more. So be careful with Ass and Hole. There might be some danger."

She waved her fingers. "Whoo, danger. Excitement and mystery. You forget I am a girl crime reporter. Used to the dark underbelly of the city." She paused and looked at me. "Wait a minute. Who hires a Zen Buddhist professor to find a missing girl?" She crossed her arms and waited.

"Well, I was a bank teller at the time."

"Clears that up," she said. She waited for more but it didn't come.

"Just saying," I finally said when it was obvious that hell would freeze over before Marci would speak first. "You might want to play it cool in there if we find these guys."

"I always play it cool." She tossed her hair and walked away, and I struggled to keep up, again. I hung back while she talked

45

to the bouncer, a big white guy with a black Stetson pulled low over his eyes. Her voice had dropped half an octave and turned husky. She had her hands on his arm, playing the bouncer. He laughed and waved her in. She turned back to me.

"This here's my . . ." she paused. "Oh, hell." She dragged "hell" out to several syllables, girl-cute and down-home. "I don't know what the hell he is, but he's with me." The bouncer waved us both in.

An old Guy Clark song played over the crowd noises, and I felt at home. Any place that played the old, honest stuff has my respect.

Only for a moment. The music changed to a rock star pretending he knew a damned thing about the South, and I looked around and saw a roomful of San Francisco pretend-rednecks digging on pretend music. A black guy, big and buff like a linebacker, jumped up on a table and yelled, "Sweet Home Alabama" at the top of his lungs. The guy wore a rebel flag t-shirt with the sleeves cut off, tight across the chest. I took Marci's elbow and shoved her in the guy's direction. She saw what I was doing and yelled "Hay-ull, yeah" at the top of her lungs.

The black guy looked down at the cute chick in the tight shirt, pointed at her, and yelled, "N-R-A."

"Later," Marci whispered and jumped up on the table with the guy.

I went over to the bar. A bored-looking guy raised an eyebrow, and I said, "Diet Coke."

"One of the hardcore ones, eh?" said the guy with a Canadian accent. "Not gonna get too high on that artificial sweetener and start shooting up the place, are you?"

"I'll try to control myself." I put a five on the counter. The guy took the five and offered no change.

I looked around and saw the young female bartenders

hustling and dancing while they poured shots and beer. The girls here put on a show like in that movie where the bartenders danced around on the bar. This guy just stood here, quiet, down at the end of the bar where the cute waitresses and noisy customers seemed to leave him alone.

"Your place?" I said.

"Naw." The guy looked at me a minute and saw the cap that said I belonged here, saw the college professor jacket that said that maybe I had two brain cells. "Manager. Owner wants someone in here that doesn't like meth or beer, can keep his head on straight. That's me."

"Like it?"

The guy shrugged. "Music sucks, but the work is predictable enough to be easy."

Kid Rock was banging on my ears. I wanted to bang back.

"If you hate the music, it's got to be a long night, every night."

The guy shrugged. "You do what you can. Every now and then I slip in Guy Clark, Johnny Cash, Robert Earl Keen, something like that. I can get away with it for a while till somebody yells for something kick-ass. That's what they come here for: something they can scream to. More they scream, more they drink. More they drink, more I make."

I raised my glass. "To big checks." Somebody in the crowd yelled, "Hell, yeah." The guy nodded. "I agree with both of you."

Marci was bumping with the black guy, playing him while he thought he was playing her. The manager noticed them.

"Saw you come in with her. Didn't last long."

I thought. "She's my sister."

"Yeah, sure. I can see the resemblance."

Marci and the black guy jumped down, and Marci led him over to the bar. He was sweating, already into the night, and Marci was starting to glow, too. Marci ignored me. This end of the bar wasn't crowded, but she turned her back to me and shoved her ass into my crotch anyway. I tried to look cool, and I sure didn't pull away.

"Got Abita?" she said to the manager. He nodded. "Two Purple Haze," she said.

The black guy started to correct her, "My daddy said to always drink Bud."

"You want Daddy, or you want me?"

The manager went to get the Purple Haze. She held the guy's hips with both hands and slowly pulled him into her until I could feel her hips grind against us both.

"Daddy can wait." The guy pushed back, and I had to hold on to the bar to keep from falling off the conga line. "I don't know if I can. Might have to get those beers to go."

Marci laughed and pushed him away, but only a little. "What's your hurry? I want to get to know you. I bet you got a real fancy place and a big job, something like construction, maybe."

He sneered. "I ain't no flunky, get bossed around out in the hot sun all day like that. I take what I want."

He put his arms around her and nuzzled her neck. His head bumped up against mine. I wanted to move away but decided to try to stay still and invisible. So I stood there with my head nuzzled against his sweaty head and Marci's body rubbing against the rest of me. At last, I thought, I've got a ticket to the Jerry Springer show. Or at least a letter to *Penthouse*.

"Oh, I like that," said Marci. "Now where's this big house you're going to take me?"

"Better than a house. Got a van, right outside in the parking lot."

She pushed him away. "I look like that kind of girl to you? Takes a hell of a lot more than the back seat of a van to get what you want from me."

"What you mean?"

"I want to go back to your place, be surrounded by all those fine things you got there."

She wrapped one long leg around him.

"Look," he said. "It's a trailer, a long ways away. And we can't go back there, at least not right now. But that don't mean I can't give you what you need."

She pulled him in. "What I need is those two big bulges in your pants. Once that big wallet of yours takes care of me, I can take care of that other bulge." She rubbed up and down, the motion catching the guy and me all at once. I was ready to pay her if the guy wouldn't. "Don't even try to tell me you're going to let a little thing like money stand in the way of true love."

"I got the money, just not right now. Take care of me now, and I can take care of you soon in real style, baby."

She uncoiled her leg, put her foot down, pulled his head away, and kissed him on the head.

"Then call me when that 'soon' happens, lover." She walked away and waved the beer without looking back.

The guy just stood there for a moment. He slowly became aware of the manager and me watching him. He pulled himself up straight and proud, stuck out his chin and said, "I ain't never paid for it in my life, and I ain't starting now." He walked away.

"That's your sister?" said the manager when it was just him and me.

I watched the black guy walk off. Marci came back and set her Abita on the bar and said, "Watch this for me," and walked off again. Now the manager and I watched Marci walk away.

"You should see the family reunions," I said. I turned back to the crowd and watched the black guy, who was talking to a skinny little white guy with a mullet and crazy eyes.

"Speaking of close family," I said to the manager, "what do

you know about my dear brother that I just met."

"Your brother?"

"We damned near shared a sister."

"I get your point." The manager leaned across the bar. "Calls himself 'Dread Clampett,' thinks it's a funny joke. See the little guy with him? The one dressed up in a *Miami Vice* look but looks like he bought the clothes in the boys' department? Two of them always shooting off their mouth. Most days they want to run a tab. No way, José. Sometimes, they have money for a few days, and I'm glad to take it.

"Guys like them, they make this job hard. Most folks come in here to play, looking for something a little different from the city, some way they can be somebody other than a little chickenshit pushed around by their bosses all day. Those two are looking for a score, but not smart enough or pro enough to do it right. Gonna get somebody hurt someday.

"Course, long as they don't do it here, no skin off my ass." He pulled out some papers and a pen from under the bar and went to work.

Marci was back.

"What'd you think of my show?"

"I don't think I'm old enough to buy a ticket."

She punched my arm hard enough to hurt. "Hey, we learned that bozo thinks he's got a big score coming soon. I think your little rich girl may be in over her head with those two."

I was still watching the two bozos. The big black guy was hassling the little skinny guy about something. The little guy shook his head and went off to the quietest corner of the bar.

"Are you jealous?" she said when I wasn't paying her much attention.

I wasn't sure what to say. "Should I be?"

"Try this." Marci leaned over, put her arms around my neck and gave me a long beery kiss. The manager looked up and raised an eyebrow. He moved down the bar, far enough to be out of the way but close enough not to miss anything.

"I don't have any cash," I said, when I could breathe again. "But I'd be glad to lie about it if it will help."

"Nothing's going to help you now."

Over her shoulder I saw the little guy talking on his cell phone, but with a bar napkin wadded up over the phone. I pulled away from Marci and pointed with my glass.

"What do you think that's about?"

"Is this a distraction?"

"No. Well, yes, it certainly is. But no, I didn't mean for it to be. That's not what I meant. Oh, just look."

She looked. "Huh."

"That's the partner of the guy that was nearly your partner."

"Huh," she said again.

We watched while the guy tried to talk through the napkin, alternately shouting and then looking around to make sure nobody heard. Finally, he took the napkin off the phone, shouted one last thing into it. He turned the phone off and threw it into a trash barrel and walked back to his partner.

"Huh," said Marci for the third time. She took out a little notebook and wrote something down. She pulled out her own cell phone and pointed it at me.

"My niece showed me how to do this." She pressed a button and a flash went off. Everyone in the bar turned toward us. The manager came over.

"Don't do that again," he said. "People don't like pictures in here. Might catch the wrong people in the wrong poses in the background, if you know what I mean."

"I know," said Marci. "I'm just trying to figure this thing out and make a call." Manager gave her a look to let her know she was now officially on bar probation, one more cute thing out of her and she'd be out. But he went back to his end, and she turned to me and whispered.

"There. Think I've got it so it won't flash." She pointed it at the ground and pushed a button. "OK." She looked up at me. "Think I'm going to the dance floor."

"I don't dance," I said. "Parts of me try, but it's not pretty."

"Then I'm still going to the dance floor."

I stood and watched her on the floor, gyrating to her own beat. She didn't dance either, but she didn't know it. Every few beats she'd strike a pose with the phone held at her side or behind her back, and snap a picture, hopefully of the two bozos.

I watched Dread harassing a busboy trying to clean up a mess they'd made. The busboy was a young Hispanic, trying to get his job done and scurry out of the way without any trouble, but Dread and the little guy were having none of it. They were yelling things at the busboy, trying to shame him because the busboy's family came here by choice, taking risks to sneak into a country they loved and wanted to be a part of. This was unlike Dread and the little guy's own families, who had probably arrived kicking and screaming as convicts or slaves, the way God wanted true Americans to start out.

I had an idea. I turned to the manager and said, "Tell her I'll see her for coffee tomorrow" and headed out the door.

CHAPTER 9

Mayor looked up when I ran back into the Western World. So did one of the two patrons in the bar.

"Hey, Klaus, that's the guy," the one I knew as Rooster said to the other patron. "The comedian I was telling you about. Comes out of the back room dressed like this character or that, goes into some rant or the other. Can't understand what he's talking about, but he's funny as hell."

"You told me the girl danced, too." Klaus was as old as Rooster, both of them with white hair sticking up in tufts like two spring dandelions planted at the bar.

"Does. Only dances when she gets a snoot full of coke, needs money for more."

The skinny girl was behind the bar with Mayor. "Told you. I don't do that no more."

"What? Coke? Nobody quits that stuff. You'll be back."

"I'm a waitress now."

Rooster looked at her like she was a bug. "Yeah, no customers in here now. Can't be no waitress with no customers."

Mayor leaned over the bar. "She's a waitress, now. Don't care what she used to be. Just like you used to be a customer. Now you're just a barfly. You want to go back to being a customer, or you want I should shoo you out the door so she can go back to waiting on the customers we don't got, which are still more important than the two we do got?"

Rooster looked back at his beer. Klaus laughed. "Showed

you, asshole. Maybe the entertainment's not so bad in here after all."

I shook my head and kept going. I ran into the back room and opened the old surplus trunk that was the only furniture in the room besides the cot, unless you counted the mop and bucket. Rummaged through the trunk in a hurry. A white silk shirt, some kind of security guard uniform, and an old dashiki hit the cot until I found what I needed. I changed into a torn pair of jeans and a clean white t-shirt, pulled on a black wig, longish hair for a guy or shortish for a girl. I thought a minute and added a fake mustache, black and droopy, and ran back out.

Rooster laughed. "That's what I'm talking about. That's one of his characters he does. Kind of like the old José Jiménez bit, only this guy calls himself Pablo Neruda, reads these effing poems about nothing. I remember once he read this one about an onion with breasts. Laughed my ass off. The whole idea was that a real poet was writing a poem just about an effing onion. Stupid wetback poet. This guy never cracks a smile, just recites it like it's the greatest thing on earth and he wishes he could make you see it. C'mon, do one now."

Mayor looked at me, his cynicism coming back strong, sure I was drunk and back to my old self. But I just waved at him and ran out like I had a purpose and everything.

I made my way to the side entrance of General Lee's and waited. After a few minutes, the door opened and a barback came out to stack a case of empties in the alley. I ducked in while the door was open.

I found a broom and a dustpan and started rearranging the dirt in one corner of the club. Kept my head down but glanced up through the wig. Marci was still over at the quiet end of the bar, the manager ignoring her and working on some papers. After a few minutes, she looked at her watch, drained her beer, and left.

Good. I didn't think she'd recognized me, but you never can tell. The two bozos were standing over a tall bar table now trying to have a conversation, but their conversation was little more than random shouts in each other's ears whenever the music paused. I worked my way over to them, randomly sweeping under a table here and there and keeping my head down.

The table next to the bozos was empty for the moment while its occupants were on the dance floor. I paused there and worked hard at getting the floor clean, listening to the bozos.

"All I'm saying is phones don't grow on trees," said Dread.

The skinny white guy pointed at his head, said something I couldn't hear.

"Ain't smart," said Dread. "Dumb. Now we got to pick up another phone at Seven-Eleven, deal with that shitty clerk don't like us. Should have kept the phone. They already got the number."

"Yeah," said the skinny white guy. I decided to call him "Mouse" until I knew a better name, because the guy reminded me of a little gray mouse: sneaky, dirty, and antsy. "And if they trace it, they find it in a trash can in a bar. Or maybe riding a garbage truck downtown. Besides, we got to stop at the Seven-Eleven anyway, get some food for the girl."

"She ain't going to like that Seven-Eleven crap. Got to be expensive for her, with a big label that says, 'No animals were harmed in the making of this meal.' "

"Yeah," said Mouse. "She gets pissed and walks out then this whole thing falls apart."

That was more than Dread could hear over the noise. He shook his head at Mouse to let him know he didn't follow a word he said and that it was all Mouse's fault. They tried to yell something else back and forth but Charlie Daniels and the Devil were fiddling full bore and their words couldn't get through. Mouse was getting impatient with Dread and the noise.

Finally he took a deep breath and yelled at the top of his lungs.

"Tomorrow, we tell them where to bring the ransom."

Unfortunately for Mouse, Charlie Daniels had come to the end of the song and the manager and the DJ were arguing about the next one, so he shouted his line into a silent bar. Didn't matter. The drunk crowd thought it was a joke, or didn't care. A couple of people yelled, "Hell, yeah." Somebody else yelled "That's what she said," and everybody that was three sheets to the wind laughed, which covered most of the place. Mouse turned red; Dread glared at Mouse.

Lyle Lovett came on informing everyone in the bar that they weren't from Texas, and I almost saluted the manager, knowing he'd won one. I decided to get tricky.

The crowd was coming back from the dance floor, laughing and stumbling by the two bozos. I put my head down and shuffled upstream against the crowd. When I got behind Dread, I hooked one very drunk woman's ankle with the broom. She went down, still laughing, and I fell with her. I grabbed Dread's backside to steady myself and put my hand in the back pocket of Dread's jeans looking for a wallet.

Good idea, but not good enough. The pocket was empty and the jeans were tight. My hand stuck as I went down, and I was left hanging in midair with one hand still stuck on Dread's ass. Dread pulled the hand out and kicked me away.

"Goddamn wetback fag. Go feel up your own kind."

The manager looked over at me and didn't recognize the new busboy. He looked at one of the bouncers for a minute. I tried to melt away into the crowd. Dread turned back to his drink, and the party rolled on.

I saw the other busboy, the one Dread had abused earlier. I worked my way over to him.

"Stay away from them. They're bad news," the busboy said in Spanish.

My Spanish is pretty good. "Everybody here like them?"

"No, man, most of the people here are good folks. Working folks, or rich people who want to feel like working folks. Most people here just want to laugh loud and work up a sweat. Those two, though, they look for trouble."

"Probably just want to get out of their trailer."

"Trailer? Man, no, the big guy, black guy, lives with his stepfather. You heard of the guy, John Clampett, all the time on TV, saying close the borders, America for white people only, South won the Civil War, all that shit. Funny how Dread worships him, always claims that he's John's son instead of stepson. Screwed up pair, both those Clampetts. Screwed up pair in here, too, Dread and that skinny white guy called Roscoe."

There. At least Mouse had a real name.

"Dread said he lived in a trailer earlier. If he's trying to impress someone, you'd think he'd brag about Daddy's place."

The busboy laughed. "Not if Daddy's home. No partying in the Clampett mansion if the old man's home. He keeps Dread on a pretty short leash. Who knows? Maybe he and Roscoe got a trailer someplace. Maybe they got a meth lab someplace out in the sticks."

I looked and saw that the bozos were gone, and I cursed myself. I'd meant to follow them out, but now I'd screwed up again. I wanted to crawl back to the Western World, put some money on the bar, and feel the warm oblivion of Mayor's liquor slide down my throat again. If I had any money. If I didn't have Russians with guns threatening me. Small matters.

The place was closing, and it was just me and the other workers. I went back to sweeping. The manager spotted me and came over.

"I know you?" he said.

"Cousin," I said with a heavy Spanish accent.

"Yeah, well, get your money from your cousin. I ain't hiring."

Chapter 10

This time, Marci was the one who'd had too much coffee. She was hunched over her laptop at the high table in the corner of the university coffee shop typing madly when I walked in Friday morning.

"Don't start." She didn't even look up. I stood there in front of her like a little boy, not sure whether to sit, stand, or run.

A cute young woman, not just someone with good features but someone trying too hard to be cute, came up and put her hand on my arm and smiled.

"I understand you're teaching the Kama Sutra this fall," she said.

"Ha!" said Marci, still not looking up.

"No," I said. "I mean, I guess that's Buddhist literature. No, it's not even that, it's Hindu. I mean—do you even know what the Kama Sutra is?"

"They said I'd like it." She gestured at the table of hipsters. The kids laughed, and she realized that she'd been played. She stood there like a cartoon character who's run off the cliff and is looking around trying to figure out where the ground went.

"Honey." Marci looked up. "This one doesn't even know how to give a good-night kiss, or even say a polite 'good night' before he disappears down his private wormhole. This one doesn't know the Kama Sutra from a kamikaze."

"I do too."

Marci raised an eyebrow at me, and the girl glared at me,

too, eager to find someone to blame.

"Here." Marci held up a tall paper coffee cup to the girl. "I'm almost done with this. Go dump it on that boy's head, the one with the Bob Dylan hair and the permanent scowl. It'll make you feel better, and he'll think you're flirting with him."

The girl took off with the cup and aimed for the boy. The boy laughed and jumped up and the scowl was gone now. They ran out the door like children playing tag.

"You can get me another one before you sit down and apologize," she said to me.

I schlepped over to the counter meekly and got two coffees, plain and black, and sat down. She kept typing.

"Is that a hate letter to me?"

"If it were, I'd be carving it on your back. I have excellent calligraphy with a knife"—she closed the laptop and looked me in the eye—"because I take my time. No, this is a book outline. Something's going on with that Russian girl, and I'm going to get a book out of it. Don't know if it's a girl-reporter-rescues-heiress book or a poor-little-rich-girl book, but I'm going to write it."

"You know it's going to be a poor-little-rich-girl book. Bored with Daddy, ran off for a couple of days with the bozos, be back when Daddy gives them some money. Everybody laughing. Except for the bozos, who will probably be targets on a skeet range."

Marci shrugged. "Maybe. Probably. Still a story. Besides, I can dream, can't I? This could be a real kidnapping. We could solve it. Book would be a best seller."

"God you're cold. She could be lying dead in an alley somewhere."

"She's not. Rich people don't lie dead in alleys. They hire someone to do that. You've seen what, a thousand murders on the TV news in the last year. How many were rich?"

I stirred my coffee, wondering if this was how a Buddhist literature professor would stir his coffee. Or a detective. I wasn't sure which I was today.

"None," I said. "A million bodies, none of them rich. Of course, keep the TV on for a while until the detective shows come on and you'll see a million more bodies, none of them poor."

"See? That's the point. People don't want to read about ordinary people. Even ordinary people don't want to read about ordinary people. That's why this will be a best seller. People already read any tabloid that has an article about Kiev Romanov. Put a picture on the cover of her in a bikini, say she's lost five pounds or, better, gained ten pounds while she was kidnapped, and you'll sell out."

I stirred my coffee a different way just to see how it worked. "So it's kind of like we've split everything into two worlds: a bullshit world where everything makes sense and crimes get solved in forty-four minutes and the world is run by clean-scrubbed faces who just want what's best for us, and then a real world that's so dreary and so beat-down that we have to spend all our time in the bullshit world just to pretend."

"You got it. That's how the rich keep people down, kind of like the circuses the Roman emperors threw to keep the masses from revolting."

"Yeah." I thought of Mother Romanov. She was a rich woman living in what looked like the bullshit world to everyone else. Right now, all she wanted was to protect her baby. I also thought of a woman living in the back of a busted Toyota on a back street close to the Western World, doing everything she could to keep herself and her two babies alive. They didn't seem that different right now. Or maybe they were. I wasn't sure, and my head hurt. I needed alcohol or caffeine or certainty and I didn't have enough of any of the three.

"So you gotta decide," said Marci. "You want to live in this crappy real world or break through into the bullshit world yourself. This book could be my ticket to the bullshit world and not having to worry about paying the rent anymore. I may have to get your purple beret back, go out into the street and throw it up in the air like Mary Tyler Moore with a big smile, have you stand on the corner and sing, 'You're going to make it after all.' "

"Sounds like me," I said.

"Yeah, what about you? You gonna find some phony-baloney way to break through to the bullshit world and be happy, or you going to stay stuck in this crappy real world?"

I thought about it. I found the right way to stir the coffee and looked up at her.

"Gonna stay drunk," I said.

She laughed. "Not me. Got my horse and I'm going to ride it into the sunset."

She picked up her coffee and blew on it. "And you can be my sidekick."

I wished I had brought the skinny girl's reading glasses. They hurt my head like everything else this morning but they would be good to hide behind now.

"Anyway," I said. "I found out where the two bozos live, and I got their names. I'm the real detective. You can be the sidekick."

Marci snorted. "Buddhist literature professor who's a detective on the side? Maybe on TV. You got some kind of quirky mental problem we can play off of for laughs, so the audience can make fun of somebody with a problem, but still think they're nice people because they watch his show?" That sounded good for a minute, but Marci didn't wait for an answer. "No, I'm the pro. You're the sidekick."

"John Clampett."

Marci looked at me across her coffee. "You mean the crazy

guy, acts like he's Robert E. Lee reincarnated? You have my attention. What's he got to do with this?"

"He's the stepdaddy of the guy you were in love with last night."

Marci looked at me and laughed. "You're serious?"

"Serious as grits and red-eye gravy."

"You don't know red-eye gravy."

"Do too. And I know that your boyfriend is Dread Clampett, stepson of John, and he lives with his stepfather."

Marci typed into her laptop. "So we got the celebrity daughter of a Russian mobster kidnapped by the black stepson of a right-wing nut?"

"Only we don't know that she's been kidnapped. Maybe there's something going on with the bozos—we don't even know that—but it doesn't exactly sound like the girl is tied up begging for her life."

"Details, details." She paused and looked up. "So you don't think this is a real kidnapping?"

I swirled my coffee, getting good at using coffee as a prop. "Doesn't sound like it. Think we got a rich girl who ran off for a few days to show Daddy she can. Maybe she's pulling some kind of scam on Daddy with these guys, maybe not. She'll sashay home soon enough, act like nothing's happened, the family and the publicity machine will kick into overdrive, and everybody'll be happy. If it can happen soon enough to keep me alive.

"Who knows? I got to go report to them in a little while. Maybe Kiev's gone home, they'll tell me to get lost. Maybe this is over."

"Bummer. No book that way. What if she's not home?"

"Then it's good for your book, but bad for me. If I don't report in, they'll come looking for me and they have long memories. If I do report in and don't have Kiev—which I don't—they may decide to use me for target practice, unless I can figure some reason they need to keep me alive."

Marci sat her coffee down and looked me in the eye. "I thought you were just a bullshit lit professor at the college." She stared at me and waited for me to answer. I didn't.

"I talked to the Literature and Religion departments," she said when she got tired of waiting. "Never heard of you."

"Very Zen."

"Very something."

"Look," I leaned over. It was time to change the subject. "I'm sorry about running out on you last night. I really was having a good time. Almost too good a time, when you decided to shoot a sex tape with Dread and me at the bar. But I had to get back in there by myself and find out what people knew. I've got some pressure on me to come up with something on this girl. Supposed to have something today."

"This book is starting to look more like a novel."

"Disguise my name when you write it."

"Do I know your name?"

"Good point."

Marci drummed her fingers on the wooden table top and glared.

"Josh," I said.

"You mean like," she was still glaring, "Josh for today, maybe something like Beefaroni tomorrow?"

I just sat there.

"So." Marci closed the laptop. "If you're not a professor and you're not a detective, you can still be a sidekick, Josh-for-today. Look what I got."

She reached into a plastic grocery bag and pulled out a cell phone. It still smelled of beer.

"Pulled this out of the trash can last night, after the skinny guy threw it away."

"Roscoe. I wanted to call him Mouse, but his real name is Roscoe."

Marci opened the laptop and glared at me while it powered up. She typed Roscoe's name into the laptop. "So I got a detective who's not really a detective chasing a guy calls himself Dread and a guy who's not Mouse. Whole lot of honesty going on here."

"Except I'm not chasing Dread, I'm chasing Miss Prima Donna."

"And we hope Dread will lead us to her."

"Only lead I've got."

"We've got."

I picked up the cell phone. "Maybe we can get a real name and address from this."

"Already tried. It's a throwaway."

I opened up the phone and played with it a minute, trying to look like a detective examining vital evidence.

"I've already been through it. Got a few numbers I'm checking out."

"I thought that was the kind of thing the sidekick did?"

"Well, the sidekick's usually smarter than the hero. We don't have that going for us."

I just nodded and stood up with my cup.

"No more for me," said Marci.

I went back to the coffeepot and poured another inch in the cup. I reached down and picked up one of the little environmentally friendly baggies used to hold carry-out muffins and brought it back to the table.

"Gonna use that to hide your real identity?" said Marci.

I took the cell phone and put it in the baggie and wrote a cryptic note with some numbers and yesterday's date on the edge of the bag. I looked at Marci and said, "Gonna use it to keep all my identities alive."

CHAPTER 11

I walked to the bank from the coffee shop. I stood in the lobby and looked around at the high ceilings, marble floors, and big columns with no apparent purpose but to get in your way. The message was clear: We are big, you are small. Be grateful that we will deal with you at all, *if* we will deal with you. Good to see that the banking crisis had humbled banks, made them grateful to the little guys who had bailed them out with their tax dollars. Of course, I hadn't actually paid any tax dollars in a long time. Still.

There was an icy blonde sitting at a big desk outside of Romanov's office.

"Mr. Romanov doesn't see anyone without an appointment," the receptionist or assistant or whatever said. She turned back to her magazine. I was sure from her attitude that it must be an important banking magazine, despite the pictures of celebrities on every page.

"Please give him this, and tell him it's Jo. No, tell him it's Josh."

She looked at the card. "It's his own business card. He's got lots of them. Don't think you can sell him one more of his own cards."

"Please."

"He don't like to be disturbed. Your ass, not mine." She stood up and walked to the door, the three steps requiring at least forty-seven separate actions from a body that was obviously complicated and clearly expensive, but still fun to watch. After a few seconds a man in a black silk suit with some kind of a shiny black shirt came out. The coat was long and flowed behind him like a cape. For a moment, I had an impression of a vampire floating down on me. He grabbed my arm and yanked me up in the air without any effort or emotion. I recognized him then as the laughing boy who shot the man at the Romanov compound.

"Told ya," said the charming young lady.

"Wait," I said. I reached down and picked up Mayor's battered old briefcase before being carried into Romanov's office.

The room was business-cold, with an expensive marble desk with nothing on it in the center. Bare walls except for a couple of pictures of Romanov with important people. An expensive black leather couch that looked like it had never been sat on.

"I got him, Uncle Sergei." He threw me down on the couch. Romanov glared at him.

"Had to look hard to find me," I said.

"Called the number on your employment application," said Romanov. "Nobody answers."

Which was true. Mayor could never be bothered to answer the phone. The only way the phone in the bar got answered was if I was sitting right there, waiting for a call back from some bogus job.

"Been out working for you."

Romanov stared at me for a long time. "This is Friday. You're supposed to have my niece."

I could feel myself starting to sweat. I wished I were back in the Western World, drunk and laughing with the old men. It took effort to stay cool and stay here in the moment in the bank.

"I don't have her, sir, but I'm making progress. I've identified two associates of Kiev's that she may have turned to when she ran away."

"You think she ran away? She's off on some kind of bullshit camping trip, laughing about how she's making her family worry?"

Romanov stood at his desk now, his control starting to fade. I heard the nephew shuffle and pull something out of a pocket.

"It's a possibility, sir. I hear Kiev wanted a simpler life. No offense, sir, but living with your family, with the press constantly hounding her, isn't very simple. It's also hard for me to believe that anyone would be foolish enough to kidnap a member of your family."

"You know nothing. You're no good to any of us." He nodded to the nephew. "Take him to the house. Get rid of him."

The nephew stood up and laughed. There was something in his hand, but I couldn't tell what it was out of the corner of my eye. I didn't want to look directly at whatever it was and give up what little control I had.

"Just so you know how stupid you are," said Romanov, "we got a call last night. Some punk says he has Kiev, will call back today and tell us how to get her back. You messed up. We got people to handle this now. Don't need you. Nobody needs you."

The nephew clamped a hand on my elbow. Romanov turned away.

"No, sir. I'm on the case."

"Not any more. You want to be fired? OK, you're fired, like the guy on TV with the big hair says. Yuri take you to house now. Call it your exit interview. Told you we don't like to be disappointed."

"I'm your best shot at getting her back. You said as much yourself."

"What you got that we don't?"

I thought as fast as I could. "You got to have Caller ID, everything else on that phone system you got at the house?"

"We got everything. So what? We got the whole call recorded, like everything comes in there. So what? Don't make you Travis McGee."

"What number did the call come from?"

Romanov looked at me. He said something to his son in Russian. The son took his hand off me and called someone on a cell phone.

I set the briefcase on Romanov's desk and took out the bag with the cell phone. I took out a napkin from the coffee shop and opened the bag carefully like I didn't want to get my fingerprints on anything, then took out the phone, turned it on, and found the screen with the phone's number. I turned it so both Romanov and I could see.

The phone display said 555-1489. The son called out, "Five five five, one four eight nine." Romanov reached for the phone, and I yanked it away.

"This goes to the lab."

"You have a lab?"

"I'm on my way there after I leave here. My techs will have fingerprints and IDs by the end of the day. If you take the phone and fire me, you've just got a phone. Keep me, let me keep the phone, and you'll have names."

Romanov thought about it. He reached into his pocket and peeled some bills off a roll.

"Don't just want names. I want Kiev. Look, there's more here than you know. This isn't just some missing girl, not even just some missing Romanov girl. More at stake here."

I should have kept quiet, but my head hurt from too little alcohol and too much caffeine.

"Yeah, got it. Big star, the publicity machine and the money machines miss her. Doesn't matter that she's Mother's little girl. You guys don't pay money out without a plan to get it back."

He looked at me. "Yeah, that's it." He stepped into me.

"Look, I give money because I'm generous. But I get things done with promises; people know if I say something, I make it happen. So know this: you're tied to Kiev now. We get her back tomorrow, you're free. Anything bad happens to her will happen to you." He paused to let that sink in. "Won't ask why or whose fault. You get the bill."

I took my time putting the phone back in its bag and the bag in the briefcase. Here I was, getting jammed up for the sake of money and power again, and not a damned thing I could do about it. I shoved the money from Romanov into a pocket and started to go. Romanov shook his head.

"Yuri will drive you," he said. I tried to think of a way out.

"I've got to take this to my lab, get them started on it ASAP."

"Yuri will drive you. Go to home, listen to ransom call."

It didn't seem like a request.

CHAPTER 12

"Why you no have car? All Americans have car." We were in Yuri's black Mercedes AMG sports car blasting along at ninety-five miles an hour through parking garage turns designed for fifteen. Heavy dark European techno-rock pounded louder than the engine. My head felt like it was made of plastic, vibrating like a cartoon character in time with the heavy bass beat.

"Because I can't afford a car like this," I shouted.

Yuri nodded like he understood and smiled with pride. He hit the ramp to street level, flicked the wheel to the right and the car made a ninety-degree turn onto the street without slowing. Car horns honked as drivers hit the brakes to make room for the black shadow.

"Black," shouted Yuri. I turned the music down.

"Yeah, I can see. Black exterior, black interior, dark windows. Very stylish."

"No, I mean it's a Black series car. If you have a little money, you can buy a Mercedes SL65." I remembered the old Pontiac station wagon I bought the first time I had a little money, remembered the coat hanger I used to keep the door closed. "It's a nice car, but not so much power. You get to be a man, you buy a Mercedes SL65 AMG. Same car, but six-oh-one horsepower. Better. But for a real man, Mercedes build a special Black series, six-sixty-one horsepower, every performance feature known to man."

"I can see where you'd need the extra horsepower to merge

onto a freeway full of F-15s, stuff like that."

"But you can't afford a three-hundred-thousand-dollar car?"

"I couldn't afford the tickets."

Yuri laughed. Or sneered. It was hard to tell the difference.

"You are a little man," Yuri said, still looking ahead. It was hard to hear over the music and the engine, especially since Yuri liked to talk in a made-up voice that was somewhere between a growl and a whisper.

"Very little. Almost invisible," I said.

"Look outside. See how other cars appear, then disappear as we go by, like in video game. They live at one speed, we live at another. You care about tickets, little things from a little world.

"I live large; not like you. I am like a god, maybe an angel of death. Actually . . ." Yuri turned to face me. The car seemed to drive itself as people swerved to get out of its way. Yuri's voice grew even deeper and more raspy. "I'm Batman."

It was hard not to laugh, but I didn't. "You mean like Michael Keaton Batman, or like George Clooney? I didn't care too much for George Clooney as Batman."

"Michael Keaton. Greatest movie ever made, first *Batman*."

"Actually, Adam West was the first Batman. So you're kind of like Adam West?"

"You laugh. Bad thing to do. No, like Michael Keaton, but real. I swoop through the night dispensing justice. No one can touch me."

"So is Yuri Romanov like Bruce Wayne, and Batman is your secret identity?"

"Don't need secret. My family is too powerful for me to need to hide. I am too powerful. I am Batman."

I just sat still, lost in a memory. "I used to be Batman. Hell, maybe I was the Batman before you."

"Maybe you the Adam West Batman."

I smiled. "Maybe I was."

"So why you no Batman now?"

"The cape gets heavy," I said. I looked out the window and realized that Yuri was right. At this speed, the world did look like a video game, all the rough edges smeared by speed, the people turned into cute faceless props by the sheer energy of the car.

"Not for me," said Yuri.

I shrugged. "Well, Caped Crusader, we need to stop by the bus station so my lab guys can get started on this cell phone."

"Your lab in the bus station?"

"You'll see."

The Batmobile swooped to the curb in front of the bus station and stopped with a slight screech of the tires. Yuri and I got out. Yuri nodded to the traffic cop leaning on the "No Parking" sign in front of the black Black car. The cop started to say something to Yuri or give him a ticket. He looked at the car and decided that anyone who could afford that car had enough juice to cause him a hell of a lot of trouble. So he just tipped his hat and said, "Have a nice day." We walked into the station.

"See?" said Yuri. "I am Batman."

We walked over to the donut counter.

"Let me have a raspberry cream," I said, after the kid behind the counter stood up. "You want anything?" I said to Yuri.

"Yeah. Coffee."

"Let me guess. Black."

Yuri smiled.

I took the donut and Mayor's briefcase over to a row of lockers.

"Here, hold this." I held out the donut wrapped in waxed paper, and Yuri backed away like a vampire from a cross. I looked at Yuri's black clothes, then looked down at the powdered sugar on the donut.

"Oh yeah," I said. "Even Batman has laundry problems."

I sat the donut on top of the row of lockers and fed one of the lockers some quarters. I opened the briefcase and put the bakery bag with the cell phone inside and locked up.

"Very smart," said Yuri. "You put phone in locker; your lab guy takes out. You never see him, he never sees you."

"That's the idea. Tomorrow, I'll come back and pick it up, along with the report. Like I said, I like to be invisible."

"But you have the key."

"He has a master."

"How does he know when you have something for him?"

"He waits and watches. Right now. Something for you and the rest of the Bat family to keep in mind. Someone's always watching." I turned and looked Yuri in the eye and stepped into his space. "See, here's the deal. Batman stays safe by being one man, bigger than everybody else. I stay safe by being invisible. But not to my friends. You never know when I have a friend watching. Like now. Maybe at the bank, too. Maybe other places."

Yuri looked around. The station was filled with people coming and going, filled with people who seemed to be minding their own business. But you never knew. Yuri saw a guy slumped on a wall opposite them, sleeping off last night's celebration. He nodded toward him.

"Is your guy?" said Yuri.

"How would I know?" I said. "I've never met the guy. Or most of the guys."

Yuri thought about it for a minute.

"You joke with me. How would he know which locker? He can't stay here all day. He can't be sure which locker he's supposed to open."

"This." I took the donut off the locker, broke it in half and offered half to Yuri. He pulled back.

I dipped two fingers into the filling and spread raspberry

cream on the locker. I took a bite of the leftover half. It was good, and I made a mental note to get another one when I came back later to retrieve the phone. It was another scam, but maybe I'd bought a little respect from Yuri and a little protection from the Romanovs.

"Ah," said Yuri. He nodded with respect but then frowned.

"What if they come through and clean up your raspberry marker?"

I did a slow three-sixty, looking all around the station, and Yuri followed with me. Neither of us could see any sign that anything had ever been cleaned here. We looked at each other and both laughed. Yuri slapped his new friend on the back, and we glided out of the station, the Batman and the invisible detective.

CHAPTER 13

I looked at Yuri and remembered my last appearance as a hero. Remembered standing at attention under the lights of a game show years ago. The lights were so bright I couldn't see the audience, couldn't see anything but the glittering uniform I once wore proudly and the gorgeous blonde game show hostess in front of me. She smiled at me with the big smile that meant she had something for me after the show, backstage. Or—and this was even more amazing to me—she was smiling because I had something she wanted. I was the All-American boy then, the star of the moment. I stared into her eyes and saw it: her need to steal a piece of the fantasy world. Even though she had stepped right off the tabloid cover, out of what every reader thought was the fantasy world, she was still begging me now. Her eyes said, "My world's all sham and sadness and you just don't know. But you're the real deal, Smiling Jack with the medals to prove it. You're clean and you're good and you're real America and I'm just an immigrant from Hollywood. Let me touch you and hold it, hold the good and the pure from where the smiles are real."

I shuffled uneasily under the lights. I was always uneasy at these appearances, uneasy for a good reason. The audience took it for modesty, and they loved that about me, too.

I won my medals in an unpopular conflict that was one of those wars that seemed to pop up in the modern American psyche like a recurring nightmare: go in with flags flying and just enough supplies to get the job done fast. Wake up years later, and find that American children were still coming home in coffins with no end in sight and no reason to keep going. The country was caught up yet again in a sad debate between those who wanted to give up now, and those who wanted to stay just to avoid giving up.

I was a TV anchor when the war started. I was a golden boy even then: the youngest of the big news anchors, flashing the confident smile that told everyone they could trust me. When the bombs went off in my hometown, I felt called to do something more than read the news. I enlisted as a grunt and learned to do as I was told and keep my head down. When the shine wore off the uniform, I found I enjoyed the anonymity. No responsibility, no need to take a stand, just get up in the morning, make cynical jokes with your buds, and drink yourself to sleep at night.

"Josh?" The game-show girl touched my arm and squeezed it, her middle finger lingering and rubbing the inside of my elbow slowly. I had drifted away somewhere. It was something I did often.

"This man," she said, gazing up at me in awe for the cameras. "This wonderful specimen of American manhood." The crowd screamed, knowing she had just said that I was one of them, and that she wanted me and therefore them. "This man risked certain death to save his whole platoon and to defend a village of grateful . . ." The girl hesitated, not sure of the proper name for the people we had defended. "A village of grateful foreigners, saved by this great American."

The medal around my neck itched and burned, itched and burned like it had the day the President put it on me. I remembered looking at the President and wanting to ask him so many questions. But the President's eyes were misty and his voice cracked with the unspoken message that said, "See, this man gives us all meaning." I knew then that there were no answers anywhere, even at the White House. After the flashbulbs stopped popping and the President left, my handler, a big-time Hollywood agent hired by the Army, led me away, talking me through the schedule of speeches and appearances for the rest of the day and just laughing when I said I needed a drink. Laughing, but making sure a shaker of margaritas was waiting in the car.

Now the game-show girl turned to me with her million-megawatt smile focused on me and me alone. Of course, she kept her good side to the camera and the audience.

"Now, Captain Josh." She used the nickname the country knew me by. "Now you've won another battle. Over the last three nights, this country has watched you answer every question right." She didn't mention that the answers were flashing on the monitor at my feet. Wouldn't have been heard if she did: the crowd was on their feet cheering and wouldn't stop.

I tried to focus but the noise and the hot searing lights reminded me of the day I won the medal. I remembered walking through the hot sun of another village, just show the flag, come home, and get drunk again. Another day to make the world safe for democracy.

Then there was the pop-pop that always sounded small and fake and far away. But my buddy's neck was spurting red and another man had a small, neat hole in his head, right where his helmet would have been if the man had been wearing his helmet.

We all dropped. The lieutenant fired wildly in the direction of the shots and screamed as he fired. Village bodies dropped as he fired at faceless people that could have fired the shots, may have fired the shots. Then we were all firing and screaming, firing in every direction and more bodies falling.

Our guns were suddenly empty and silent. One by one, we could hear the cries of the dying. I stood up, careful and dazed.

"What have we done?" I asked but no one knew the answer. There was an old man sitting on the ground right in front of us, miraculously unhurt. But unimpressed, too. His face was just tired. He didn't care anymore who won or lost, or who lived or died. All he wanted was a dollar to buy food the next day. Because the world was too great and proud to give the man a dollar, it gave him a war. He would accept that, too.

I looked past the old man. A barrel of an AK-47 was waving loosely in my direction from behind a wall. I pointed my rifle at the AK-47, then realized I was out of bullets. Bluffing, I ran toward the wall.

There was a kid behind the wall. A scared kid gripping the rifle like he'd seen everyone else do. The kid pulled the trigger and a single shot went off harmlessly in the air, the sound echoing through the quiet while the kid grinned.

I ripped the AK-47 from the kid, broke the magazine off, and shook the rifle as hard as I could. The kid looked down. For the first time, he saw his mother's body lying in the dirt, dead from a chain of events that had started from his own silly action and then blossomed to an awful fruition by the faceless men in uniform around him. The kid stood in the dusty field and looked down and knew that the best thing he had ever known was gone. The kid looked up at me. I looked into the kid's eyes and saw that, next time, his shots wouldn't be accidents. He would strike back, and the cycle would be repeated forever.

The lieutenant was on his feet now. He looked around.

"Collateral damage. No one can ever know about this," he said. A Humvee with embedded reporters was coming up now. "We need a story." He looked at me with the smoking AK still in my hands. "We need a hero."

★ ★ ★ ★ ★

The game-show girl turned back to the crowd, waiting for them like a teacher waiting for a bunch of children to get quiet before she would give them their candy. When they quieted a little, she turned back to me. I tried to smile but my mind wasn't there anymore.

"You've answered almost every question. But we have one more question, the hardest question of all. Answer this question right, and a grateful nation will proudly salute its newest millionaire. Before I give you the question, I have to ask you one thing." She held up her hand for the audience to be quiet, but it did no good. They were on their feet screaming, and nothing would sate them now except raw meat.

"DO—" she screamed and the audience screamed.

"YOU—" I saw a woman crying in the front row.

"WANT—" the game-show girl dragged the word out like a carnival barker.

"TO—"

"BE—"

"A—" the girl paused and I saw a sea of faces red and screaming, demanding that I give them what they wanted, what they all wanted.

"MILLIONAIRE?"

The answer to the final question was flashing at my feet. All I had to do was smile and play the game. But that answer was their answer and not mine. They weren't offering anything; they were buying. For the first time in a long time, my answer was as clear and hot as the lights were now and the sun had been in the war.

"No," I said. I walked off the stage—a suddenly silent stage in a suddenly silent studio—and out a side door. The next day, I woke up in the back room of the Western World wearing a pair of old gray coveralls with my head shaved. Mayor was shoving a mop at me.

"You're going to work your ass off until you pay your bill," he said.

CHAPTER 14

Yuri pulled the Black SL65 up in front of Mother Romanov's house. Two of Yuri's brothers flew out the door of the house as Yuri and I tried to go in.

"You don't want to go in there," one of them said to Yuri. We stepped into a living room the size of a cathedral and decorated with the same restraint. A young blonde girl wearing a black bikini bottom and clutching a towel to her breasts ran across the room to a staircase.

"I'm wearing black," she yelled back over her shoulder. "I'm showing respect."

Mother Romanov rolled into the room like a tank into Red Square. "Put some clothes on. I'm tired of looking at my children's store-bought ta-tas." She chased the girl to the stairs and yelled after her. "And no black. Your cousin is not dead."

A couple of the boys stuck their heads through the door.

"You!" she yelled at them. "Go find her. Now."

"But Mother—"

"Now."

She turned on Yuri and me. Yuri threw up his hands. "Hey, I always wear black."

Mother waved him away.

"Josh!" She grabbed me and hugged me hard and cried.

"You alone I can trust. You must save my baby."

I was seeing stars from lack of oxygen before she released me. Funny, I thought, feels kind of like being drunk. I tried to hug her back to maintain the high, but she was ready to talk now.

"These spoiled children with their guns and toys will never find my baby. I have hope for you alone. You have heard, they have called and want to sell us our girl?"

"I know that, Mother. I have been working. We have the phone they used to call you. We are getting closer."

Mother's eyes grew wide with hope. "Better than the men who claim to work for Sergei and my husband, Rudi. They strut, they go outside and fire their guns and brag about what they will do when they catch these men. But they too lazy and too gun-proud to do any real work. Even now, while kidnappers demand money for Kiev, Rudi—my husband, Kiev's own father—he yell, we no pay, we find them, pay them with bullets. Sergei little smarter, he at bank getting money, he say, give them money, get Kiev, *then* kill them. He hire you. You find Evie."

"That's what they hired me for." I was still steamed at Sergei Romanov's comment that this was more than just a mother with a missing daughter, pissed that they had jammed me up for some bullshit business thing and I was ready to walk away.

She led me into the kitchen. A young Hispanic woman bent over the stove, cooking something that smelled sweet and spicy. Two men sat by the phone. They were older than the Romanov children but younger than the parents. The men looked up and showed no expression.

"So," said Mother Romanov to them, "you welcome our guest, no? Maybe he do your work for you if you be nice to him. Maybe Rudi let you live if he get Kiev back all right."

Both men rose slowly, like they'd been doing one pointless thing after another all day. The first guy was all flash: too-expensive gray leather jacket and a too-fake scowl. The second guy could have been a CPA: dark gray suit that was nice but not intimidating, white shirt, and narrow tie. A CPA, except that he moved with the grace of a big cat and had a big cat's bored expression that said he was deciding whether to eat you or save you for later.

"Vodka?" he said. He poured a big tumbler full from a bottle on the counter and shoved it at me.

High-quality vodka looked good, but I recognized the gesture as a challenge disguised as a friendly offer: drink enough vodka to knock out a pro wrestler, and we'll treat you like a man. I couldn't remember anymore what good vodka tasted like, but knew how good it would feel.

I looked hard at the vodka but said, "No, I'm here for work."

The thug in the leather jacket snorted. The pro, the one who looked like a CPA, left the glass on the counter. He went over to the table with the phone and sat back down.

"See?" said Mother, "He doesn't stay drunk when he works for me." She turned to the Hispanic woman. "Bring him Russian tea. Me too." She led me out onto the patio. The pool was empty. Today, there were no hilarious boyish games of shooting fake pigeons and real people. We sat down at a table. The Hispanic woman brought two tall clear glasses of hot tea. I took a sip politely. The tea was so strong and so sweet I wasn't sure I shouldn't just have taken the vodka.

"You heard?" she said. "They called and wanted money. They said they would call back today and tell us what to do. Sergei called, said you had something, but I thought you had something small. If you know the kidnappers, Rudi's men can persuade them. Rudi's men are not good at many things, but they are good at persuasion. If you know the men, Kiev can be home tonight."

I held up my hands. "I don't. I have the phone, and a little more. My lab is trying to trace the phone back to its owner."

Mother's face fell. "I can't believe anyone would try to steal anything from us, much less something as precious as my daughter. You saw how Rudi's family deals with anyone who disappoints them."

I nodded and thought, that's why I need to keep something in reserve. If I give them the names of the two bozos, they'll crash in, kill them, and probably kill the girl. And then kill me.

"It may not be a pro," I said. "Maybe just a couple of small-time guys who don't know much about Kiev's family and thought they'd pick up some easy cash. Kind of like a guy who tries to rob your husband of pocket change only to realize that he'd made a mistake when he sees himself surrounded by a bunch of your boys."

"That would be a mistake."

"So is this. But the good news, Mother, is that if they've made one mistake, they will make more. Maybe they made a mistake when they called you. Did you take the call?"

"Yes. They said they needed to speak to Kiev's mother and I thought, oh no, she's in trouble with the police again."

"Do you remember anything about it? Anything at all?"

"Better. We have top-notch security here, or so they say." She waved her hand like swatting away a fly. "All phone calls on the house lines are recorded to protect us and to show police that we do nothing illegal." She paused. "On the house phones, at least. But you can listen to the call yourself. Come."

She stood up and started for the house. I touched her arm to stop her for a minute.

"One more thing, Mother. I'm sorry to ask it, but I wouldn't be doing my job if I didn't ask it."

"So ask."

"I don't know Kiev. Is there any chance that Kiev was not kidnapped, but that she may be doing this with some friends? Just kind of a joke?"

The muscles in Mother's jaw tightened. She muttered

something that I did not understand and marched off toward the house. She turned and looked back.

"Kiev is not just my baby. She is the one my heart go out to. This is a powerful family: we strut, we demand attention. But it's pretty easy to be a Romanov. The world caters to you in every way.

"Every way except one: you can't be yourself. I'm the Romanov Mother, now that Rudi's mother is dead and Sergei's wife has gone back to Russia. Sergei and Rudi are the loyal sons, Father Andre is like some Greek god far away.

"So it's like being an actor all the time, or maybe like being in a fancy cage, you know? For all of us except Kiev. Even when she's getting in trouble, and I'm mad at her for the trouble, part of me want to say, 'Do more. Make us all mad.'

"I think she's crazy some, my Kiev, but she's trying to break out and be herself and not just play some half-assed role that the world gives her, you know?"

I did know, and I knew the price you paid for trying to break out and I knew that sometimes you just wound up in the back room of a bar. But I knew.

"So yes," said Mother. "Yes, Kiev could have done this. And Kiev could have got herself into more trouble this time than she can get out of."

She reached over and touched my cheek. "Maybe you understand Kiev some. Maybe you make up your own role, sometimes pretend to be what you are not." I started to protest, but she held up her hand and said something in Russian. I didn't respond. "I knew you weren't Russian. I think you not even sure yourself who you are, but you know who you don't want to be. Like Kiev. You brother and sister, make me your Mother, yes? Now you go find your sister."

She turned and I followed her into the kitchen.

"You," she said to the pro in the gray suit. "Go play phone call for Josh. He solve crime."

The pro stood up and assumed I would follow him. Yuri drained the last of my vodka glass. Yuri and I followed the pro to the end of the kitchen through a door that could have been a pantry but led to a stairway heading down. At the bottom was a room that looked like a rec room with one guy in it watching TV. The guy looked up at the pro and Yuri and nodded. He reached into his pocket and pressed a fob about the size of a car remote control and a hidden door at the end of the room opened. As we walked through the door, I noticed a small video camera over the door. I looked back and saw the guy in the room walk over to the computer without taking his eyes off of us until the door closed behind us with a quiet whoosh.

CHAPTER 15

We walked into what could have the reception room of a large, tasteful law firm. The room was small but expensive, with a single desk, very modern, and a young girl, also very modern, with hair like platinum parenthesis marks and pale white makeup. She smiled up at us from behind a clean desk of pale wood.

"Good morning, Mr. Branch, Mr. Romanov."

Yuri smiled but the pro, the one she'd called Branch, just walked by the girl.

"Tell Jackson we're coming to see him," he said without looking at her.

At our backs we heard, "Yes, sir."

We walked into a long hall with private offices on one side and bays full of people in cubicles on the other.

"How big is this?" I said.

"You don't need to know," said Branch.

"What do all these people do?"

"You don't need to know."

Most of the rooms had small discrete signs with numbers, names, and job titles. As we walked, I read a few even though I was sure I didn't need to know:

310
J. Karamov
Accounting

312
M. Ackerman
Federal Accounting

332
J. Randov
Home Operations

333
J. Whitefish
U.S. Operations

We came to an office with the door closed and just the number, 415, on the door. Branch opened the door, and we went into a big dark bay with video screens on all the walls and men in gray working at computers. It looked like a dozen command centers I had seen years ago: square-jawed men in uniforms striding around purposefully and talking tough to hide the fact that it was all a show.

A tall black man met us at the door.

"Jackson," said Branch.

Jackson nodded back. He was wearing gray like the others, but while the rest of the men in the room had gray cargo pants and gray t-shirts, he had on gray dress pants and a gray cashmere turtleneck and jacket.

"Romanov wants this guy to hear the ransom call," said Branch.

"What's his interest?"

"Romanov wants this guy to hear the ransom call."

Jackson shrugged and motioned us into a private office off to the side of the bay.

"You guys want something to drink?" said Jackson. Branch shook his head. Yuri said vodka and then changed that to orange juice. Jackson said to me, "How about you, new guy? Vodka?"

"Diet Coke."

Jackson said to a guy standing beside him, "Yeah, get me a Diet Coke, too."

Yuri and I went in the door; Jackson and Branch hung back outside. They came in a few seconds later.

"What's your name?" said Jackson.

"Josh."

"Josh Whoever?"

"Good enough for me."

Jackson scowled. "What's your last name?"

"You don't need to know that."

Jackson scowled some more. Branch shrugged at Jackson. "Romanov," was all Branch said. Jackson still wasn't happy, but he turned to the man at the console in the office and said, "Bring up the ransom call, but hold it till I get back." Jackson left.

"He's not happy with you," Yuri said to me. Yuri's eyes were a little bloodshot, and his voice was a little giggly.

"Nobody is," I said. I turned to Branch. "What's that guy do?"

"He's in charge of security."

"Security for the Romanovs?"

"Just security."

Jackson came back in, followed by a guy with a tray of drinks in clear glasses. Jackson took his and drained it in one swallow. Yuri did the same. I shrugged and followed suit. Everybody turned to the screen.

"Play it," said Jackson.

I felt the need to get tricky, partly because I didn't trust things here and partly just to see if I could get away with it. I took my fingernails and pushed Jackson's glass to one side, to the empty spot waiting for my glass, and set my own glass down where Jackson's had been. I turned back to the screen.

The big screen went blank and we could hear a phone ringing.

"Hello," said a polite female voice. I looked back. The guy who brought the drinks put some kind of a clear plastic cover over Jackson's glass, the one he thought was my glass. I smiled.

There was loud music in the background on the tape. Charlie Daniels was playing the fiddle, and a man screamed hello in a muffled voice. I wasn't sure about the voice, but the music sounded like General Lee's.

"Hello," said the female voice again.

"Yeah." You could hear the caller better now; this must have been when he moved to the quiet corner. "I need to speak to Mrs. Romanov." The voice was muffled and muddy now; he must have the napkin over it.

"Mrs. Romanov cannot come to the phone right now. May I take a message?"

"Yes. No. Tell her this is about her daughter. Tell her this is important."

The screen glowed with some kind of squiggly-line chart of the voices, as well as a printout in the bottom as the security system logged the call.

"Just a minute."

Charlie Daniels played on. The voice I assumed was Roscoe's muttered to itself.

I heard Mother Romanov pick up the phone.

"Hello? You tell Kiev she can get herself out of trouble this time. No lawyers. No money. No nothing—"

"Lady, I'm not the police. We have—"

"I don't care what you have. She is not our problem. She is twenty-three, old enough—"

"Lady, your daughter is in trouble."

"I no care."

And now there were a few seconds where they both just talked at each other without anyone trying to listen. Finally, we heard Roscoe screaming clearly.

"Lady, your daughter has been kidnapped. I have kidnapped your daughter."

There was silence for a few seconds, Mother stunned and Roscoe probably looking around the bar frantically.

"Kidnapped?" said Mother.

"Yes, kidnapped. We're dangerous people, so listen."

"You can't kidnap my baby. You know who her father is?"

"A guy with a lot of money. He's going to give some of it to me."

"You no know who my husband is, else you not do this."

"Well, I did it. Listen to me now. Tell your husband to get one million dollars. No, make that three million, one for each of us. Have it ready. I'll call tomorrow and tell you what to do. No cops."

"Cops? You no know my husband."

"No cops or your daughter dies."

"You no know my husband."

There was a click and the line went dead. The technician looked up at me. "You want to hear it again?"

"No," I said. "I got it."

A guy in gray stuck his head in the door and waited until he caught Jackson's eye.

Jackson nodded to him, turned to me, and said, "Good. Now I want to hear some things from you when I get back. Excuse me."

Jackson went to the doorway with his back to us in the small room. I eased back enough so I could hear.

"What do you mean, blocked?" said Jackson. He was irritated.

"Just what I said. I ran the prints from that guy Josh's glass like you told me. It comes up 'access blocked' like it would for one of us or a CIA guy or some other kind of dark federal op. I'm telling you, this guy's somebody."

Jackson's voice went down to a growl. It was too quiet to tell what he was saying, but loud enough to know Jackson didn't like what he was hearing. Finally, he dismissed the guy with a gesture. When the guy turned to go, Jackson said, "Hey" and turned the guy back around with that single word. The guy stood there, irritated but dutiful, doing his job and showing he knew his place. Jackson said two words: "Get more."

Jackson came back into the small room and said quietly, so that everyone had to strain to hear, "We've got to go upstairs. Romanov's here; wants to see the new guy."

Branch said, "Which Romanov?"

"Both of the sons. Let's go."

Jackson leaned to Branch. "Why are we taking crap from the Romanovs on this?"

"Word from the top. This is personal. Don't push the Romanovs on this one."

Jackson led the way out. As we approached the door out of the security bay, he grabbed me by the arm and pointed at a small box above the door.

"Look up there."

I looked up. "I'd have smiled if you told me you wanted my picture."

"I don't have to tell you anything."

We went back up through the kitchen and out into the formal living room. Sergei Romanov was sitting on a big couch, red satin with gold embroidery. Across from him another guy I didn't know sat on an identical couch. Both of them had assistants next to them. The room was full of sons and flunkies and hangers-on. But between the two couches sat a single chair, set up a little higher, with arms of gold and a tall headboard. That chair was empty. Sergei gestured to a small couch next to' his and said, "Sit down, Josh."

A couple of boys got up from the couch and I sat down.

"Rudi, this is the guy I told you about," said Sergei to the man at the other couch. "Freelancer, sort of. I brought him in to give us another set of eyes. He got the phone the guys called from yesterday."

Jackson was trying to look calm, but his body language looked like a man ready for a fight.

"Josh, you heard the call, right?" said Sergei.

"Yeah."

"And you got the cell phone the call came from, right?"

"Yeah."

Jackson stood up even straighter.

"You've got the phone?" he said.

"Yeah."

"Where?"

"My lab."

"I want that phone, here, now. You're wasting time, time that might be critical to this man's daughter's life."

Rudi nodded.

"You're right, we're wasting time," I said, and turned to Sergei. "That's what guys in these big organizations do: waste time, and justify it with big brochures and uniforms and letterheads and everything. When this is all over, they'll produce an after-action report, maybe even a cool multimedia presentation; explain why nothing was their fault. It's what big marching organizations do."

I turned to the Romanov boys in the room.

"You guys, of course, are the other side of the coin. You want to go in shooting and prove how tough you are. At the end of the day, you'll feel really cool, kind of like a Russian Justice League of America, till one of you looks down and says, 'Oh, gee, we shot Sis.' "

I looked at Rudi. "You want Kiev back, I'm your best shot. Not family, not the gray shirts. I know what I'm doing."

There it was. First time in years I'd heard myself say that. I wondered where that came from. Wondered if I could take it back.

Sergei looked at me and back to Rudi.

"You work together. Get Kiev back. What else you both know?"

Jackson gave his report. It was crisp. It was professional. It didn't say anything useful other than the fact that they had traced the cell phone number back to a disposable phone bought in a convenience store. The clerk who sold the phone was in the hospital recovering from questioning, but he had nothing to tell them.

Sergei turned to me, and I shrugged.

"We asked around. Somebody heard somebody yelling into a phone in a bar and then the yeller threw the phone away. We picked it up. We got lucky. We're working on a few other things. I'll let you know.

"But I got to tell you, you're missing the important thing here. Listen to the phone call again. Guy thinks he's being smart, calling from a bar. Finds out it's too noisy to talk, mistake one. Middle of it all, he changes his demand, mistake two. Says there are three of them, although you can't rely on that.

"These aren't pros. These are kids, bozos. Everything this guy," I gestured at Jackson, "is doing will never find them. All the searches of Romanov enemies, all the analysis of government databases ain't going to find these guys."

Jackson glared. "We want the name of the bar, and the name of the guy who supposedly tipped you."

"Why? So you can roll up in a line of black Hummers, bust the place up, rough up the staff? All that'll do is scare away anybody who can help us. We got feelers out. If anybody saw anything useful, we'll know it. We'll know it, as long as you don't break it all apart."

Sergei said to Jackson, "Do it his way. He's the only one here making sense." He turned back to me. "But you stay here and work with Jackson."

Yuri said, "He stay here. I make sure."

The phone rang, and everyone froze. Jackson said, "We let it ring three times; give us as much time as we can get." Jackson got up and stood by the phone. "The rest of you go to the media room and listen." Everyone else broke for a door at the end of the living room. I stared at Jackson for a second and then followed.

The media room was a small theater with red velvet seats and a small stage at the front of the room. I walked into the room just in time to hear Jackson's voice coming through the speakers. "Romanov residence," he said.

"Get the old lady," a voice replied. It was muffled, but it was Roscoe.

"We have no old ladies."

"Don't get smart. Either she's waiting for me, or this call is over. You got one minute."

There was a long pause followed by Mother's voice. "Yes?"

"Do you know who I am?"

"Yes."

"Have you called the police?"

"Of course not."

"Then listen: you want to see Kiev, do this. Come to the Aquatic Park tomorrow noon at the Ghirardelli building. Wear a red dress and carry the money in two Target shopping bags. Sit down in the little amphitheater and eat your lunch. We'll take the money, and you'll have your Evie."

"No, wait. I need to talk to Kiev."

"Tomorrow." We heard the tone as the line went dead.

"I want a copy of that," I said.

"You can listen to it here." Jackson had come in and stood behind me.

"No. I want my people to have a copy."

Sergei nodded. They all started to talk at once. I went out to the kitchen.

"Mother?" I said. Mother was still standing with the phone in her hand, like a mom who can't turn loose of their child's hand on the first day of school. I took the phone and hung it up.

"Could we have two cups of tea?" I said to the Hispanic woman. She nodded.

I put my arm around Mother and led her out to the patio. Sat her down and pulled up a chair beside her.

"Mother, these men are not professionals. We will give them the money tomorrow, and we will have Kiev back." I prayed I was right, and not just because they would kill me if I were wrong.

"He called her 'Evie.' "

"He was just trying to be tough. Believe me Mother, these guys are not tough."

"No, he called her 'Evie.' Only I call her that. They know Kiev. They have Kiev."

The face that looked like a tank to me earlier had tears in it now.

"Mother," I took her hand. "We will get her back." I paused and was surprised when I heard myself say, "I will get her back."

She looked up at me and smiled when she believed it was true, and I hoped it was, too.

"You no stay here," she said, and the tank was back in her face again.

I nodded. "I need to go to work and not be trapped here with the gray shirts."

I looked back at the house. Yuri watched us from the kitchen. Over by the house, a gardener in brown coveralls trimmed a bush. "And I can't take Yuri with me." Mother nodded. We talked for a minute. I motioned the gardener over, and Mother talked to him. Mother went into the house, threw her arms around Yuri, and started crying hysterically.

Yuri was proud of himself. Drunk as he was, he was still able to comfort Mother and calm her down after a few minutes. He was a man, and he could hold his vodka and still be a good son.

Mother went back to the patio. Yuri watched her back and the back of my brown corduroy coat as the two figures finished their tea.

Yuri was feeling protective of Mother now. After a few minutes, he took two more hot teas out to the patio and sat them down on the table and smiled at Mother. The gardener sitting next to Mother, wearing my jacket, smiled back. Yuri stopped smiling.

I eased the landscaping pickup through the back gate and onto the road. It had been years since I had driven a car, and the brown gardener's uniform was a little too tight. My pulse beat fast in my neck. This matters. They can keep their goddamned money and threats, I thought, but Mother matters. This matters.

CHAPTER 16

I walked into the Western World, and Mayor shook his head at my dirty gardener clothes. The way kids dress today, Mayor's look seemed to say. I ignored him and went to the bar. Mayor took out the cheap bottle and my tumbler. He poured the tumbler half full and looked at me.

"Not today." I pushed the glass away. Still looked good, sitting there on the bar waiting for me, but I pushed it away.

Rooster was at the bar by himself. He was in drinking his breakfast.

"C'mon," Rooster said. "Mayor won't put anything but sports on this crummy TV of his. Gimme one of your stories. That's what you know how to do, stay drunk and tell stories."

I looked at Rooster and realized that this was the first time I had seen him sober. When I was sober, that is. Still hadn't seen Rooster sober.

"Once upon a time there were these three bears."

"C'mon, man, you're a barfly. What the hell you got to do but tell me stories?"

The glass looked good. "That's the hard part. Don't know what to do or how to do it."

Rooster laughed. "That's why you're here. The crappy world out there don't need us. Try to do something to help, you'll just screw it up and the world will kick you in the ass for trying."

"Maybe you're right. They've got armies and pros."

"Let them handle it. All you got is little stories. All I got is

. . . I forget. Give me one of your Josh stories. Funny things about what you wanted as a boy, fishing in the Gulf. Oh—I know—tell us one of those lies you used to tell about that Pat Leary girl."

I felt tired and useless and ashamed for promising Mother I would bring her daughter back to her when I had no idea how. "Sorry, Rooster, no stories in me today."

Rooster pointed at the glass. "The stories are in that glass. Drink it up. Pour the story into you, let it percolate like you was a coffeepot and the story will come back out. And I won't have to sit here and squint at this two-inch black-and-white excuse for a TV and try to figure out if I'm watching baseball or the Olympics."

I looked at the glass. Rooster was right. It was all in the glass. All the funny stories. The way I felt OK when everybody was smiling. Nobody to save, and nobody to run from. The only world that made sense to me was in the glass, waiting for me.

"There was that time Pat and I went crabbing for the first time." I smiled and put my hand on the glass, but the glass stayed on the bar.

"What I'm talking about," said Rooster.

"Thought you had a job," said Mayor. He waited to hear how I had screwed up this time.

"Yeah, I do. I guess. If I can do it. If I can live through it." I looked at the glass and looked at Mayor. "On the one hand, the smart thing may be just to stay here and lay low. Stay drunk. The Romanovs have their own private army to handle this. The kidnappers say they'll ransom the girl tomorrow. Maybe I just stay here, let it happen, and everything will be all right." I looked to Mayor for guidance.

Mayor just shrugged. Answers cost extra, and he wasn't handing out any for free.

"But that's the problem, too: the Romanov's have an army," I said. "Armies just screw things up and people get hurt. The Romanovs and their army have a lot of guns and a lot of itchy trigger fingers. If I don't do something, they'll just end up with a field of bodies, including Kiev's and probably mine, with Mother crying off to the side. Just like before."

Mayor leaned over. "What story is this?"

I shook him off. "Course it will all be accidental or incidental once the official report comes in and it turns into a heroic story. But we'll all still be dead."

"So find the girl and save her yourself," the skinny girl said without looking up from her book.

"Yeah. That's the plan. Course, that's about as far as I've got with the plan, and I need something more. Now, today, before the shooting starts tomorrow."

She looked at me over the top of her reading glasses. "Used to be, only thing I had was coke and tricks, and a guy who let me hang around a bar and another guy stayed drunk in the back. Now the drunk in the back is stumbling around trying to be a real live human being. He can do it; I can do it. Now I'm reading a book. Hurts my head. Don't understand all the words. But I'm reading a book with no pictures. And I'm going to read more."

"So I should read?"

She slammed the book closed and glared at me. "You should do what you're goddamned capable of doing. And that's a hell of a lot more than drinking this." She snatched the glass out of my hand and poured it down the sink behind the bar. Mayor yelled "Hey!" but she ignored him.

"You might be that girl's only chance. What if you're wrong and somebody's holding her out in the woods somewhere and she's crying and praying, 'Please just let me get out of this and I swear I'll be a better person?' What about that, Mister Smartass?"

Mayor and I exchanged looks.

"So this is Kiev Romanov, reality TV star we're talking about here?"

The skinny girl waved us both away.

"You got to do what you can do."

"And how do I do that?"

She shrugged. "Damned if I know." She held up the book and waved it in my face. "One page at a time, buddy. One god-damned page at a time."

We looked at each other a long time before the skinny girl put down the book and went back to reading.

"You're right," I said. I stood up from the bar stool. "I need to get to Kiev before they do. I made a promise to Mother. Ain't going to keep it standing here."

Mayor held up a hand.

"I got a place you need to start."

"Any place to start is better than I got now."

Mayor reached under the table and came up with an old grimy canvas purse with a big opening.

"You're in charge," he said to the skinny girl.

"I'm reading." She turned away so we couldn't see her face.

Mayor shrugged. "OK. Rooster, you're in charge till I get back. Stay out of the cash register."

Rooster threw up his hands. "Hey, I'm a customer."

"Think of it as a self-serve bar." Mayor came around the bar and jerked his head toward me. "Come on."

"Where we going?"

"Going to teach you how to be a detective." Mayor walked out the door.

CHAPTER 17

The guy at the shooting range off of Embarcadero Street looked up as Mayor walked in carrying an old purse, with me in a gardener's uniform a step behind. Sure, this was San Francisco and he had seen stranger things, but he kept his eye on Mayor as we walked up to the counter.

Mayor put the purse on the counter. He reached in and pulled out an old revolver, rusty and dirty, and waved it around. The guy behind the counter pushed the gun out of his face.

"Hope that thing's unloaded."

Mayor thought about that a minute. He broke the gun and dumped the bullets into the purse. Only five came out. Mayor reached over the counter and borrowed a pen, pried the last bullet out, and held the gun up so the guy could see it was unloaded. The guy looked at the filthy gun like it was a dead rat.

The guy said, "You need ammo?"

Mayor thought about it. "Yeah, I guess so."

The guy fished a box from a cabinet and sat it on the counter.

"The good kind," said Mayor.

The guy just stared at Mayor.

"But cheap," said Mayor.

The box still didn't move.

"Target?" the guy said.

"Naw, we don't want to shoot anyone. We just want this guy to practice."

The guy looked at Mayor without any expression and waved at a wall with posters of people with targets printed over their hearts. "I mean, what kind of target you want us to set up. We got Bin Laden, a wide array of politicians. Favorite one looks like a generic mother-in-law. For twenty-nine fifty, you can bring your own photo in and we can print a personalized target for you to fill full of holes."

Mayor hesitated. The guy said, "How about cheap?"

"Cheap is good," Mayor said. The guy gestured to a generic outline of a man with a target over the heart. A kid took it down from the wall and went to set it up. Mayor paid the guy. The guy handed us two sets of headsets to protect our ears and waved us to a booth.

The booth had a small counter. Beyond the counter was the range with grimacing cartoons of every kind of real and imagined bad guy known to man. A panel slid up from the floor with our target opposite us. It looked lost and ghostly among all the pictures of real people.

Mayor set the gun and the purse and the bullets on the counter. I looked at the first gun I'd seen since the Army and thought of all the small-arms training I'd had and didn't want to show now. Didn't want to remember it, for that matter. Stay in character here. Just be a doofus with a gun, and let Mayor straighten me out.

"So the bullets go in pointy-end first?" I asked.

Mayor pulled the big hearing protection headset off, motioned for me to do the same, and said, "What?"

"You put the bullets in pointy-end first?"

Mayor glared at me like I was an annoying kid pulling at his pants leg. Right now, Mayor regretted being a Good Samaritan.

"Yeah. We put these big earmuff things back on. I'll load and fire six rounds. We take the earmuffs off, you ask me questions, and then we'll let you fire six rounds. OK?"

"OK."

The range was sleek with stainless steel surfaces and efficient machines designed to project an air of competence and security and make every man at the range feel like a square-jawed James Bond. I looked around the range, distracted when I should have been paying attention to what Mayor was doing. There were a couple of guys in suits imagining they were blowing the boss's head off, and a couple of guys in jeans and military shirts shooting at targets of Arabic men. One guy looked back at me with a crazy look, scowled and clutched his gun box closer. I didn't want to know what he was shooting at.

Mayor tapped me on the shoulder and didn't need to say, "Pay attention, numb-nuts" because the look said it all. I smiled back and my look said, "I'm paying attention," like a little boy with a stern father. Mayor balanced a little unsteady with his feet apart and both hands on the gun. He looked kind of like the guys on TV, or more like a guy who learned to shoot by watching the guys on TV. Still, not too bad for someone with no training.

Mayor turned loose with six quick unsteady shots. Two of them hit the generic target. We took off our earmuffs.

"Is that good?" I said.

"Hit the target two out of six shots. Means I killed the guy twice. Good enough for me. Besides, this place is bigger than the bar."

"Might have hit a couple of customers."

"Got more customers."

I shrugged.

Mayor broke the gun and dumped the shell casings into a disposal box. He handed the gun to me and said, "You try it."

I looked at the gun a minute, then stood there clicking the cylinder in and out of the body of the gun a few times, like a kid with a toy. Mayor glared.

"I want to get back to the bar sometime today. Rooster's robbing me blind while I'm down here."

"Gonna shoot him with this?"

More glaring. I picked up a bullet, tried to load it backward and found out that, yes, they do go in pointy-end first. Loaded all six and snapped the cylinder into the body of the gun. Mayor motioned at the nearly pristine target.

I decided to try a couple of things. I turned sideways to the target and held the gun out at arm's length, looking cool like the punks on TV. But my hand was unsteady like that, and the gun waved all over the place. I held the gun down at my side, like I was Matt Dillon. Pulled it up fast and realized that the gun was pointing at the ceiling.

I looked at Mayor and realized it was time to get serious before Mayor took the gun away and beat me to death with it. I imitated Mayor, kind of like Mayor imitated every cop he'd ever seen on TV. Feet apart and holding the gun with two hands, I sighted down the barrel and pulled the trigger.

The earmuffs kept the sound out, but they didn't keep the explosion from traveling up my fingers and arms and leaving both of my arms tingling. The gun had kicked up like a frightened animal, and I found myself pointing back at the ceiling.

"Jesus." I wasn't sure if I said it or Mayor said it.

I lowered the gun and tried to squeeze my arms and hands tighter, force the gun to do what I wanted on the next shot. It kicked harder that way. I remembered my training and loosened up, used my arms as springs to absorb the shock. I was able to squeeze off the last four shots that way. One of them hit the target.

"Pretty good." I said, taking off the earmuffs.

"Good for the bad guy."

"Hey, you killed him twice. I killed him once. Once is good enough."

Mayor sighed. "Yeah. You killed him, long as he's one of those notorious killers who happens to have his heart in his shoulder, which is the only thing you hit."

"I don't know, Mayor. Don't think I need this thing. All Romanov's guys, they got like a whole arsenal. If I get to the point where I need a gun, I'm dead already. I got to get out of here and do something more than shoot paper dolls."

"Look, I'm trying to help you here. You're going to be a detective; you need to carry a gun. They got guns, you don't have a gun. You think that's fair?"

"No, guess not." I paused and looked around. "Doesn't seem like much of a reason to have a gun, just because all the other kids have guns. Look around here at all these posers playing Billy the Kid and Rambo. There are good reasons to own a gun; good reasons not. I look around here and I don't see a lot of those good reasons, for them or for me. What's the point?"

Mayor took the gun away. "Sometimes I think you're smarter when you're drunk."

Marci walked up.

"Now this is my idea of a date," she said.

I remembered calling her cell and asking her to meet us. I didn't remember saying anything about a date. Looking at her, I wished I had. She had on a thin pink top, and a denim skirt that looked about as wide as my hand. I didn't remember her legs being that long.

"What's this?" She picked up Mayor's gun.

"It's a revolver," said Mayor. "Be careful. You want to see what you can do with it?"

"With this?" She broke the cylinder, dumped the casings into the box. She pulled back like she was going to throw the gun at the target. Mayor stopped her.

"Hey, hey," he said.

"Only way this piece of crap will hurt anybody is to throw it at them," she said. She looked at it like it was a spider. "You ever clean this thing?"

"It's not for show."

She looked at him now like he was the spider. She motioned for us to put the earmuffs on.

"Let's see what I can do." She put Mayor's gun down on the counter. Mayor and I put our earmuffs on and looked at her.

Fast, she reached between her legs into the little skirt. A million thoughts went through my mind, but none of them were about the tiny automatic that came out in her hand. My eyes were still on her skirt when the last of the five shots echoed in the air.

The manager hustled over to warn us about the forty-seven rules we had just broken.

Mayor and I looked at the target, at the five neat holes in the chest. Mayor turned to Marci.

"She carries the gun."

CHAPTER 18

I set two coffees on the corner table at the coffee shop. Marci reached over and moved her cup to make room for her laptop.

"Still don't get why we had to go by the bus station to get the cell phone," she said.

"Look, they can't just think I'm one guy; they'd eat me alive. They gotta be worried that someone has my back, and they gotta believe I know something they don't know."

"So they think the dirty old bus station is your lab?"

"Yeah, sort of," I grinned at her. "Like you're my assistant. Kind of a matched set."

"We settled that. You're the assistant."

"Trust me, you find Kiev Romanov and return her to Mother, and you can have this job and all its fame and fortune, and I'll go back to the bar."

"Professor Nirvana works in a bar?"

"Yeah. More proof we're all pretenders. Any more, my strong suit is getting drunk and sobering up, and Mother Romanov expects a hell of a lot more. We don't get Kiev back and I may never get back to the bar."

"What do you mean? Poor little rich girl's run away from home. She'll be back when the credit cards run dry."

"I need to catch you up."

So I did. After I talked for a minute, Marci took out a notebook. After a couple of minutes, she opened her laptop and typed as fast as she could.

"Slow down," she said. "Let me get all that I can about these gray shirts. Give me as many names as you can remember from the office walls."

I rattled off what I could remember.

Marci talked without slowing her typing. "There was one story they wouldn't let me write, back when I was on the paper. It involved the Romanovs." She paused her typing and looked up at me. "There was always talk about how much the Romanovs got away with. Most people thought they had some kind of juice in the DA's office. I said something about that to one of the assistant DAs one day, and she almost took my head off. It looked like something bigger than the DA and the state of California was protecting them."

We talked until Marci thought she had it all down. She closed the laptop and looked up at me.

"Let me get this straight: Romanov thinks you're a detective because you worked in his bank, and Mother thinks you're going to save her daughter because you've convinced the whole damned family that their shadow army can't do it?"

I nodded.

"And you've got absolutely no idea how you're going to do it."

I nodded again.

"For a man who complains about bullshit, you're pretty good at it," she said. "You do know, if this doesn't work, you're dead."

"Yeah. Bad thing is, that's not the hard part for me. I don't mind so much getting killed. Remember what Socrates said about death? Either it's like a big sleep, and he didn't fear it, or it's like going someplace where he could talk with all the great minds from history, and he would welcome it? Well, to me, death looks like a big bar: either I'm getting drunk and forgetting everything, or I'm getting sober. Either way, it's all right by me."

"Like I said about you and bullshit."

"Yeah, I guess. But the problem here is Mother. This goes wrong, she won't be dead, she'll be worse: she'll be in hell, in hell every day for the rest of her life.

"And I'm right about them not being able to solve this themselves. The boys are the Russian version of the Little Rascals: cute sons and thugs who just like to shoot people. I don't know what the gray shirts are good at, maybe overthrowing small countries' governments, I don't know. But I've never seen anything touched by these swaggering military types that didn't go bad and then get papered over to tell us that it had been good."

"So that leaves the girl reporter and her trusty assistant," said Marci. "Actually, maybe I'll make it a bunch of assistants in the book. A literature professor, a detective, and a drunk. Good enough?"

"As long as we get Kiev back alive, I can be a circus clown for all I care. We got to get something going."

One of the slacker kids, the girl from the other day, caught my eye and came over with a big smile.

"Professor, I just wanted to tell you that I think the police are looking for Kiev, too. A couple of guys who looked like detectives came by here this morning asking about her."

"Describe them," said Marci without looking up from her typing.

"You know, kinda like all you old guys look. Bored. Settled. Trying to look like they own the world and the rest of us are just in the way. But trying to be cool, you know, gray sport coats over gray silk t-shirts, kind of a dark *Miami Vice* thing."

Marci and I looked at each other for a second. "These guys are closing in," I said. "We've got to get to Kiev first before they get to her and screw things up and maybe kill her."

"What makes you so sure these guys are going to screw things up?"

"It's what they do."

"And what makes you so sure we won't screw it up worse?"

I turned my coffee cup around and said, "I'm not."

She looked at me hard and made up her mind about something.

"OK. So what's next."

"Yeah, well, we don't have a next."

"Hey, we know where they live."

"We know where Dread lives, sort of. What are we supposed to do, knock on the door, say, 'Excuse me, did your son happen to bring home anything extra from school, like a missing heiress?' We need more."

Marci turned the laptop around. "Look at this."

"The South Rises Again," said the notice in the on-line paper. The article promised a grand party for any like-minded people with money who came to the Clampett mansion and wrote a big check for the New Confederacy Foundation.

"That's tonight," said Marci. "At the stepdad's house. How do you look in gray?"

CHAPTER 19

We went back to Marci's place after a trip to a costume store.

"Don't get used to it," she said, looking around her living room. "One more month without a paycheck and I'm coming to your place."

You have no idea what you're asking for, I thought. I looked around Marci's place. It was a pretty standard urban apartment with one bedroom and a living room and a small kitchen area. Except that it looked like it was a storage shed for a sporting goods store. There were two bikes on a rack on the wall where any right-thinking American would have a flat-screen TV. I kicked at something in the pile of clothes and felt the give of a wadded-up wetsuit.

"Triathlon stuff," she said. I looked around the room. Clearly, room cleaning wasn't one of her sports.

"Let's see what we've got here." Marci took the two costume bags from me and separated them. "I think my friend George at the costume store did good."

I wanted to go back to the costume store run by Marci's friend and play some more. Every new costume in the place gave me an idea for a new scam. If I could just survive the next few days, I would go back there and beg the guy for a part-time job, something that would let me borrow costumes. With a treasure trove like that, I could hide out forever.

"Let's see what George came up with for you," said Marci.

"Surprised he let you borrow these."

"He owes me. Likes to think he'll owe me again someday."
She held up a gray Colonel Reb costume against me, took the
broad-brimmed hat out of the bag and put it on my head.

"My, my," she said. "All this and you still lost the war?"

"It was a long time ago. Yankees had no appreciation for
sartorial splendor."

"I do." She looked me straight in the eye and held it longer
than usual. I felt uncomfortable but didn't want to break the
stare. Marci had the healthy-animal features of an outdoor girl:
strong lines, clear, tanned skin. But she had the eyes of a little
girl, fun and mischievous. I realized I'd never really looked in
her eyes, maybe never really looked into anybody's eyes like
this, and I felt like I was falling into them, into a clear blue
pool, chasing at the little gold flecks that seemed to turn into
magical creatures the farther I fell.

Just as I was hooked, she broke away. Her expression clearly
said, "Gotcha!"

"And I, sir, am going to be positively fetching." Marci pulled
my costume away and held up the white hoop skirt against her
body. I'd fetch, I thought.

"I wish the neckline were lower," she said, and looked back at
me. When I reacted, she looked away this time.

"Do we have a plan, or we just fumble around and see what
happens?" she said.

I hesitated, then realized she was talking about tonight at the
Clampett party, changing the conversation from the topic I
thought we had been discussing without words.

"Don't know. Don't know how to plan these things. I guess
we just get in there and hope someone says, 'Oh, that's Dread's
room back there. He's got a girl locked up, but here's the key.'
Maybe they'll give us cab fare, too."

"You pay the cab fare," said Marci. "Remember, I'm the one
that's out of work."

"Yeah, well, being a fake professor doesn't pay too good either."

"Too well. No wonder you're a fake professor. How about detective?"

"I'm not licensed, so there's not a lot of money there."

She smiled. "Is there anything you are good at?"

I knew it was a joke, but it hit me wrong, and I wondered the same thing myself. Right now, I missed the outside world with all its bullshit and sloppiness and pretence. Missed it because, once in a great while, you'd get just a brief moment like the one I'd just shared with Marci. No posturing, no getting or giving or taking, just a moment falling into someone else's eyes. I wanted more of that but felt ashamed and unworthy for all the things I had done and not done. For a moment, I thought of just leaving and going back to the Western World. Stay drunk until they all came for me.

I looked up at her, unable to carry the joke anymore. She looked into my eyes this time. She saw the doubt and the simple human plea.

"Time to get changed," she said.

"Where?"

"Here," she said. She reached up and slid the corduroy jacket off of me. Reached up again and unbuttoned the top button of the shirt from Goodwill, and I felt like I was already naked. Naked and sober all at once, for the first time in a long time.

CHAPTER 20

Marci and I climbed onto the bus, dressed in our full Confederate regalia. We sat down on the long bench seat up front, the only one long enough for Marci's hoop skirt. Across from us sat an older black woman in a business suit.

"The glamorous life of an unpaid literature professor and an unlicensed detective," Marci said.

"I like to think of myself as a nonconformist."

"Yeah, well, I'd like to think of you as a nonconformist who could afford cab fare."

I looked back in her eyes again and thought, yeah, I wish I could afford cab fare right now, too. Cab fare, and other things to give to you. I remembered all the times in the Western World when I preached about how I could live without money as long as I had free beer. Skinny girl would sit and gaze at me with admiration, this holy man who rejected the world and its materialism. Mayor would just look at the calendar and calculate how many more days he'd have to listen to this crap.

I looked over at the black woman and felt like I needed to apologize.

"It's a costume party," I said.

She didn't seem to feel the same need to accept an apology that I felt to make one.

"I just didn't want you to think that we bought into that same pathetic idea that the Old South was just people in cute costumes with funny accents and that the oppression of your people was no big deal."

"My people came from Jamaica," the woman said. "My father still works at the consulate. I grew up here in San Francisco. Never picked cotton or baled hay. Wouldn't know a buckwheat cake if it came up to me and said, 'Howdy, ma'am.' "

Marci put her hand on my arm, like an old husband and wife with the wife saying, "Please, honey, let's not make a fool of ourselves." And like an old husband, I ignored her and plowed on.

"I just wanted you to know that we don't support the things that keep people like you in the American underclass."

She pulled the cord and the bus stopped. She stood up and looked at me like I was a pitiful child.

"I'm a judge. I'm going to meet the mayor and a couple of congressmen for dinner. I ride buses because sometimes you meet interesting people." She looked at me again, a little harsher. "Sometimes."

She started down the aisle, then thought of something and stopped with her back to us. She held her hands up, fingers out. She danced as she walked with her hands going back and forth while she sang, "Here come the judge, here come the judge, order in the courtroom, 'cause here come the judge."

Marci looked at me. "I may have misjudged you," she said. She laughed and put her arm through mine.

"So we're at the arms-linked-in-public place now?" I said.

"We're wherever we want to be," Marci said. She looked straight ahead but smiled.

"Imagine that," I said. For the first time in a while, I was at a place that didn't suck and didn't involve degradation. Imagine that, I thought again.

The bus got to our stop and we got off, with Marci's skirt crinkling and swishing down the steps. The bus pulled away and we stood alone in the middle of a neighborhood of high fences and big houses. Marci fumbled with her purse.

"I've got the map I printed in here somewhere," she said. I put my hand on her hand.

"Be a pro," I said. "We're money. Money doesn't pull out a map or ask for directions at the convenience store. Money *knows*. Our limo just dropped us off. The driver's gone around the corner to wait for us, probably at an expensive bar because we're so rich that even our driver has more money than he can spend. We put our noses in the air and march right in because we already know everything."

"Like where we're going?"

"Yes." I pointed to the end of the street, to a big white house with thirty-foot columns.

"Lucky guess," she said.

"I'm lucky tonight. Go with it."

She smiled back at me.

We marched up to the house, just two rich people in love. We were met at the door by a tall black butler wearing tails.

"Oh, our dear friend John will want to see this." I took out an envelope and handed it to the butler. When dear old John Clampett saw the money pledged on the fake company purchase order, he would want to see this. When his accountant saw that the company was fake, he'd want to see me, but of course I'd be gone by then.

"Tell him his good friend Colonel Balderdash from Mississippi offered this with his sincerest hopes that it will further our noble cause. We are so grateful to have the opportunity to put our excess money to something worthwhile like this rather than wasting it on something liberal like clean water or food for starving people."

Marci elbowed me but the butler really didn't seem to care.

"Very good, sir," he said with a heavy English accent. He led us into a ballroom a little bigger than the state of Kansas but still a lot smaller than the Romanov's. We were at the top of a staircase with the upper landing making a small stage on which to present the incoming guests. A few faces looked up expectantly, sure that they would know the newcomers because all right-minded rich people know each other. Their faces stayed frozen in place when they saw that they didn't know the newcomers. There's nothing that makes rich people more cautious than other rich people they don't know. Might be someone trying to take their money. Better yet, might be someone whose money they could take. What fun.

But there was something wrong. Everyone except for Marci and me were in expensive business suits and gowns. No costume party. The room froze, and the polite stares masked the little wheels turning in people's minds as they thought of the best way to casually decimate these stupid newcomers who were in over their heads.

Marci laughed and reached halfway down to her hem and ripped. She laughed while she ripped, her actions saying, "I'm so rich I tear up expensive clothes just for the hell of it, everyday." She ripped her gown into a short skirt, wriggled out of the hoop petticoats, and turned back to the crowd.

"It's a joke, y'all," she yelled. Her smile said to the crowd, no, you're the stupid ones who don't get my joke. The crowd laughed, still not sure if these newcomers were prey or predators, but taking no chances.

"Now, Strom, that hat just looks ridiculous." Marci yanked the hat off my head and sailed it across the room. It landed in a punchbowl, and Marci laughed. Another mess for the servants to clean up. More fun. The crowd laughed, too.

I smiled a big, toothy, imperious smile. Strom, I thought, I like that touch. This girl could be a pro.

CHAPTER 21

I wasn't the only one admiring Marci. A tall man with swept-back gray hair and an elegant tux and no tie came up the stairs bearing a skinny glass with something green stuck in it.

"Julep, m'lady?"

"You must be our illustrious host," said Marci, simpering as if she'd never seen his picture during her Internet search. "I have been dying to meet you." Marci took the drink and smiled a four-hundred-megawatt smile. I faded into the background to let Marci work.

She leaned into Clampett. "Perhaps we could prevail upon your good nature for a tour of your lovely home? I am always on the prowl for ideas for my home back in Jackson."

"Ah, a Mississippi girl. How could I say no? May I, sir?" John Clampett put his arm out and Marci took it. Clampett turned to me with a big toothy smile that clearly said that he had just taken something from me and done it with impeccable manners and grace. I smiled back.

"However do you do this?" I said. I waved around the house. "I mean really, sir, how do you do all this?"

"Natural superiority," Clampett said without dimming his smile. "Same as all of these fine people here. Superior genes, superior values, superior lives. That's the American story."

"God bless America," I had a big smile, too.

"All the foreigners in this country do nothing but steal from real Americans. I find creative ways to bring money back to Americans from foreigners."

I affected my very best knowing leer and said, "Like Russians?"

Clampett smiled. "Particularly Russians."

Clampett led us through the front hall to the dining room. He pointed out antiques and artwork, proud of his money. At the end of the dining room, he turned away from a pair of big double doors and started back to the rest of the house.

"Why, John." Marci clung to his arm. "What's behind those big doors? I always want to see big things."

"Oh, honey, that's the kitchen. Just servants and all that."

"Oh, I would love to get some ideas for decorating my kitchen."

"I'm sorry. I have strict rules about associating with the servants. I speak to the butler, he speaks to them. We have to be careful with whom we mingle."

Marci giggled a long throaty laugh. "I only mingle with the very, very best." I didn't know "very" had that many syllables.

So we went up another long curving staircase and strolled elegantly from one overdecorated room to another. The walls looked like someone had randomly thrown liquid money at them and the money had stuck in the form of paintings that were old, expensive, and bad and the rooms filled with furniture never meant to be sat in.

"Why, John, how many people live in this great big old place?" said Marci.

"Just me," said Clampett. "Tragically, I am a widower." Then he was smiling again. Or still, I wasn't sure which.

"Although I would dearly love to share it someday with the right someone," said Clampett. "It's so hard to meet that kind of girl out here in San Francisco. Out here, everybody mingles with everyone and nobody stays true to their class and breeding. Not like back home in the South."

I was pissed at that. I had spent time in the southern US. I had cheered at football games in Tuscaloosa, screaming my head off between a black farmer and a bank president with Pakistani heritage, all of us wearing red "Roll Tide" shirts. I was pretty damned sure that Clampett's capitalized South was, literally, gone with the wind. But I kept quiet and let Marci work.

"I'm sure you will find your belle," she said. "But these things take time." She pulled away from his arm and walked down to a big picture window looking over the back of the property.

"Look at all this."

Clampett walked over and took her arm back. I hung back and looked around to get a feel for the place.

"That looks like an apartment building over the garage."

Clampett laughed. "A little smaller. That's where my stepson from my first marriage lives, with a friend of his. Many in the liberal media consider me to be a racist, but they never even look at Dread. Dread was my late wife's child from a previous marriage. Dread is half Negro. Despite that, I have raised him as my own. I treat people fairly as long as they stay in their place." He turned toward Marci, his eyes moist and pleading. "I love everyone. It hurts to be misunderstood."

I jerked my head at Marci, trying to get her to distract Clampett so I could get away and get a look at Dread's place. She ignored me. She knew how to do her job without being told.

"Why, John," she reached up and wiped an imaginary tear away. "You are so sensitive." She leaned up against him and brushed her breasts against his arm.

"Why don't you show me your bedroom now?"

Clampett's eyes grew wide. This was like winning the lottery without even buying a ticket.

"I'm sure my brother can amuse himself." Marci hugged Clampett and looked at me over Clampett's shoulder. She cut her eyes toward the window and mouthed, "Find something fast."

"Brother?" I thought as I watched the two of them walk away. I hadn't meant for her to be *that* distracting.

CHAPTER 22

I drifted through the big house and smiled at everyone until I found a door to the backyard. I walked around the garage to a set of wooden stairs in the back. The stairs led to a second-story window that was unlocked, and the window led to what I hoped was an unoccupied set of rooms.

My scams had never included breaking and entering, and I was shaking. I pulled myself over the windowsill and landed in a pile of dirty clothes and sat listening for any signs of life. Nothing but some heavy breathing that I recognized as my own. I crawled to the side of the bed and felt what I hoped was a flashlight. What I found instead was a big automatic, something that looked like it had been carved out of a single piece of steel. It looked better than Mayor's ancient revolver, so I stuck it in my pants, adding robbery to my résumé. The gun in the pants thing looked good in the movies, but here in real life, I realized that I didn't want the gun to accidentally go off pointing where it was, so I took the gun out and wedged it into a coat pocket.

There was a little mini Maglite on the nightstand. I took that and turned it on. In the closet I found nothing but more dirty clothes, some boots, and a hunting rifle stacked in a corner. I went to the door and took a deep breath.

Carefully, I eased half of my face around the doorjamb. The next room was a small living room with a kitchen at one end, with a couch and a couple of chairs that had once been expensive but had been mistreated to the point of being junk.

No one was in the room. There was a door to the outside, another door that opened to a bath, and another closed door. I crossed the room, looked in the bath, and opened the other door just a little. Another bedroom, also empty. I eased in and looked around. No one there. I stepped in and swept the room with the flashlight. There was no sign of Kiev in the room. No sign, for that matter, that any woman had ever been in the room: muddy camouflaged hunting clothes lay in piles, the desk in the corner was piled with old mail, and the room smelled of mud and body odor. I looked at a couple of unopened letters and saw the name Roscoe Dewar. I sifted the mail and found nothing obvious.

There was a noise back in the kitchen, and I jumped. I crept to the door and saw nothing, but heard the same noise coming from the freezer of the refrigerator. Ice maker. Some detective, I thought. I wondered what Travis McGee or Harry Bosch would do here.

"Not what you're doing," I said out loud without thinking. I shut up and went back to work.

There wasn't much in the refrigerator. The milk was past its expiration date, but that could mean nobody had been here in a while, or it could mean they were slobs. I had plenty of evidence of that already.

I looked in the bathroom. Again, no sign a woman had ever been there, or ever would be. The floor was stacked with old hunting magazines, and a few magazines with women on the cover.

I looked at the women. The women looked fake: plastic bodies and plastic smiles for the camera. I thought of Marci, thought of what happened a few hours ago and tried to make sense of it all. Even before I had walked away from the world, I was never sure what first-time sex meant with a woman. Back then, every time had left me wondering. Was this love? Fun? Should I send flowers or make a joke? I remembered one time long ago. After the lovemaking, I sat with the girl in her kitchen drinking coffee and peeked over the top of my mug trying to read her expression. She was doing the same thing. She laughed and then I could laugh.

"Hell, I don't know," she had said. She was still wearing my shirt. It was open, but not much. "Maybe this is the start of something. Maybe it's the end. We'll find out. Either way." She sat up straight so the shirt fell back. She gestured with her coffee cup. "Ready for another cup?"

That was the start of something good, maybe the best something I ever had before I dropped out. But it had ended, of course. Everything ends, and you wonder what it meant. Wonder what any of it means, all the high words and pretense and promises and tears. I thought about the skinny girl and her advice: one goddamned page at a time. I caught a glimpse of myself in the mirror. "More bullshit," I said out loud.

I shook myself and went back to work. I was halfway through Dread's room when I realized what was missing. Other than one rifle in Dread's closet, and a bunch of dirty camo clothing on the floor, there was no hunting equipment to speak of. Almost. Back in Roscoe's room, I found a camo knapsack that smelled of animal blood and sweat. I picked it up and looked inside. Empty, with a rip down the side. I said to myself—not out loud this time—the boys have been packing. They threw this on the floor when they realized it was ripped.

There was a set of stairs that led down to the garage. I went down there hoping to find a trap door to a secret room, a map, anything. All I found were two sets of oil stains where two poorly maintained vehicles had sat.

No girl, no leads, no hope. Frustrated, I went back upstairs and gave up. Taking the torn knapsack, I scooped up everything I could get from Roscoe's desk, dropped the automatic in, climbed back down the stairs, and hid the knapsack in a hedge by the street.

The party downstairs in the big house was going strong when I got back, and I wondered how the private party upstairs was going. I hurried up the stairs and smiled at everyone and muttered to myself. At the end of the hall, I found the door Clampett had referred to as his suite. The door was closed. I cracked it open and listened.

"Oh, I am so clumsy," I heard Marci say.

"I believe you've had enough," Clampett said, and I gritted my teeth.

"Oh, please, darling. Just one more glass of champagne will really put me in the mood."

"You've already had three glasses, not to mention the one you spilled."

"A gentleman would go downstairs and get a lady one more."

I shut the door and looked around for a hiding place and didn't find one in the hall. There was a statue of Robert E. Lee outside Clampett's door, apparently standing guard. I jumped beside old Bobby Lee and came to attention.

The door opened and Clampett came out, eyes down, walking fast, He marched past the General and me and headed down the stairs muttering under his breath. I opened the door.

"Why, darling," Marci started, then saw it was me. "You! Where the hell have you been?"

"Trying to be a detective."

"Find anything?"

"Said I was trying. Give me an A for effort."

"I thought I was going to have to earn my own scarlet A if you didn't hurry up."

We headed out and down the stairs. Coming up was Clampett, this time with a whole tray of champagne flutes.

"You," he said, looking at me and stopping. He turned to

Marci. "Honey, what went wrong?"

"Natural superiority," said Marci as she brushed by him. "I have to be very, very careful with whom I mingle."

CHAPTER 23

"You didn't sleep much last night," Marci said. We were on an early morning bus to the Romanov's.

"No." I took another sip of the giant coffee I'd picked up from the convenience store at the bus stop. So far, the coffee hadn't helped my mood.

"Look, Josh, you said it yourself. Kiev is playing a scam to get a little of her own money. The bozos are amateurs. They will just show up and take the money and run. By afternoon, we'll be sitting at the Romanov family reunion. Expect the positive."

"Never been good at that. At least not sober. Marci, you don't know how these military groups can screw things up. I don't want to do that again, and I don't want Mother to be the one crying on the battlefield."

Marci let that go. "You find anything in the backpack you picked up?"

"No. Random bills and shit. Nothing that says, 'Go here to pick up kidnapped girl.' "

Marci sighed. "Then we've got no choice but to go along for the ride today and put on our happy faces."

"This is my happy face."

Marci dropped it and looked out the window. We got off at the stop by the Romanovs' and walked up to the little guardhouse. One gray shirt stepped out to escort us up the driveway while another said something into a Bluetooth headset.

Jackson met us at the door. "Where's your car?"

"My people dropped us off."

Jackson stared at Marci.

"This is my assistant," I said. Marci glared but said nothing. We walked into Mother Romanov's house behind Jackson.

"Where the hell you been?" Yuri said. I pushed past him into the house, trying to look tough.

"Detecting," I said.

It was still early in the morning. I wanted to be here before they planned the drop.

Jackson looked at Marci. "Can she handle herself?"

"I trained her myself," I said. Jackson wasn't impressed, but Sergei, sitting on his couch, nodded, and Jackson said, "I guess that will have to do."

I pushed through the crowd of gray shirts and Romanovs into the kitchen, where I knew Mother would be.

"Mother, how are you doing?"

Mother sat in a chair, ramrod straight. A technician in a gray t-shirt was fitting a Kevlar vest on her.

"We get her back," Mother said. It wasn't a question.

"We get her back," I said.

"You go back there." She waved toward the living room. "Boys plan. You listen. No mistakes." She looked up at me, fierce and demanding. "No mistakes."

I nodded and turned to walk out. I turned back and kissed the top of her head.

Jackson was questioning Marci when I walked back in.

"What's your name, Missy?"

She started to answer but I cut her off. "Sheila," I said. "From Vegas."

Marci's mouth tightened, but she kept quiet.

"Sit," said Sergei. He waved us to a couple of chairs worth more than Marci's apartment. Yuri stood behind us. He pulled back his jacket and leaned forward so we could see his two black automatics, one on each hip.

"Run through it again," said Rudi.

Jackson nodded, and a tapestry slid away on a wall. The screen behind it lit up with an aerial shot of Ghirardelli Square and the Aquatic Park.

"The red figures are my men. They are already in place, or will be soon. We will have a chopper from eleven-thirty on. We have an office in the Ghirardelli building set up for you gentlemen." He nodded at the Romanov brothers. "You can see everything from there. That will be the command center. I'll be there. You'll know everything as soon as we know it." The brothers nodded back.

"How many are armed?" I asked.

The men in the room looked around. It was as if I had asked how many were wearing pants.

"Everyone but you and Sheila chick," said Jackson. "You stay here."

I looked at Sergei.

"They come," he said. "But they don't need guns."

I stood up. "No one needs to have a gun if they're trigger happy," I said. "No shots until we have Kiev. No guns drawn. If a guy comes and takes the money, let him go. Don't spook them. We want Kiev."

Jackson sneered. "We're the pros here. We run the show."

I said, "Your kind of pros are good at killing people. So are your boys." I nodded at Sergei and Rudi. "This isn't the time to prove how tough you are. Nobody shows a gun, anyway, anyhow, until we have Kiev."

Jackson and I faced each other in the center of the chairs until Sergei nodded.

"Of course," he said. "Nothing until we have Kiev."

I reached into my jacket and pulled out a picture of Dread

and Roscoe that Marci had taken in the bar. I handed it to Sergei.

"These are the men that made the original call. Watch for them. Nobody touches them until we have Kiev."

Jackson looked at the picture in Sergei's hands.

"We need to know what you know."

I glanced at him and then focused on the screen to show him how unimportant he was. "You know what you need to know. Watch out for these two. They may be the only ones, but they may not."

"He's holding out on you," said Jackson to Sergei.

"Leave him alone," said Sergei. "He's got more than you." He handed the print to Jackson. "Nobody touches those two until we have Kiev."

I sat down and realized I was shaking. I liked fading into the background and wanted to fade away here. It had been a long time since I had been the one standing up. Being drunk was a lot more fun.

They went over the plan a couple more times, but they were just killing time.

At eleven A.M., Jackson said, "Time to get the family down there."

CHAPTER 24

Jackson motioned at me. "You ride with me. And keep quiet."

Yuri said, "No. They ride with me. They go nowhere without me." Jackson shrugged.

Marci and I followed Yuri down to the garage. Black Escalades were loading everybody else up. Yuri walked past to his SL65.

"You've only got two seats," I said.

"She ride on lap. Pretend you lovers."

It was a tight fit. Every bump bounced Marci against my lap. I thought of the old Mae West line, the one that went, "Is that a forty-five in your pocket, or are you just glad to see me?" Right now, I wished it were a .45.

We parked in the Ghirardelli parking lot and walked over and milled around the entrance of the beautiful old building, blocking the tourists coming out with bags of overpriced chocolate. Mother stood by herself, looking sad and old as the two heavy shopping bags with money stretched her arms like some cartoon figure. She stared down the sidewalk that ran around the building to Aquatic Park. Rudi went over and hugged her, and then stepped back with the crowd. Mother started around the building on her lonely walk to the little amphitheater by the water. She looked back and motioned at me.

"Him. I want him with me," she said.

Jackson started to object, but Rudi cut him off.

"Mother want, Mother get."

I took the shopping bags.

"Soon," I said.

"Soon," said Mother.

We walked around the building and forced ourselves to look straight ahead and be casual.

The amphitheater was a set of concentric stone arcs that led down to a small stage by the water. There was a small park with trees on a rise to our left. I didn't have to look to know there were gray snipers in those trees. I hoped they hadn't drunk as much coffee as I had today. Or as much alcohol as I had in the last few years. We came to the top arc.

"Here," I said. I brushed off the step for Mother.

"Thank you." Mother sat down. I put the shopping bags between us and sat down.

We looked out on the water, the bay beautiful and sparkling but also dark and menacing, the old prison at Alcatraz framed in the center of our view. A couple of guys in wetsuits swam by. It was a warm fall day, hot and clear by San Francisco standards. Tourists walked by. A couple of joggers came and went. Two guys in business suits walked by, arguing about something or maybe nothing. Mother jumped at the sight of every one of them.

I looked at my watch. Eleven-thirty. Too early for anything to happen. I leaned back and looked around for the gray shirts, half expecting them all to be standing at attention like toy soldiers, but they were well hidden. I thought of the plans I had seen, and mentally counted the guns I knew were trained on me. I looked down at the amphitheater, just rows and rows of steps out in the open. Not much cover there if shooting started. There was a ledge below the next row. I decided that was where I would put Mother at the sound of the first shot. I moved us both down a little so they were closer to the ledge.

Mother was nervous, making small random noises and fidgeting with her hands. She was not used to sitting still. I gestured out at the bay. "I grew up on water like this. My dad was a waterman. All my family were."

"Tell me about your family. Make time go by," said Mother.

So I did. When I finished, I looked over at Mother.

"You poor, poor boy," she said.

I realized there were tears in both of our eyes. Some of what I had said was even true. I wasn't sure if the tears came from the true part, the made-up part, or even why I felt the need to make things up.

I looked back at my watch. Twelve-ten. I stretched and glanced back over my shoulder and saw a man in black in a tree with a rifle resting against the branch. The man pointed the rifle at me, and flicked the barrel to tell me to turn around. I ignored him and thought about waving just for the hell of it. I looked up the path at a couple of joggers. I watched them, but they ran by.

"What time?" said Mother.

"Twelve-ten."

"So could be anytime."

"Could be. Tell me about Kiev."

"No, then I would cry more. Now we talk about nothing important, keep our heads clear. I will talk about Evie when she is here."

So we talked about nothing as much as we could. I tried to explain football to Mother; she tried to explain borscht. I tried to make her laugh. Sometimes I did. Sometimes it was a forced, polite laugh. Once, it was real, when I talked about an old tire swing that had broken with me in it and dumped me in a saltwater creek and how I had come screaming out of the water with a crab locked onto my nose. She laughed hard, but the laughter started to dissolve into tears, so I pointed out a sailboat going by and taught her the names of the sails and talked about the lines on the boat and any other meaningless thing I could think of. I realized that this was the opposite of the world I railed against: a world where high-sounding and important words often mean nothing. Today the flow of simple words meant everything.

"What time?" Mother said.

"Twelve-thirty," I said.

Mother swore something in Russian under her breath. I couldn't understand the words but knew the meaning.

I told Mother jokes, anything I could think of. At first she laughed at some, argued at some, telling me this thing or that were stupid. Eventually, her emotions began to disengage and she just sat there repeating, "Yes, yes, very funny."

Then she was talking, but I realized she wasn't talking to me.

"No," she said. "No. I don't care. I stay. We stay."

She turned to me and tapped her earpiece. "Rudi say, is one o'clock. They not come. He say we go. I tell him no."

I watched as she scanned the faces of everyone who went by now. I decided to try to use that to distract her.

"Nah, that's not him," I said, pointing my chin at a man walking along the water. Mother had been staring at the man, pleading, please Mister, come ask me for millions of dollars, and give me just one thing back.

"Look at his feet," I said. "Look at how big they are. That guy used to be a circus clown, back with Ringling Brothers. See the lines on his face? How deep they are? That's 'cause he never could get all the makeup out. No way he could turn to crime. Imagine. He'd go to rob a bank, and they'd laugh at him. He'd probably take out one of those fake pistols, pull the trigger, and a little flag with the word, 'Bang' would pop out."

Mother laughed a little. "He run out to getaway car, no get in because there already forty-seven clowns in car." And we both laughed, probably just so the other one could see how relaxed we were. Bullshit, of course, but bullshit that held us together.

So we made the time go by, making up stories for everyone we saw, while hoping we already knew the story. One after another, the stories all walked on by.

I saw a guy in a business suit that didn't fit well. I said the guy was a plumber who liked to dress up and come down to the water, but I was hoping the ill-fitting suit might mean he was our guy. Mother started to laugh, but then the guy turned and came toward us, focusing on something on the ground at our feet but ignoring us. He walked up the steps, and I felt Mother tense and look behind the guy to see if Kiev was out there somewhere. I tried to stay loose. The guy got close, looked up, and smiled at me, and I moved away from the bags to let him get to them. He paused in front of us, bent down, and picked up a beer can some kid had left.

"We've all got to do our part," he said, smiling and throwing the can in the trash as he walked away. At that moment, I hated the environment.

"Just a plumber," said Mother.

She turned to me and said, "Show me pictures of your family."

I said, "I don't have any."

"No pictures?"

I wanted to say, "No family," but I knew that would lead nowhere good. So I made up more stories.

After a while, Mother put her hand on my arm.

"These are not real," she said.

I started to argue, but she said, "What time?"

I looked. "Two o'clock."

Mother's mouth tightened into a line and she stood up. "Rudi right. We go now."

CHAPTER 25

Mother Romanov stood up and pushed the shopping bags at me. "You take," she said and walked up the hill. I followed.

Yuri stood slumped by the door like a pile of black laundry. He looked at Mother, but she didn't look back, just followed him to a conference room with a big window overlooking the bay and the park. A couple of Jackson's men scanned the park with cameras with telephoto lenses and made entries in a laptop computer while the rest of the family and Jackson sat around the table.

"We want to know where you fit in," Jackson said to me as soon as the door closed.

Rudi held up his hand. "No. First we take care of Mother." He turned to a young woman, one of the daughters. "You take Mother downstairs, have cup of tea."

"No," said Mother. "I stay. I hear this."

Rudi started to argue, but realized that guns and thugs and private armies were no match for Mother. He shrugged and motioned to Jackson to continue.

"This was a setup," Jackson said to me. "You're the wild card here."

I looked at him. "So you think I conspired not to get three million dollars from you guys?"

"I don't know your game. But you just happened to show up the day after Kiev was kidnapped, volunteered to help find her even though you're no detective. You know more about this

137

than you let on. You conned these folks into doing it your way with bags of money waiting for you or somebody working with you. Something went wrong, and now we're going to do it our way."

I turned to Sergei. "You were there. Did I volunteer to find Kiev?"

Sergei shrugged, "I don't know anymore. But Jackson's right; something doesn't add up here. When you took the bags from Mother, every one of us thought you were about to run."

I looked over at Marci. She sat in a chair in a corner guarded by a gray shirt. She looked stressed and confused.

"This doesn't make any sense," I said.

"Something doesn't make sense," said Jackson. "We're going back to the compound and find out what."

Sergei shrugged again. "Look, you can't ask us to believe you now. You spend all your time trying to fool everyone. You're a bank teller, but you're not. You're a detective, but you're not. You're a gardener, but you're not. Maybe you're a kidnapper, too. Maybe not. We'll see. People tend to tell the truth once Jackson finishes with them."

Sergei stood up. "Let's go." One of Jackson's men came over and took my arm. Another took Marci's.

Yuri stepped into the center of the room and pulled the sides of his jacket back. He stood there in full Batman pose.

"They ride with me," he said.

"They ride with us," said Jackson.

"They ride with Yuri," said Mother.

Jackson started to argue, but Rudi shook his head.

Jackson stared at Rudi and saw that Rudi wouldn't back down in front of Mother. "OK, you get him there. But once we're back, he's ours. We question him, our way. No more backtalk. Remember who's running who here."

Rudi gave him a look but said nothing.

We marched down the stairs and the tourists in the Ghirardelli shops stared at this odd sad group. Out front, there was a line of black Escalades with Yuri's SL65 crouching in the middle. A gray shirt handed Yuri the keys and they got in.

"What have you got me into?" said Marci, wiggling onto my lap.

I thought about asking how I got her into it. Yuri revved the engine, mad at being boxed in between two Escalades.

"Yuri, we've got to get away from all this," I said.

"You mean you've got to get away from this. Or maybe you just want to get away with this, whatever this game is you're playing."

"The game I'm playing is getting Kiev back safe. Jackson's just going to strut around and show how tough he is. That won't get Kiev back."

"We're going to get Kiev back."

"Not this way. Look, those guys don't have a clue, and you know it. You trust them?"

The Escalade ahead pulled out, and Yuri followed.

He laughed. "Does dog on a chain trust the man pulling the chain? They jerk us around, do what they want. They show up one day and tell my grandfather how things are going to be, and he and my father and my uncle say OK. Don't know why. Now they stay in basement and pretend to work for us. But when gray men tell father what to do, he do it." Yuri goosed the SL65 and tapped the bumper of the Escalade in front of him and leaned on the horn. The Escalade ignored him.

The two Escalades kept him boxed in as they pulled out in traffic. One guy in a gray shirt stood in the street holding up traffic until the entourage got out.

"Look, these guys are pros. They have contacts," said Yuri.

"Then why don't we have Kiev now? Look, Marci and I are the only ones on the trail here. I'll tell you something else: I started off thinking this was something Kiev cooked up herself. But she should be here now. It could be that she's got herself in real trouble."

I leaned around Marci to Yuri. "You don't need an army to find her. They'll just get in the way, stumble around, and shoot things up. Afterward, they'll give a great briefing on why it wasn't their fault that your sister got shot, and they'll find some way to blame you Romanovs yourselves for getting in the way. You know it."

"It wouldn't be the first time they've screwed up and then blamed us."

"Let Marci and me go. When we've got Kiev safe and sound, we'll call in the troops."

Yuri was irritated at being boxed in by the Escalades.

"I feel like dog crap. I'm supposed to be Batman, and I can't even protect my own sister."

We were coming up beside an on-ramp for the Bayshore Freeway. Yuri jerked the wheel and slammed the gas. We were halfway up the ramp, the speedometer needle spinning past 100, when the Escalade behind us pulled onto the ramp to follow.

"You better be right," Yuri said.

CHAPTER 26

The black SL65 became airborne as the ramp leveled off at the freeway, flying, literally, like a bat out of hell. I looked down at an older couple in a Subaru beside us and below us on the freeway, and the man stared back at the black shadow flying next to him while his wife stared straight ahead, her mouth moving as she told some story that he was barely hearing now. Yuri landed the car in the lane to the left of the Subaru, cut across two more lanes of traffic, and was gone. I imagined the man in the Subaru trying to interrupt his wife, telling her about the flying car, and having her say something like, "John, don't you interrupt my story with your nonsense. You're supposed to be paying attention."

There was a crash behind us. I turned and saw two Escalades wrapped up in a pile with a truck and a handful of cars. For a moment I thought about asking Yuri to turn around and go back to help, then realized there was nothing we could do.

"Don't worry, they fix." Yuri cut across a police cruiser and disappeared into traffic so fast the cop probably wasn't sure what he had seen.

"Yeah," I said. "The gray shirts keep a couple of spare arms and legs in their magic toolbox, maybe something to bring a mother back to life before her kids know she's dead?"

"Money fix everything. You see. Gray shirts make sure this never make the news. Poppa write big checks. Money fix everything."

"Yeah," I said. Maybe that was the fundamental bullshit of the world: money fix everything. Reduce every product and service to a dollar sign, even monetize medicine and politics, and then money fixes everything. Everything except the broken bodies of the people run over.

I knew I had a hand in this, too. Maybe if I'd gone to the police. Maybe if I'd just given the names of the bozos to the Romanovs. Maybe, maybe. My head hurt and I wanted to be in the back room of the Western World, just conscious enough to be aware of the skinny girl rubbing my head and saying, "Poor, poor Josh."

Instead, I heard Marci say, "Where the hell are the seat belts on this thing?" As if there were a seatbelt-for-two in the seat she was sharing with me.

"No need," said Yuri. "Drive good, have no wreck." He swerved across two lanes to an off-ramp. An old Camaro, carefully waxed and probably on its way to a classic car show, crashed into a wall to avoid them, but the SL65 was unscathed. Yuri slowed to 125 as the car hit the surface streets.

"See?" said Yuri. "Drive good, and trust in Jesus." He touched a religious medal hanging from the mirror.

"Oh yeah," said Marci. "I remember that lesson from Sunday School. Think the Bible reading that day was from Crap 7:19."

I said, "Speaking of bodily functions, you don't stop this thing soon, I'm going to anoint your fine Corinthian leather with holy water."

Yuri looked at me with fear in his eyes for the first time today. He jerked the wheel into a deserted construction site with a battered Porta-Potty.

"Take time," Yuri said. "They catch up, we have more fun."

Since more fun probably meant more people killed, I hurried as much as I could. When I stepped out, I saw Yuri standing with his hands on the roof of the car, his feet back and spread wide. Yuri looked up at me and grinned.

"Don't ask," he said.

Marci stood behind Yuri. One of Yuri's automatics was in her right hand. She pulled the other one from his belt with her left hand.

"We've got to do this," she said to me.

"Better for the book?"

She thought a minute. "Probably. But that's not what I was thinking. This guy is going to get us or someone else killed. I don't want to die. We've got to find the girl, get her back home, and get these guys off our backs."

I shrugged, "I trust my driving more than his."

"I'm driving," said Marci.

"I'm driving."

"I've got the keys. And the guns."

"You're driving."

She turned back to Yuri, who was still smiling. She gestured with one of the automatics.

"Any more of these?"

"Of course." Yuri grinned.

"You're going to make me pat you down?"

More smiles from Yuri.

"Search carefully," he said.

She looked at me for help.

"No way."

She found a small revolver in the back of his belt and a pop-gun on one ankle.

"Bet you take these off when you go to Weight Watchers," she said.

"You missed a spot." Yuri grinned.

"Anything you're hiding there I'm not interested in."

"Here. I show you."

Yuri reached into his pants. Marci wanted to look away but

couldn't. He pulled something out of his pants that looked like what a man would normally pull out of his pants.

Waving the object in front of Marci, Yuri said, "See? This make you look good in tight pants. Also, you press here, fire one shot, out the end."

Marci said, "Typical man, one quick shot and done." She opened the door and got in. "We'll leave that one with you, long as you don't point that thing at me."

Yuri grinned. "I count to one hundred, then I come after you."

Marci shook her head as I got in. She cranked the engine with her left hand, still pointing one automatic at Yuri. As she put the car in gear, Yuri yelled at the sky.

"Batman returns! One Mississippi, two Mississippi . . ."

The SL65 fishtailed out of the lot. Gravel flew around the shouting figure in black as Marci struggled to get the car under control.

CHAPTER 27

Yuri's counting had barely faded behind us before I tapped on the tach.

"You're getting into the yellow," I said.

"I know how to drive." Marci pushed the clutch in and the engine raced a little until she ground the car into third and popped the clutch. The tires chirped, and I was pushed back into the seat by the acceleration.

"I can see that. Drive a lot of fast cars?"

"Not this fast. I got it, though."

Marci drove as carefully as she could drive a rocket ship, trying to attract as little attention as possible. The car fishtailed a time or two when she shifted gears, and stops were almost instantaneous until she got the feel of the brakes, but she didn't kill anybody, which was a big improvement over the previous driver. We zoomed past a crumbling brown warehouse and onto a big commercial street. A motorcycle cop pulled up beside us in the left lane, glancing at us but pretending not to stare while he kept pace.

"Stay cool, stay cool," I said, even if I wasn't cool at the moment. "He doesn't know about us. The gray shirts didn't tell the police. We're not caught."

"Oh, hush," said Marci. "I know how to handle this." She chirped the tires just a little coming up to a red light. She licked her lips and pressed the window button. The dark window came down with an expensive whine and allowed a square of the outside world to intrude into the car's isolated interior.

The cop looked in, a little bored. He got a look at Marci and was less bored. He flashed a big smile.

"Nice car."

Marci smiled back and licked her lips. "It's my boyfriend's." She jerked her head at me. She gave the cop an ambivalent look that said, "Yeah, I'm his toy now but he's a bore and someday I may want to party with somebody like you." She looked into the cop's eyes and rubbed her hand up and down the shift lever. "I'm just getting the feel of it."

"I think it likes you," said the cop. He leaned forward so he could see me. "Lucky guy," he said. The light turned and the cop sped away, showing off a little.

So this is what it's like, I thought, calming down. Expensive car, good-looking woman. People on the street think you've got everything, and got it good. I thought back to when I had been on top and wondered what things would have been like if I had just followed the script and given the right answer that day on the game show. Even then it all seemed surreal, like a role I had to play.

I remembered people arguing about my schedule like I wasn't even in the room with them. Remembered the publicity guy saying he didn't see Josh this way or that way and me thinking, what the hell does he know about me. But even back then I realized that I had no real argument for the publicity guy, no real idea how I saw myself. I was just an empty figure playing a role. Maybe same as now.

Marci pulled into a parking garage beneath her apartment building. She put the SL65 in a numbered spot and pulled up the parking brake.

"This is where I kept my Honda until I had to sell it," she said.

I paused a minute. "Mind putting it over there, by the wall next to the stairs?"

"Why?"

"Don't know. It's a little more hidden."

"You just like being tricky for no reason."

I shrugged and she moved the car for me anyway. We climbed the stairs to the lobby and took an elevator to Marci's floor.

It was the same messy place we had made love in less than a day before. Marci stepped through until she found a large gym bag.

"This'll do," she said. "It has workout clothes, a spare outfit, and makeup. I always felt like some kind of tough loner agent walking to the gym with this bag on my shoulder. Imagined that the bad guys would jump out of an alley and I would have to run for my life and live out of this bag. Be careful of what you wish for, I guess."

The giant bag made Marci look like a little girl lost. I walked over and put my hand on her cheek.

"We may be gone for a while," I said.

"You think? You've got an army and a mob trying to kill us. Unless we find that girl, and get her back, I may never come back here. Not in one piece, anyway."

"I'm sorry. Look, maybe you could go away someplace."

"And do what? Become a nobody like you? I've got a life. They can find me. People know my name. I've got an agent who says he'll read my book outline, if I ever get a book outline. I'm going somewhere. Was. Now what? You think I can put on a fake mustache, go be some bullshit professor like you?"

She looked over and saw me reaching down, picking up a green sparkly dress that looked like an expensive something she deserved.

"One more thing you've got to leave behind. I'm sorry," I said again. She brushed my face.

"It's not your fault," she said.

147

"I'm sorry," I said again. There were tears welling in my eyes, and I couldn't make them stop. She looked at me, not sure if I was sorry for the mess we were in or for something much more.

"We can make it all right," she said. She kissed me on the top of my head and put her arms around my neck. For a few minutes, it was all right.

"We need to go," I said after.

"Oh, they won't find us anytime soon." She climbed out of bed naked. I looked at her and thought it might be good to stay longer. But no.

"These guys are pros. It will take them a while, but they'll get here soon enough. We don't want to be here then."

"Ah, spoilsport," she said. She kissed my cheek and pulled on her panties. "But you're right. We've got to get out of here, find that girl, write my book, and be rich and famous."

She was happy now, like a little girl. I looked at her, amazed at how fast she had changed.

"What got into you?" I said. She looked at me, and we both laughed. It was an old joke, only funny in the five minutes after sex when everything seemed funny and warm and good.

She picked up her big bag and then saw an Irish sweater on the floor.

"Maybe this, too." She put it in the bag.

"This." She picked up a Stanford rain jacket.

"And this." She picked up the green dress.

"Jesus. We're not going to the prom anytime soon."

"Memories." She smiled at me.

"Well, we need to get out of here before you find any more keepsakes. Let's take this, though." I picked up the knapsack from the Clampetts'.

"Oh!" said Marci. She picked up the messenger bag with her laptop. "Got to have this. Got to write my book and be rich,

rich, rich." She kissed me again.

She looked up at me. "Thank you, Josh."

I wondered what to say to this new girl that had taken Marci's place. "Sorry" had worked before. I didn't know what to say now.

CHAPTER 28

Marci locked the door to her apartment as we left, and I laughed at her.

"Jeez, Louise, you think that's going to slow the gray shirts down? Think they'll knock politely on the door, see that it's locked, and take their rocket launchers and flamethrowers and go home?"

"Habit. I protect my stuff."

"Good luck with that."

She kissed me in the elevator, and I could still smell the sweat on her.

"You should have showered before we left," she said to me. She buried her head in my neck and nuzzled. "But it's good." She thought a minute and then said, "Probably me too. Maybe I'll get a shower at your place later."

I didn't say anything to that.

On the stairs to the garage I held up something and said, "I'm driving." She turned, and I dangled the keys to the SL65 in front of her.

"Children. I'm not going to let you kill me. I'll sit on the hood until you give me back my keys." She ran on down the stairs, and I stood there smirking.

The idea was just to tease her, then let her have the keys back. Every silly flirtatious thing seemed funny now. She disappeared through the garage door. I was on my way down when I heard her yell, "Josh!"

Then I heard another voice amplified through a speaker, "Put your hands up where we can see them."

I froze and looked around. A side stairwell led down to some kind of maintenance room. The door was open, and I went in.

The room was dark, and I was afraid to turn on a light. I reached into the knapsack and fumbled until I found the Maglite. Turned it on and saw shelves of supplies and a couple of mops. There was a second door on the other side of the room.

I went to the door and turned off the light and put it back in the pack, cracked the door and looked out. Marci stood by the SL65. Behind her was one of the gray shirts with a gun to her head.

I ducked back into the room and looked around and tried to think of some way to improvise a weapon. There was a mop. Maybe I could break the handle into a sharp point and turn it into a spear. Thought of the hundred ways that could go wrong.

I thought about facing reality and just giving up. Let them beat the crap out of me, sure, probably Marci, too. But eventually they'd turn us loose, and eventually I'd be back in the bar listening to Mayor say, "Slow down. Don't drink that stuff so fast." And then I'd be drunk and laughing at nothing again.

I remembered something, reached into the knapsack and pulled out Dread's automatic. I popped the magazine and checked it. Full.

I looked out the door. The guy was still behind Marci. Over by the main entrance there were three Escalades blocking the door. Between them, Jackson and two other gray shirts were walking over smiling.

I eased out of the door with the gun in one hand and the knapsack in the other, creeping along the floor and watching the dark shadows of Jackson and his men through the tinted windows of the SL65. I raised up into a crouch and pressed the gun against the small of the back of the guy behind Marci.

"Hand the girl the gun or you'll be popping wheelies in your wheelchair tomorrow," I said.

The guy stiffened and hesitated, but it didn't matter. Marci swung her gym bag into the guy, spun around, and snatched the gun out of his hand. She put one foot in his back next to my gun and shoved the guy out and onto the pavement. Before he hit, she slid across the hood of the SL65, firing wildly at Jackson.

"Drive," she yelled, opening the door and throwing her bag in the back. She got off another quick couple of shots. One of Jackson's men fired back.

Jackson slapped the man in the back of his head. "Asshole, you kill them, the Romanovs will kill me."

I jumped in the car next to Marci.

"I've always wanted to do that," she said. "It looks so cool in the movies and it really, really is."

I looked at her with my mouth open while the engine cranked.

"Let's hope it's not the last cool thing you get to do."

I floored the car and it fishtailed toward Jackson. Jackson yelled to his men to shoot out the tires.

"Keep them down," I said to Marci. But then I lost control of the car and we went into a slow motion spin, Marci hanging out the window and trying to shoot at the men but just spraying bullets around like a lawn sprinkler out of control.

"You're not making this easier," she said.

"I got it now."

"Sure you do."

I got the car pointed away from the Escalades and toward a smaller gap on the other side of the garage.

"Not sure if that one goes anywhere," said Marci.

"They know that?"

"Thought double-naught spies knew everything."

"And yet, we're still loose."

"Barely."

Two of the three Escalades were cranked up and coming behind us now. I slowed the SL65 down.

"What the hell are you doing?"

"You said that gap might not go anywhere, just leave us trapped. Besides, we can't let these guys follow us out of here."

The two Escalades were gaining on us now, the drivers inside probably gloating.

"Hold on," I said as we passed a concrete pillar. I counted, "Oh shit one, oh shit two, oh shit three." On three I reached down and yanked the hand brake hard and threw the steering wheel over at the same time. The car spun around. Halfway through the spin, I released the brake, straightened out the wheel, and hit the gas.

The driver of the first Escalade looked up and saw the SL65 roaring full speed right at him. He jerked the wheel, and the Escalade plowed into the pillar with a crash.

"Not bad for an amateur."

"I meant to put him into the other guy."

The second Escalade was making a wide circle to come back for us. I turned inside him.

"These big honkers carry all their weight up front. Means they don't have much traction on the rear." I pushed the front of the SL65 just behind the back tire of the Escalade. The Escalade spun into a wall.

"Yuri's not going to like you bending his car."

The third Escalade was coming toward us, but the exit was clear.

"You're faster," she said. "He can't keep you away from the exit."

"Yeah, but if I just outrun him, he'll be on our tail. We need to buy some time. Let him think we messed something up in the collision with the last guy."

I goosed the engine a couple of times and then almost let it die. The Escalade caught us in the middle of the garage and mashed into the bumper of the SL65, trying to push us into a wall and trap us there. I pushed down on the clutch and revved the engine like it was dying and let the Escalade push. I stood on the brakes harder and harder. The other driver was having to give the Escalade a full throttle to keep the two vehicles moving.

Just before the wall, I jumped off the brake and stomped the gas hard. Popped the clutch, spun the wheel, and pulled the SL65 away, scraping the wall with the rear of the car. The Escalade's 400 horsepower slammed the big black SUV into the wall. I gave the SL65 one turn, and we were out the exit and onto the street.

"How'd you do that?" said Marci.

"Drive good, and trust in Jesus."

CHAPTER 29

When the garage faded behind us, I said, "A long time ago they gave me a free weekend at Skip Barber's driving school for free publicity. That SL65 is the second-fastest car I've ever driven."

"They gave a professor in Buddhist literature a weekend at a performance driving school? The only questions here are how many things you're lying about, and which ones."

"You've seen me drive. Ask me anything about Buddhist literature."

"I'm busy right now."

We rode along together in silence for a little bit.

"One thing that's true is that the gray shirts are on to us. They must have a GPS on this car. If we don't do something fast, they're going to keep popping up at every corner," I said.

"On it." Marci pulled her cell phone out of her bag and dialed a number. She talked low so I couldn't hear her, but there was a lot of giggling. She clicked the phone closed and looked at me with a triumphant smile.

She directed us through the city to a garage painted to look like graffiti but much more expensive.

"Not here," she said. "Go around to the back."

The back was an alley filled with old motorcycles, pieces of expensive cars, and a line of camera trucks that said "The Real Deal" in dramatic print on their sides. I knew the name from a TV reality show about a garage that juiced cars for movie stars and street toughs.

A guy dressed like a gang-banger leaned against a roll-up door. Looking bored, he slid the door up and then slid it back down as soon as we were inside. As my eyes adjusted, I saw another guy standing inside. This part of the building was kind of a long tube that connected the door we had just come in to another door like it on the far side. The guy waved his hands to guide us a little this way, a little that way until he held up his hands for me to stop. He cut his hand across his throat, and I cut the engine.

Two guys rushed in from each side with floor jacks. Marci and I bounced up into the air in a single motion. Another guy slid under the car. In a few seconds we heard two quick "frip" noises, and the guy slid out. He held a small metal box up to my window.

"They make my job too easy," he said. He clipped a small battery onto the two leads of the GPS. "There, now their baby's alive again. All we got to do is find a ride to hitch this thing to so your friends will have someone to follow." He looked around through a glass panel into the main garage and saw a police officer standing at the counter. "Ah, the illustrious Officer Johnson of the San Francisco Police Department. Likes to come around to try to catch Johnny in something dirty. Like there's anything illegal Johnny could do that would make more money than the reality TV show they film here. Think we've found a home for the GPS."

He motioned for a guy to open the exit door, then walked out and slid under the black-and-white police cruiser parked outside. He crawled back out and gave me a thumbs-up.

The jacks slammed the SL65 down, and a guy banged on the hood for me to go. I cranked the engine but someone tapped on Marci's window. She slid the window down with an electric whine.

"Babe." A man leaned in and gave her a long kiss. Too long, as far as I was concerned.

"Where you been?" he asked.

"Around. Where you and the actress been?" Marci said.

"Aw, I told you not to read those tabloids. I told you we broke up."

"When?"

"Last night."

They both laughed. I looked at him and wondered if I was going to get an introduction. Guess not. The guy had Hollywood muscles and Hollywood hair but street tats up and down both arms.

"What's that?" Marci asked about a big square bandage on one bicep.

"Producers made me remove the 'FU' tattoo. We're moving to a more upscale market, and they didn't want to scare the families watching at dinner."

"So they got you doing a family-friendly version of your famous *Garage to the Stars and Dope Dealers*?"

"Yeah, something like that." They both laughed, conspirator's laugh, only good between the two of them. "More money in it."

"To success," she said.

"The best revenge," he said, and she reached through the window to give him a high five. He banged on the fender, pointed at me, and said, "Get her out of here."

I squealed the tires and threw Marci against the door as we turned onto the street.

"Hey," she said.

"Hey yourself."

We drove in silence for a little while.

"You're jealous." She smiled at me. Not just a happy smile but a triumphant one.

"Am not." I thought about it. Thought about all the times I had spent talking with the skinny girl about how important it was to stay free. And the way the skinny girl would kind of look off and say, "Yeah. Free. Not owned by anyone or anything. Wouldn't that be nice. You keep dreaming, kid. I'm betting on you, and I'm getting good odds." Maybe I was jealous. So what?

I said, "We got more important problems. Staying alive. Finding kidnappers. I could go on, but by the time I listed them all there would probably be guys pointing guns at our heads."

"You shouldn't be, you know. Jealous. Johnny and I are just buddies. Well, yeah, there's that, too, I guess, the sex thing. But I mean really, our biggest thing is Best Revenge."

"What's that, a band?"

"No, a support group. You know, like the saying, 'Living well is the best revenge.' The founder says that you've got to get your mind focused on being successful. Then you'll be successful and you'll get your revenge on all the ways the world has tried to keep you down."

"But aren't you just giving in and going along and becoming a part of the bullshit?"

"Bullshit with money ain't bullshit."

" 'The rich are very different from you and me,' the man said." I shrugged and turned onto a four lane in a better neighborhood.

"Right he was."

"Yeah. I like Hemingway's answer better."

We rode along a little bit.

"OK," I said. "But to be successful, you've got to write your book. And to write your book, we've got to get Kiev back and stay alive."

"Yeah. So what do you think went wrong?" Marci scooted sideways in her seat to face me. "Girl got away? If she was kidnapped, and then escaped, she ought to be home soon. Girl got killed? We're all screwed. Kidnappers screwed up and will call again?"

"Don't know. For Mother Romanov's sake, I hope Kiev's just at Macy's shopping for shoes. Only thing we know for sure is that the bozos are in on it. We need to find them."

She thought a minute.

"You got Wi-Fi at your place?"

"Not exactly."

"Then I need to go someplace before we go there. Drop me at the coffee shop."

"Not a bad idea."

CHAPTER 30

Officer Johnson was pulling out of a donut shop when the black Escalade cut him off and another Escalade pulled up and blocked him from behind. He jumped out of the car with one hand on his microphone as the other reached for his gun.

"Code Thirty. Officer in danger. I'm blocked in by two black Escalades at Dynamo Donuts on Twenty-Fourth."

Jackson got out of the trailing Escalade. He put his hands up to the officer to say, "Calm down." A gray shirt beside him said, "The signal says it's here," and then shrugged. Jackson motioned him to the police car.

There were sirens coming closer now, first one and then several. Jackson motioned to Officer Johnson.

"I apologize, officer. We'll have this taken care of in a minute." Officer Johnson kept his hand on his gun.

The guy came out from under the car holding the GPS.

"The old switcheroo," he said. Jackson didn't smile.

Officer Johnson took his hand off his gun and reached for his cell phone. Jackson pulled his out first.

"New version of the fast draw," said Jackson. He pressed a speed-dial number and muttered a few words into the phone. He hung up without waiting for a reply.

"You'll get a call in a minute," Jackson said to Officer Johnson. "This never happened."

Officer Johnson's phone started ringing as the Escalades drove away.

CHAPTER 31

I parked the car in front of the Western World. There was one little window in the bar that wasn't painted over or covered with dirt. I figured if I stood at just the right spot I could keep an eye on the car.

A kid came out of the shadows by the bar.

"Watch your car, Mister." He looked at the car. "Whoa. That's some ride. I got me some tip coming when you come out. Be soon, too. This ain't the kind of place a man like you wants to hang out. Nothing in there match this."

"Yeah, sure."

Mayor and the skinny girl were inside at their same poses in their same positions, like a painting that doesn't change. Mayor looked up like he had seen me just the other day. Which he had, but it seemed like a long time ago.

I looked around and was surprised to find that I wasn't surprised at the sameness. I felt like everything should have been changed by the last few days. I had been rich, or at least had money in my pocket. I had a girlfriend, or at least had a girl who would sleep with me without taking money. Fancy weapons, fast cars, big houses—but this broken-down bar was still the same. The Western World had dirt and meanness and lying and broken people—but no pretense. Here, I was who I was. Except, of course, that I couldn't tell anybody about my history or where I had come from and even I didn't know or care where I was going, particularly when I was in here. Small matters. Every home has a window that's a little cracked, or a piece of furniture that needs replacing. You accept it, and I accepted the limits here. Maybe even loved it because of its limits.

I took a deep breath and savored whatever it was the place had. Mayor looked up to see who had come in; people never came in here just to take in the fine sour air of a cooped-up bar. He took out the jug of cheap stuff and set it on the bar.

"Ready?"

"Very. But I can't. I got to tell you guys what's going on. You know, like in case something happens to me, you can go to the police or something." I thought about that even as I said it. I imagined Mayor at the police station, looking more like somebody who ought to be in a lineup rather than reporting a crime. Mayor tells the cops this barfly hangs around the Romanovs, trying to find one of the biggest celebrities in the country just because the Romanovs like him and trust him. Oh, by the way, there's this secret government or not-government army living in the basement. The cop shrugs, and Mayor says, you don't believe me, I got a character witness. Goes out and comes back in dragging the skinny girl. She says, of course I'll back up anything Mayor says. Just let me get a fix first.

I laughed. Mayor laughed, too, although he probably hadn't seen the story in his head the way I had.

"Anyway. You got to hear this. There's this girl."

"Oh good," said the skinny girl. She closed her book and took off her reading glasses. "I love a romance. You don't tell many of those."

"No, this isn't a romance. Well. I don't know. Maybe. But that's not what I mean." I looked around for something to change the topic. I looked at the cover on the skinny girl's book. "High school algebra?"

"Yeah," she said. "I think it's a mystery. Any case, it's a mystery to me. But I was good in math. In school, back before everything started happening. So I figure, if I was smart once, I can be smart again. I keep reading this thing, over and over. Each time, it makes a little more sense."

Mayor picked up a glass, the same glass he always picked up and polished when he wanted to play the role of fatherly bartender. "So how many times you figure you're going to have to read it before the light comes on?"

She laughed. "I don't think I can count that high yet. But I ain't going to stop till I get there."

Mayor looked at her like a proud poppa. Right answer.

The skinny girl turned to me. "We now return to our regularly scheduled story."

"Oh yeah. So there's this girl. Actually, there are two girls."

Mayor leered. "Now it sounds like my kind of story."

"Except I haven't even met one of them."

"Now it sounds like her kind of story."

"No. There's this rich girl who's disappeared. Maybe kidnapped, maybe hurt, I don't know. There's these rich guys think I can find her."

Mayor frowned. "What did you tell them to make them think that?" Parent figures never stick up for their kids. They say they do, but they always want to know how something was your fault. Of course, in this case, it was my fault.

"That's another story. Anyway, some of them think I can find her. Some of them think I took her. The ones that think I took her have more guns. Actually, they all have a lot of guns."

"Now we're back to my story," said Mayor. "Wake me when we get to the part where the superhero who's been masquerading as a bar owner saves the day. And gets the girl. Girls."

"Well, yeah, see, there is this girl. Woman. Whatever. She's helping. I really like her. I think she likes me." I paused and realized how middle-school those two sentences sounded. But I didn't know what else to say, even to myself.

"Oh good," said the skinny girl. "Now we're back to my story."

"Yeah, except, unless I find the girl. First girl. Unless I find the first girl. I mean 'we.' Unless we find the first girl, I'm going to get myself and the second girl killed. Well, I'm not going to get her killed. She got herself into this and thinks she's going to get rich off of this. She gets herself killed, she can't blame me."

"So you may be about to die," said Mayor, leaning over the bar. "And you're worried about whether this girl's going to be mad at you."

"Yeah."

Mayor jerked his head at the skinny girl. "This one's right. It is her kind of story."

"Joshie's got a girlfriend," she sang.

I thought. No, that wasn't right. My head hurt, and the jug on the bar looked real good.

"What Josh doesn't have right now is a place. This girl thinks we're going to stay in my place."

Mayor threw up his hands. He could see he had made a mistake getting involved and treating these two as something more than the barflies they were.

"Don't bring her in my place. Don't bring a bunch of guys with guns in here behind you, neither. This ain't your home and it's never going to be your home." Mayor picked up a towel and started polishing the bar, looking at the talk show on the TV with the sound turned down.

"I got a place," said the skinny girl.

I thought about what kind of place the skinny girl might have. Imagined bringing Marci there.

"Thanks. That's nice of you. I'll figure out something."

"No, really. There's this real nice place up in South Beach. Nobody lives there, I swear. I got the keys to it. You can have it for as long as you like, nobody will bother you, nobody will even know you're there. Really. Kind of like a honeymoon for you two."

I looked at her. "I don't know."

She reached across the bar and pulled out her purse and unloaded the contents on the bar.

"Oh yeah, here." She pushed a key across the counter. "That's the address on the tag."

I looked at it. "This means a lot. Thanks. I owe you. I'll bring the key back in a few days."

"Throw it in the bay when you're done with it. You owe me a happy ending."

Mayor chuckled a dirty laugh. The girl hit him in the shoulder, too hard to be funny.

"I've had all of those comments I'm ever going to take."

I went into the back room and opened the trunk. I took out some of the costumes and wigs and stuffed them in a bag and walked out into the bar and to the front door. As I touched the doorknob, I felt like I needed to say goodbye to the place where I was nobody and I was everybody that I ever would be, all at once. I turned back.

Mayor didn't look away from the TV. The skinny girl said without looking up from her book, "Remember. A happy ending."

Out on the street, I was the rich guy with the hot ride again. The kid had a crowd around the car.

"That's him," the kid said. "Probably a movie star down here getting the feel of a crummy bar for his next movie. You'll recognize him when you see him on TV."

I reached into my pocket for something to pay the kid, pulled out my last bill. It was a hundred.

"No, man. You don't owe me. I been charging these guys a buck just to touch the car. We took turns polishing it, just for you, 'cause you something big and famous and rich, like we going to be." The kid looked at the bill and laughed. "Oh, I get it. That's Hollywood money, anyway, something from the movies. They don't make no hundred dollar bills. I ain't stupid." All the kids laughed.

I recognized a little one in the back.

"Here. Give this to your father. He used to work at a bank, before he wound up on the street. He helped me out and gave me a tip on a job at a bank once. He'll get a laugh when he sees this fake bill."

The boy took off running with the bill before the bigger kids could take it away from him.

CHAPTER 32

Marci looked at the young black hipster strutting to her table at the coffee shop.

"Hey, momma, got you something extra sweet here."

"Beat it," she said. "I got a boyfriend who will kick your ass."

"So you think I can kick somebody's ass?" I grinned down at her.

She looked up bored. When she recognized me, she was irritated.

"Very funny. So you think you're my boyfriend?"

I had a mental image of myself and Johnny from *The Real Deal* in a commercial hyping a heavyweight fight between us, both of us snarling and talking trash. Maybe the fight would be more like a heavyweight fighting a middleweight. Light middleweight. Even I wouldn't bet on myself. I shrugged and sat down.

"Found anything?"

"Not really. Our boys applied for hunting licenses up in the mountains a while back, but they gave the San Francisco house as their address."

"Maybe I need to go back there."

"Maybe." She closed her laptop. "What now?"

"First thing, we got to get rid of the car. Even without the GPS, that thing's too noticeable. Particularly for guys who have choppers out right now and can tap into any street camera."

"You know they can do this?" Marci said.

167

"See it on TV all the time. Must be real. Your boyfriend will tell you everything on TV is real."

"He's not my . . . yeah, he's the Real Deal all right. Says so right on the title. So how do we do this, just walk down to Friendly Fred's Used Cars and trade this thing in?"

"Yeah. I used to work for a guy. Well, for like a day. The guy paid me a bundle to keep quiet about what I saw."

"Will he recognize you?"

"Did you?"

"Yeah, well, frankly, I'm bored with you right now. And tired. And stinky. They say be careful of guys who won't take you back to their place."

"It hasn't exactly been your usual date, so far."

"Yeah, well," she stood up. "Let's go see Fred."

We went out to the car. Marci shooed away the teenage boys the car was already starting to attract, and we got in. I reached back behind the seat and pulled out a long jet-black wig.

"Here. Put this on."

"Eww, I will not. This thing needs to get washed."

"So do you. Put it on. This guy's white-white. He thinks everybody black or Chicano are street hoods and can be trusted to be as dishonest as him. You can't pass for black, but wear the wig and throw a little Spanish around and he'll trust you to be dirty."

She pulled it on.

"Yeah," I said. "Besides, it makes you look pretty skanky. Help give me some street cred."

"*Hombre*," she said with a passable accent. "You want your señorita to wear this later?"

I looked at her and laughed. Thought about it and said, "Maybe."

She looked at me. "So, you know, I never thought to ask. What exactly are you?"

168

I cranked the car and pulled away from the curb. "You mean do I have a Republican or Democratic voting card in my wallet? Saved by Jesus, or am I a hard-core atheist? Surprise, no. I'm nothing. I'm a proud member of the nothing party. I trust nothing."

"No, no. Don't go off on one of your rants with me. I get it. The world sucks and you'll have no part of it. I read the pamphlet you gave me the first day, the one with the title that said, 'Don't read this because nothing's worth reading.' Got it. No, I mean what are you? Doesn't matter, but I just want to know. I thought you were white, but I guess that's just because I'm white and everybody assumes everybody else is the same as they are."

"I'm American."

She thought about it. "So that's why you don't believe in anything."

We had to go out to the suburbs. Even Marci had to admit the SL65 stood out like a sore thumb here. We pulled past a Burger King and a bank advertising that it was local in over three thousand locations nationwide and into a car lot with a building like a big red and white diner. "Comfort Cars," the sign said. A guy came out in a cheap blue shirt, clip-on tie, and a white apron. Again I noticed the shoes. Too expensive to wear an apron. I remembered that the guy was rich but put on working-class airs to show he was just like you.

"Come on in, folks. Let me whip you up a plate of the best ham and eggs you ever had, all for free. We sell cars here, but we give away love. Love is food, good home food. You can't have enough of love, food or home.

"Of course, if you want to look around at some of these cars while I'm cooking for you, that's all right, too. I'm all about cooking and serving the Lord and his children, but we do sell cars."

The ham and eggs were stacked up in the back room next to the microwave, little bitty packages from China that could be heated up in fifteen seconds. Still, it sounded good right now. I couldn't remember when I had eaten. I leaned on a car.

Fred brightened. "That one you've picked out is a very fine choice, sir, and an excellent deal for today only. I can tell you confidently that you will be much happier in this than what you drove up in." Fred looked at the SL65 for the first time and his mouth dropped.

"I've never seen one of those before. The Black model?"

"Black model, man."

Fred tried to find something wrong. "Needs washing. Got dents."

"Needs more than washing. Needs a new home. Hoping you could help me out."

"I don't buy cars."

I wanted to ask where all the cars on the lot had come from, but that wasn't the point now.

"Don't want to sell. Just trade. Straight up."

"Straight up?" Fred looked down to make sure he hadn't wet his pants.

This was too easy. "Yeah, straight up plus a thousand bucks. For that one."

I pointed over to a 1969 Chevelle SS 396, tricked out with fuzzy balls in the front window and a Day-Glo orange paint job.

"That's my pride and joy," said Fred. "Best car on the lot. Full hydraulics, speakers alone are worth more than most cars here. How about a nice pickup truck?"

"Yeah, I'm sure the 396 is a big draw to the moms and pops who come in here, just looking for something to get them to work. You make money by selling them a piece of crap that puts them further in debt so they gotta make payments to you and payments to the mechanic down the street."

"That's America, my friend."

"I ain't your friend. I leave here, you don't know me, never saw me. Got it, mother?"

Fred looked at the SL65. "Don't suppose you've got the title?"

He looked at me. We both laughed.

"We'll take our ham and eggs to go," I said.

CHAPTER 33

"So you think this will fly under the radar better than, oh, a Camry or maybe the Ford he had on the lot."

"I know the guy. The Camry or the Ford would fall apart before we passed the Burger King. He figures the people who buy those cars, they can't sue. Guy who buys this car, though, he might come back and bust a cap in old Fred's ass. This car is in good shape, or he wouldn't have it out there."

Marci laughed. "Say it again, 'Bust a cap.' I just want to hear you say it. You been watching MTV or something, think you know how to talk tough."

"No. I learned it watching *The Real Deal*. Learn a lot from that show."

Marci didn't say anything.

"Besides," I said. "Did you see the trunk? We can live there and have room for your relatives to come visit."

Marci was still sulking.

"Here, get into this." I turned on the stereo, just barely cracking the volume. The car shook so hard from the bass I was surprised the building next to us was still standing.

"Jesus," said Marci. We stopped at a light in traffic, a little old lady in a black Hyundai next to us.

Marci looked at all the switches on the dash. "What's this?" she flipped one and the car started bouncing up and down in time with the bass. Marci puffed her lips out and started bobbing her head in time with the music.

"I'm a mean bad girl, I can hurt you, too," she sang. Or rapped. It was hard to tell which. "And if you don't believe it you can just go—"

I put my hand on her mouth and gestured to the lady next to Marci. The woman gave us a dirty look but kept quiet. The light changed. The woman turned the NPR in her car up to full volume and pulled away.

"See," I said. "That's what this car does for us: drops us into another universe, makes us kings there. People respected us in the SL65 because it meant we had money and power. People will respect us in this because they think we have meanness and power. Same bullshit. We tell ourselves it's all about right and wrong, but then we bow down to power and money."

"Yeah, well, I just want a shower. You think this will fool the Russians long enough for us to clean up and rest?"

"They aren't going to be looking for this. Or that." I pointed at Marci with her wig.

"I'm a bad Momma."

"Yeah, well, don't count on that rap career taking off. Thought you were a writer."

"Society page."

We cruised along a little with the windows down and music up, feeling cool.

"So what's your place like?" said Marci.

Good question, I thought. Gifts from the skinny girl often had the incomplete sweetness of a handmade valentine from a three-year-old. Heartfelt, but so bad that when you said, "Aw, you shouldn't have," you really meant it. I had a vision of driving up to the address and finding a do-it-yourself car wash with a maintenance shed in the back.

"You'll see." I tried to smile but felt like it just came out as an awkward baring of the teeth.

The street that the skinny girl's place was on was nice. The block was even nicer, with a big bayside marina behind all the buildings. We crept along, one big rich building after another.

"When are we going to get to your neighborhood?"

I glanced at the discrete little marble sign by the big driveway, snuck a look at the tag on the skinny girl's keys. It matched.

"Now."

"So why'd you have to look at the tag on your keys?"

I ignored her and pulled into the big arcing driveway, looking for a place to park. No place here. At the top of the hill there was a dark burgundy awning. A middle-aged white guy in a designer uniform stepped out and smiled down at me.

"Need directions, boy?"

I was irritated and offended. I stepped out of the car and handed the guy the keys.

"Have our stuff brought up to"—I looked back at the tag— "suite fourteen-twelve."

The guy looked at me, his face now an unreadable pleasant mask.

"Fourteen-twelve?"

"That's right." I peeled a twenty-dollar bill off the roll from Fred's car lot and handed it to the valet. I looked at the ink from Fred's bill to be sure it didn't rub off.

Marci climbed out and looked around.

"Wow," she said. "I didn't know San Francisco had a view of the bay like this."

I wanted to say I didn't know about this view either, but I showed nothing. We stepped into the lobby where we were met by a young man in the same uniform.

"Good evening, Mister . . ."

"Havens. Richard Havens. Good to see you again."

We walked past him to the elevators.

"So they think you're Richie Havens?"

"They do now. The kid's too young to know Havens."

"Everybody's too young to know you. Who were you pretending to be the last time you were here?"

"U Thant."

"May I call you 'U'?"

"You can call me Ray, you can call me—"

The elevator opened at the fourteenth floor. I was hoping for a sign showing suite numbers, but there was nothing. Marci was too impressed to notice any hesitation I had.

"Wow. Fresh flowers at the elevator stops. I'd settle for a little Lysol at my building."

"I hadn't noticed," I said. I took the hall to the right hoping for something. The suite entrances were set back from the hall in little individual alcoves. The tiny brass signs by the entrance doors had a single number too small to be read from the hall. Nothing to do but walk down and read it. 1492. Well, that was a good number for a history class, but I felt like I was about to flunk here.

"This it?"

"No. Just checking on a neighbor." I walked away quick before Marci could ask what or why. I made a long walk to the end of the hall.

"This it?"

"No. Just wanted to show you the view from this window."

"Wow. You're telling me that Buddhist literature professors get to look out this view from their apartments?"

I walked away. "No, just wanted to show off."

A left, a right. Nothing but proof that there were people in the world with more money and taste than I would ever have.

"Look," said Marci. "You win. I'm impressed. But I don't need another statue or picture window. I need a shower. I'm stopping at your apartment or the next fire hose, whichever one you get me to first."

I was imagining Marci showering in the hall and wondering

where that might lead when a bellboy came out of a tastefully disguised elevator entrance with our luggage. Well, with Marci's gym bag and laptop, the bozo's old hunting pack, my used bag of used clothes and a cardboard box the bellboy found in the back of the SS 396.

"Ah, there you are," I said, following the bellboy as he turned away from us in the hall. When the bellboy turned into a foyer a little bigger than the others, I pushed ahead and pulled out the key. I read the plate as the key slid in the lock. 1412. Thank God. I opened the door and went in.

I stepped into the doorway of what looked like a living room out of an old Doris Day–Rock Hudson movie. Expensive, modern furniture. A beige-pink carpet thick enough that I had to look to find my shoes. There was a click somewhere inside the walls and music came on, slow smooth smoky jazz so quiet and clear that you swore it was barely playing right beside your ears.

"Sir?" said the bellboy. I was blocking the door. "Sorry." I stepped in and to the side, plenty of room for all of us to come in without crowding the entranceway.

"Wow," said Marci again. It was a bigger "wow" than the others.

"Shall I take your bags into the dressing room, sir?" said the bellboy.

I didn't know what a dressing room was. "No, here will be fine." The bellboy opened a door to the coat closet and set the bags inside. The coat closet was bigger than my live-in closet at the Western World. Maybe I'll ask Mayor to remodel, I thought.

I reached into my pocket and pulled out another twenty.

"No thank you, sir. The staff appreciates the regular tip you give us at Christmas. We're not encouraged to accept tips on an everyday basis."

"Of course not," I said. Marci looked at me.

The bellboy left. I opened the closet and pulled out the cardboard box from the SS 396.

"Any idea?" I said. Marci shook her head.

The box was filled with handguns and ammo.

"Between this and Yuri's guns, looks like I need to find my NRA shirt," said Marci.

"Take this with you to the convention." I held up a plastic bag with a white powder.

"Shit." Marci jumped back. "Get rid of that. I don't want to add jail to all the trouble we're in."

"No. People in places like this don't go to jail. The management politely taps you on the shoulder, takes the bag and suggests you switch to a good cabernet. The cops put the bag on a street bum and arrest him."

"Yeah, well, do something with it. Which way to the shower?"

I hesitated. "Why don't you explore?"

"Careful what you ask for."

I realized she was right.

CHAPTER 34

I was standing in a shower in the front bathroom that I originally thought was a dining room when I heard Marci's voice coming over the music.

"Hey," her voice said. "What you got here?"

I dried off and tied the towel around my waist, and wandered off to find Marci. She was naked and dripping, standing by a big open drawer in the bathroom off the master bedroom.

"How'd you do that?" I said.

"Do what?"

"Talk over the music."

She looked at me. "Intercom." She pressed a button and said, "Earth to Josh. Return to base." Her voice floated out with the music.

I looked at the intercom. "Always wondered what that button did."

"You are such a flake. Now you going to tell me you didn't know you had these?" She pointed into the drawer. It looked like the box they had inherited from the car, with a scary collection of weapons. I looked closer and saw that these weapons were all sex toys of one kind or another, although some of them looked pretty scary, too.

"Look, ah," said Marci. "I like fun too, but some of these—no. Don't even ask. What kind of woman even—" She started to pull one of them out, but I stopped her.

"Hey, no problem. I like the toys we've been using." I thought

178

a minute about an answer. "Those aren't mine. I inherited them."

"You mean somebody died and this was your legacy?"

Well, it wasn't a very good answer. "No. I mean. No. What I mean is they were here from the previous owner."

"You mean this building doesn't even clean stuff out for new tenants?"

"Yeah. Something like that." I needed a change here. "Besides, it's hard to take you serious when you're naked."

"Funny." She reached out and pulled the towel off of me. "It's easier to take you serious when you're naked and not talking." She reached in the drawer and pulled out something that looked like a blender. "Maybe I'll try this on you."

I tried to imagine what the thing did. Maybe it came with a manual.

"Yeah. Well, no. I mean, I'd love to, but I got to get dressed. I got to go see if I can find out where our bozos are. I'm going back to Clampett's and see if anybody there knows anything."

She put the thing back in the drawer. "I need some rest anyway. Maybe I'll hang around here and work on the book." She took a thick white robe out of a closet and wrapped it around herself.

She looked at me. "So where do we think we are? Still think this is a joke by Kiev?"

"No. Maybe at first. I don't know. Why the ransom call, if she just wants to get away? I can't believe she just needs money. She could probably find a million dollars in the sofa cushions at home."

"So the bozos have her?"

"They made the call. Your scout troop at the coffee shop says they know each other. But what went wrong? All they had to do was show up, take the bag with the money, and say, 'Here's Kiev.' "

Marci walked back into the bedroom with the music flowing around her like a soundtrack. "Course they'd have been dead within an hour, unless the Romanovs or the gray shirts wanted to play with them like a cat plays with a mouse," she said.

"Yeah, but they didn't know that. I don't think these guys realized what they were dealing with."

Marci took out her laptop.

"Hey, you've got Wi-Fi here."

"Of course," I said, trying not to look surprised.

Marci was hunched over. "Cool. What's your password?" I panicked, but Marci saved me. "Never mind. You've got a public network that's open."

"OK." She looked up. "Save that for later. Lets see what we've got." She started typing away. "Girl disappears. How long's she been gone?"

I thought. "Let's see. The bank robbery was Tuesday. She had been gone three days then. So six days now."

"Six days." Marci typed and looked up. "What bank robbery?"

I shook my head. "Never mind."

She looked at me hard for a minute. "OK, I'm learning with you. Ninety percent of what you say is true one minute, fake the next. You're so full of bullshit I can't tell. So the bank robbery is just made-up bullshit?"

"Yeah. That's it."

"OK. Then the bozos." She looked up. "You think I should organize this thing into an outline or something?" She didn't wait for an answer. "I've got more stuff on the gray shirts than I know what to do with already." She looked back at the laptop. "Oh. Forgot to tell you about that. I called some folks while I was at the coffee shop, and got some stories about the gray shirts that will make even a paranoid like you scared. Of course, the people who told me the stories said I couldn't publish them and stay alive. I need to write it down anyway and see how much of it winds up in the Kiev book." She paused. "I don't know when I'm going to be able to show something to the agent. I don't want to wait until I've written the whole thing."

"Maybe you should wait until Kiev is at least safe."

"No, the time to pitch the book is when it's still ripped-from-the-headlines. I told you, this is my ticket." She looked at me. "Not like you care, remember? All you think is that the rich live in some kind of privilege bubble, nothing bad ever happens to them. And who cares if it does, anyway? You've got all that tough working-class loner bullshit, but look at how you live up here."

"It's not all bullshit. Well, it is." My head hurt again. "Look, Mother Romanov is real and she's hurting. That rich bullshit celebrity is also her little girl, and Mother remembers when Kiev scraped her knee and all the money and all the power didn't equal one little kiss-it-better from Mother. Mother's sitting somewhere suffering right now. This may be a book to you, and all of it may be bullshit, but I'm just one person right now who's been asked to help by one other desperate person, and I'm not going to let her down."

Marci looked at me. "I love it when you're full of bullshit."

CHAPTER 35

Josh was gone when Marci heard a tapping at the door.

"Let me in." She heard a quiet voice. It didn't sound like Josh, but she wasn't sure. Besides, you never knew with Josh.

"You've got a key. Let yourself in."

"I gave you the key, Josh."

Marci hesitated and decided to take a chance. She opened the door to a thin, disheveled woman. They stared at each other for a second.

"Oh," said Marci.

"Oh," said the skinny girl from the Western World. "I thought Josh was here with you."

Marci drew herself up to show she was in charge of the situation.

"Apparently not. I thought you might be Kiev Romanov."

The skinny girl thought of the beautiful young celebrity.

"Apparently not," she said.

They stood there a few seconds longer.

"Well, where are my manners?" said Marci. "Come into my home." She stood back and gestured.

"Your home?"

"Well, my boyfriend's."

"Your boyfriend?"

Marci wasn't backing down. "Yes." They stood at the doorway a few more seconds. Marci said, "And you are?"

"The formal resident." The skinny girl walked in like she

owned the place. She could learn to play this game.

"You mean 'former.' "

"No, it wasn't nothing like that. I never got married or nothing."

Marci shook that off without trying to understand it.

"I just left something here and had to come back and get it. I didn't think Josh would mind."

"So you knew Josh was here?"

"Well, of course, silly, why would I come here if you and Josh weren't here? Then I'd just be tapping on the door of an empty place. The empty place would be laughing at me and going, 'We ain't going to answer the door 'cause we're just an empty place and not a person.' " She smiled at Marci like an indulgent mom who had just explained something obvious to a child. "Silly goose."

Marci never had liked being called silly. "I think I know what you left here."

Marci led the skinny girl through the apartment to the master bathroom and pulled open the drawer with the sex toys.

"Here's your stuff. Josh doesn't need it."

The skinny girl stared into the open drawer a long time. Her face had the sadness that a face has when all the tears are gone but the sadness remains.

"No," she said. "That is not mine." She looked at Marci and dared Marci to challenge her.

"Well, it certainly is not Josh's."

"No."

"Or mine. You don't think I'm the kind of girl for these, do you?"

The skinny girl looked into the drawer for a long time. "Some of these things they make, they don't make the kind of girl who is the kind of girl for some of these things they make."

Marci started to correct the grammar but couldn't find

enough grammar there to correct. She stared at the skinny girl.

The skinny girl closed the drawer gently but firmly.

"I'll show you what I forgot."

"You didn't forget these?"

The skinny girl thought about the words. "Some things you don't forget."

The skinny girl walked back into the master bedroom. The bed was a massive thing that looked like it had been carved out of a single piece of black wood. There were four posts like tree trunks that curved up and joined into a canopy of individually carved leaves. The skinny girl crawled under the bed on one side.

"There was this maintenance guy named Tony. I got him to come in one day, make me this little place in the bed frame. Probably thought I wanted a stash for my drugs."

There was a click.

"There." The skinny girl climbed back out with a child's diary in her hand. It was pink, with a pale blue unicorn on the cover.

Marci looked at the book and thought about what she could learn from it.

"So those are your memories?" Marci wished she had found it first and copied whatever sections on Josh were in there.

"No. Memories are things you want to remember. These are things I want to forget." The skinny girl looked at the cover and traced the unicorn lazily with one finger.

She stopped tracing and looked up and her mouth was tight. "But if I ever need to," she said, "I can damned well remember."

"What do you remember about Josh?"

"That's not in here. Of course Josh is not in here. Silly."

The skinny girl got up from the carpet and brushed herself off carefully, like she didn't want anything to stick to her. She looked at Marci.

"Is Josh in your book?" the skinny girl said.

Marci tried to understand what kind of book this woman thought she had, and how Josh would fit into it. "I'm a writer," she said. "A real writer. I might write a book someday. Josh might be a character in it." She thought a minute. "A minor character." If Josh had been there, she would have said "a very minor character" for his benefit. But he wasn't, and she still wasn't sure what was going on with this girl.

"Good. I wouldn't want him to be in a book like this."

"What's in that book?"

"I don't think it's the kind of thing a nice person like you wants to read. You are a nice person?"

"Well, yeah. I guess. I still don't get why you thought Josh would be here."

"I gave him the key."

"You gave him the key?"

"Well, of course. How else would he get in?"

Marci had no answer for that.

"So you came to see him?"

"Of course not, silly. I came to see you."

Marci stared at the girl.

The skinny girl said, "Let's go make some tea."

CHAPTER 36

I stood in the doorway of the kitchen of the Clampett place. It was late; dinner was done and the staff was cleaning up. People buzzed around, too busy with their own lives and jobs to pay any mind to the new guy standing in the doorway with his white shirt and white pants, looking like any of the house staff I had noticed when I was here before.

Except for one guy. I saw an old guy, black like everybody there, standing by the sink and eyeing me. I looked away. My plan was to drift through the kitchen into the rest of the house and look for anything that would tell me something about Dread and Roscoe. I didn't plan on getting hung up in the kitchen.

"You looking for work?" The old man stepped out and blocked my path.

"No, I'm just—" I started. The old man stared at me hard trying to decide something. "I already work here."

"No you don't. You're looking for work, or you're looking for trouble. If you're looking for trouble, I can call people for that. If you're looking for work, I can use some help over here. No pay except for a plate of food after the dishes are all clean, but the food's good."

"I'm looking for work."

"All right then."

The old man turned his back to me and walked away. I had a feeling that the slow pace and the back turned were all an act, that the man had his eye on me every step of the way. We stopped at a stainless steel double sink.

"I'll wash. You rinse and stack."

The man picked up a dish and started without waiting for my agreement. He moved slow and deliberate, but the dishes came out so fast it was hard for me to keep up with the rinsing.

"Name's Harry."

I thought a minute. "Jeremiah."

"Jeremiah was a bullfrog. Also a prophet. Which are you?"

"Is there a difference?"

Harry laughed. "Maybe not."

Harry paused, scrubbing a nasty pot. I took the break to reach up and adjust the temperature of the rinse water.

"No, don't do that," said Harry. "See, long as the rinse water's red-hot, the dishes will dry themselves. Cool it down to suit you rather than the dishes, and we'll be here all night drying with a rag. Gets the dishes a little cleaner, too."

"So the dishes are more important than my hands?"

Harry smiled but turned so I shouldn't see. "The job's more important than your hands. God made your hands to do the job, not the other way around."

I said, "You know, they make machines to do this. If the owner here wasn't so cheap, we'd be drinking a beer and watching the machine work."

"True. Mister Clampett's cheap. And arrogant. Figures the world would be a better place if all us colored folks were off happily doing some kind of menial labor at his direction. Probably should be singing, too, some kind of old gospel tune."

Harry held up a dirty plate and showed it to me. There was some kind of an ugly brown sauce covering the pattern of the china.

"But that's his problem. Shame on him, shame on the world when it thinks like him, but it's his problem and their problem. Not mine."

He scrubbed the plate clean and passed it to me. I held it under the scalding spray for a minute.

Harry said, "Now hold it up."

I did. The plate had a beautiful, intricate gold flake pattern I hadn't noticed.

"We took a piece of dirty crap and made a thing of beauty out of it. That's a rare moment to be treasured. Lots of people work fancy jobs for big money, strutting around about how important they are. But at the end of the day, a lot of them go home and wonder if they've done anything at all."

Harry passed me another plate.

"I used to have one of those jobs," he said.

I barely had time to rinse the plate and stack it before a handful of silverware came my way.

"Now I clean plates. Don't clean them for Mister Clampett's reasons. Clean them for my reasons. See?"

We worked in silence for a minute. I pushed a pan back at Harry.

"You missed a spot," I said. Harry smiled and hit the spot while I held the pan.

We fell into a rhythm. Harry started humming something, a little tuneless nothing made up of riffs from random old jazz standards. I picked it up and harmonized, then took the lead for a few bars and passed it back to Harry. I looked over. Harry's face was still set in a serious mask, focused on his work. But his eyes were smiling.

I felt a sense of regret when the last plate was stacked. Harry wiped his hands on his apron and said, "Let's go get that food now." We walked back to the prep area of the kitchen. Most of the workers were gone, but there was a light-skinned young woman at a big stove.

Harry said, "The folks in the front of the house had a seven-course meal tonight that will be written up in the paper tomorrow. There's plenty left, if you want some. Or you can have a plate of Sarah's eggs. She's from Jamaica, knows stuff to put in eggs you've never dreamed of. You want the eggs."

"I'll have the eggs, if you don't mind," I said to Sarah.

"Nice manners for a white boy," she said. Harry and Sarah laughed.

"How'd you know?"

"You're white," she said. "I'm white. Harry's black. Only folks like Mister Clampett think we all look alike, if our skin is a little dark."

She pulled a pan from a rack.

"I had to lie to get this job. Had to pass." She and Harry laughed again.

I looked at them both. "You don't mind working here, working for somebody like Clampett?"

Sarah waved, "He's just deluded. Look around you. Working folks like us, white folks, black folks—we built everything you see here. It's our world. Folks like the Clampetts just get to live in it."

She sat a plate of eggs in front of me. The eggs were that good.

"You could have washed those dishes yourself." I looked at Harry.

"No, I wanted to get done and get home."

I looked at Harry. "You could have washed those dishes yourself."

Harry looked back and saw that I wanted a real answer.

"They leave me that station for myself. Sometimes I work it alone, use the time to think and try to sort things out. Sometimes I find a kid at a homeless mission my church runs, bring him in and give him a day's work. I don't need the pay so I give it to him.

"Tonight I was going to work it by myself. Saw you standing

there and said, 'That boy's up to something. Maybe here to rob the place, maybe something else.' So I took you under my wing to keep an eye on you." He looked at me waiting to know if he had guessed right.

I said, "So you're like some kind of guardian angel, sent to keep me out of trouble?"

Harry laughed, then got serious. "Yeah. That's what I am. That's what everybody is. You look for opportunities to be a guardian angel, or you wander through life wondering who you are. You've got to have a mission."

I thought about that.

"And what if you don't have a mission?"

"Then why are you here?"

"I don't know the big answer to that one," I said. "But I know why I'm here tonight. I'm trying to find Dread Clampett and Roscoe."

Harry gave me a long sad look. "Those boys will get you into trouble."

"I'm already in trouble." I told Harry the story.

"I told you I used to have another job before this," said Harry. "I was a cop, a homicide detective down in LA. I had one case that became famous. They wrote a book that became a movie and I got a lot of press. And money." He sighed. "I know of the Romanovs. Bad folks. Don't know why they're not all in jail. I'd like to say you should go to the police, but I'm not sure they could help much."

"So where do I go?"

"I don't know. Hard for me to believe that Dread and Roscoe planned and executed an actual kidnapping. They're trash, and they're mean, but they're talkers more than doers."

"They made the call."

"So they made the call. Let's follow the facts. What facts you've got, anyway. The girl was missing for several days before the call. That doesn't make sense. Kidnappers would want to move right away. On the other hand, there was a ransom call. Two ransom calls. One might be a prank or just stupidity. But not two."

Harry thought a minute. "I can't believe those boys are that stupid. They don't know how dangerous the Romanovs are, but even without that, you get arrested for kidnapping, then you've just thrown your life away. Even Daddy Clampett couldn't fix that."

"Maybe they didn't figure to get caught."

"No one ever does. That's the kind of thinking kept me in business for thirty years. OK, so there was a kidnapping or a fake kidnapping or whatever. The girl's gone and somebody asked the Romanovs for a pile of money. And then something went wrong."

"How wrong?"

"We don't know."

"How long's it been since Dread and Roscoe have been around here?"

"They were here Thursday night," said Harry. "Haven't seen them since. Don't mean much. Roscoe has some kind of hunting place up in the woods. Personally, I think they just go up there to hurt things, kind of a big boy version of pulling wings off of flies. They stay gone a lot, just show up when they want money or want to live like they got money."

"But this doesn't sound like them to you?"

Harry sat for a minute. "No, but that doesn't mean much. Half of all crime is pure stupidity, and those boys have plenty of that. Maybe they kidnapped the girl. Maybe she was partying with them in the woods, bragging about all her money. Maybe they got the idea they should have some of that money."

I looked at Harry.

Harry shrugged. "Or maybe not. Look, if you need a place to

hide, let this blow over and hope the girl comes back and the Romanovs forget about you, you let me know. I got a place. I still got friends down in LA. We can come up with something."

"And if she doesn't come back? Or doesn't come back alive?" I said.

"Then it will take them a long time to forget."

"Mother will never forget," I said.

"Russian women can be like that."

"So I got to find this place in the woods."

"Like I said, it's Roscoe's," said Harry. "The bills and things for it won't be paid out of accounts here. I'll check around tomorrow when folks are here, but I don't know what I'll find out."

"Thanks for anything you can come up with." I stood up to go.

Harry put his hand on my arm.

"Be careful. Mean plus stupid equals dangerous."

CHAPTER 37

Marci and the skinny girl sat at the kitchen island finishing their tea.

"So that's why I had to see if you were good enough for Josh," said the skinny girl.

"Thanks for talking to me," said Marci. "The stuff you told me about Josh, is all that true?"

The skinny girl smiled at Marci. "Sweetie, you don't know me well enough to call me a liar."

"Yeah. Well, OK."

"Look, Josh is special. He's meant to do great things. A lot of people don't see it, but I do."

"I know," said Marci. "He puts up all this bullshit about being outside of the system, but he's just jealous. You and I are on the same side with Josh. Josh needs to live for success. Someday, Josh will have all this for real." She waved at the apartment.

"So you think Josh wants all this?"

"Everybody wants all this, deep down. We're all just afraid we don't deserve it. Once we get past that, we can see that we deserve success."

"There's more to success than money and power."

"Remember what Mae West said? 'I've been rich and I've been poor. Rich is better.' "

"Sometimes rich costs more than you think."

"That doesn't make sense."

"That's the point: sometimes you have to go somewhere where things make sense."

There was a scratching at the door. They heard a key go in and the lock turned.

"Speak of the devil," said Marci.

The door opened and a man in an expensive suit walked in, followed by a mountain-sized guy in a leather jacket with a bulge on his hip where a gun would be.

"You got that right," said the skinny girl when she recognized them.

"The doorman said you looked less strung-out than usual," said the guy in the suit. "He made a nice payday by calling me when he saw you."

"I'm not strung out," said the skinny girl.

"Yet."

"I'm not getting strung out."

"We'll see."

"Jason, I'm done with the life."

Jason and mountain man both laughed.

"And yet, here you are, back in my place."

"Ain't your place," said the skinny girl.

"I paid for it."

"No. You got your name on the deed, but I'm the one who paid for it."

"We both made a lot of money in here. I found the guys. All you had to do was lie on your back and think of England."

"England's an awfully ugly place, if England was what I was thinking."

"Get ready to do some more thinking. You were a favorite. Some of those guys still want me to call them when I've got you back. And now I've got you back." He looked over at Marci. "You a client of hers?"

Marci straightened her back. "I don't do that."

Mountain man laughed. "Get used to that line, bitch. See how much good it does you."

Jason nodded at Marci. "We've lost a lot of girls. We can use you."

Marci bit her lip and didn't say anything. She did move a little farther down the kitchen island and put a little more distance between herself and the skinny girl. She noticed that the mountain man had his gun reversed with the butt sticking out of the jacket. It looked tough but it meant than he would have to reach his right hand around to his left side to draw the gun, take an extra second. She eased over another foot until she was almost at his side. Neither of them paid a lot of attention to her.

Jason nodded and mountain man pulled a little cellophane packet out of his pocket.

"Told you, I don't do that anymore," said the skinny girl.

The guys laughed again.

"There's that line again," said Jason. "Get's funnier every time. Look, we just want to have fun and get back in business. The high rollers like you. They want to come back here like they used to and have fun like they used to. That's all this stuff is: powdered fun. You used to laugh all the time when you were using. We just want to see you laugh for us."

Mountain man stepped across and shoved the packet at the skinny girl. She knocked it out of his hand and the powder spilled all over the floor.

He looked at her cold and calm. "Now you get to snort it off the floor."

He reached out for her with his right hand. Marci jumped and kicked his elbow and there was a loud crack. She stepped across and kneed him hard in the groin once, twice, three times before he knew what was happening. She grabbed him by the shoulders and smacked his head against Jason's. She reached over and pulled the gun out of his belt.

"Get out," she said. Looking at the gun, they didn't argue.

As the door closed behind them, she turned to the skinny girl.

"Think I'm good enough for Josh?"

"You'll do."

Chapter 38

Marci was asleep when I got home. I showered to get the dish-washing smell off and climbed under the covers of the big bed. She was on her side turned away from me, the sheet off from the waist up. I lay there for a minute too keyed up to sleep and watched her. I tried to comprehend where I was, and none of it seemed real here in the big room with the big bed. None of it except Marci. I moved over and spooned against her, feeling comfort and certainty against her skin.

"Don't wake me," she said in a sleepy voice. She pushed back against me.

"Don't wake me much." She rolled over.

Marci was in the middle of not waking up much when I said, "Look, we've got a problem."

"We don't appear to have a problem. Other than your think-ing I'm your personal toy, someone you can just wake up anytime you want a little fun."

"No. I mean, I don't think that. Well, I'm not complaining. Oh." I jumped out of bed and pulled the white pants on.

"Because I am, you know." Marci stretched and smiled, sleepy-sexy sitting up in the bed naked. "Your toy. Anytime. You don't need that drawer."

"I told you, that's not mine."

"I know. I thought I was going to give those things back to their owner tonight."

"What's that mean?"

"Never mind. I'm not supposed to tell. Confidential sources and all that." Marci was still half-asleep and smiling, caught up in the moment of just being a rich guy's girlfriend in his big expensive apartment.

"Something happen here tonight?"

Marci thought. "I got a lot of work done on the book."

I shook it off and hoped I would remember to ask Marci later what all this meant. But I needed to get the important stuff out now.

"No. I mean we've got problems with Kiev."

"Oh." Marci finally woke up all the way from her half-dream of the good life and remembered they had more things on their plate. She stood up and picked up the white robe from the back of a chair and slowly pulled it on. I wished I had waited a few minutes on this conversation.

"I talked to a guy tonight. The bozos like to hurt things. I still don't know what's going on. Maybe it's still just a joke. But maybe bad things are going on and maybe we're the only ones that can stop it."

Marci sat down in an overstuffed wing chair by the window. "And if we don't stop it, then bad things will be going on for us soon."

"Yeah." I walked over to the window and looked out at the night. For a moment, I thought I saw black Escalades rolling up the street and black speedboats coming across the bay, even a black helicopter or two hovering in the air. I stepped back from the window before the snipers or my imagination got me.

I told Marci what Harry had told me.

"But I don't know where to go from here. Nobody there knows where Dread and Roscoe might be. We don't even know if the Romanovs have had another phone call. This whole thing might be over but we can't count on it."

"Oh." Marci hopped up. "I got something." She walked out

to the dining room and I followed her. "I went through the stuff in the knapsack. In between other things." She smiled, and I wondered again what I had missed. "Mostly just crap in the knapsack, but I did find this: an electric bill in Roscoe's name. I looked up the town. It's a little place up in the Sierras. There's no ski resort or anything else close, Google doesn't even show a restaurant for the town. Kind of place somebody might have a little hunting cabin or trailer."

I took the bill and stared at it, as if the address would mean anything.

"Only forty dollars for last February. Sounds like they had the place shut down for the winter, just pay the minimum amount. Maybe you're right. Maybe they just go up there in the spring and open it up, take their guns and girly magazines. Maybe we could sell them the toys from the bathroom."

"The owner might object." I looked at her but right now we had to figure out how to stay alive and keep Kiev alive.

"Never mind," we both said at the same time.

"Look," I said. "Have we got a map anywhere around here? We need to figure how to get up to this place."

"Silly." I wondered where Marci had picked up that word. "Nobody uses maps anymore."

She dug around in Roscoe's old mail until she found her laptop buried under a Soldier of Fortune magazine. She turned it on. "Get me some coffee."

I didn't like being ordered around but I did as I was told. In the cupboard I found a bag of an expensive Hawaiian blend. I remembered one time when the skinny girl brought a bag of this same stuff into the Western World. Mayor and the regulars spat it out and demanded she make a fresh pot with the cheap-shit coffee they were used to. I wondered where the skinny girl was now, wondered if she was using again, dancing on the low table with the regulars bored and half watching, occasionally trying to touch her and getting their hands slapped for their trouble. I missed her dancing. Sure, there was the sad, exploitive side of things: watching her too strung out to care, doing what somebody else wanted just to beg for a buck to buy more stuff to slowly kill herself. But the skinny girl always brought something more. A part of her danced just for herself, far away and untouchable. She danced with her eyes closed, mostly. Sometimes, when she danced, she would open her eyes and smile at me, and we would share a little moment beyond the bar and the drugs and the alcohol and the bullshit.

I imagined her reading a book now, pushing the silly reading glasses up as she struggled with a big word. I imagined her looking up from the book with that same look.

I took the coffee back into the dining room.

"Here," said Marci. "Look at this. Here's the town. Here's the route we take to get to the town. That's the easy part, maybe six hours or so."

I looked at the words beside the map. "Says, 'six hours thirty-three minutes.' "

"That's crap. Nobody drives the speed limit."

"We will. We get pulled over for one speeding ticket and the gray shirts will know about it before the cop's done writing it up."

"You're paranoid, you know it?"

"I'm alive."

She looked back at the map. "The hard part's going to be getting up the mountain and finding their trailer. It doesn't show up on the map or on satellite photos. Here's the area of their land." She turned the screen around and showed me. "Only thing going in is this dirt road. Don't know how far we can get up that."

I said, "Not to mention that we don't have survival gear or surveillance tools. Not to mention little questions about what we do when we get there. Or what we do if we get there and there's nobody home."

"Details, details. Look on the bright side. We get there, we rescue Kiev, get the Romanovs and gray shirts off our backs. I write my book and stop talking about success and get to live the good life, and we live happily ever after."

I looked skeptical.

Marci looked at me and sighed, knew she needed to add something to appeal to me. "And Mother Romanov gets to have Christmas dinner with her whole family gathered around the table. Maybe she'll even let Kiev say, 'God bless us, every one.' "

"Yeah. That would be nice."

"OK," said Marci. "But we still don't know how to do this. We don't have any of the stuff for this. Except for guns. God knows we've got guns. And sex toys. And I'm not going to go climbing around in the woods with a dildo for a compass, hoping like hell that the damned thing points north."

I winced. "Yeah, thanks for putting that image in my head."

"No problem."

We sat and thought.

I said, "We know people who have stuff for military operations."

Marci looked at me. "Those same people want to kill us."

"What'd you just say? Details, details."

I thought some more. "We know Yuri."

"Oh good. For a minute there, I thought you were talking about somebody with a grudge against us. Like somebody mad because we took his pride and joy and left him on the side of the road. Somebody who, by now, probably thinks we're holding his sister hostage. Somebody who's a murderous psychopath who kills for fun and thinks he's got superpowers."

"Yeah, there are a couple of problems."

Marci saw that I was actually thinking about how to do this.

She rolled her eyes and waited.

"I've got Yuri's cell number. You have a phone. The problem is that the gray shirts can look and see where the call comes from."

"Yeah. That's the only problem I can see here."

"Come on. Yuri's got access to all the woods stuff we need. We'll trade him his car for it: tell him where the car is in exchange for the gear."

"Yeah. I'm sure he'd be glad to give you a bullet."

"Come on. It doesn't hurt to talk to him. We need to find out what's going on at the Romanov's anyway."

She sighed. "Look. You figure out how to keep them from tracing this back here, and I'll supply the phone. Still think this is crazy, but it can't hurt. Well, maybe it won't hurt. Besides, it will make a good chapter in the book."

"How about this? See, look, if we just go outside and walk around somewhere, they'll trace it back and be all over the neighborhood. Driving somewhere else means we have to risk someone being able to identify the car, which we don't want."

"OK, so what then? I didn't bring my spaceship."

"We're going to take advantage of being rich and spoiled. We need you to put some clothes on, leave some clothes off, and think about how drunk and horny you are."

CHAPTER 39

Even at three A.M., the concierge was standing at his desk look-ing sharp. Which was more than could be said for Marci and me. The concierge watched us stumble across the lobby toward him in a not-very-straight line. Ah yes, the happy couple from 1412. A well-known suite. Still, he kept the smile on his face. Drunken assholes sometimes tipped very well.

"Can I help you, sir?"

"Yes. Yes, my good man. Yes."

I stood there a minute like I had lost my train of thought. The concierge kept smiling.

"This lovely young lady." I waved at Marci with a flourish. "This lovely young lady. My niece." I paused. "I think." Marci gave me a look. "This young lady would like to rent one of the boats from the dock behind the building. The dock that goes out to the bay."

"Into," said Marci. She wasn't drunk enough for bad gram-mar.

"Into the bay," I said.

"You want to rent a boat?"

"A big boat."

"Yes sir." The concierge got a pained look on his face. "I'm afraid those boats aren't for rent, sir. They belong to people who live here. Some of them even live aboard their boats."

"Surely the management here has a boat to rent for a substantial sum. Charged to the suite, of course."

"Of course, sir. There are only a few boats owned by the management. We use those for charters and harbor tours, you know."

"Certainly I know."

"But they're not for rent, sir. Particularly at night."

"Ah." I turned and winked at Marci. She leaned on me, and the man's unbuttoned shirt she was wearing came open.

"Whoopsie," she said. She and I laughed, and the concierge pretended nothing happened.

"I know what you're saying." I reached into my pocket and pulled out a twenty. I put it in the palm of the concierge. The concierge looked at it like it was a rat turd he had to clean up. So much for drunk assholes tipping well.

"Sir, I'm sorry, but it is after three. Perhaps if you came back in the morning the light would be better for your boat ride."

I pulled the roll out and took a handful of bills off.

"And I'm not authorized to rent the boats."

I pulled more.

"You'll have it back by morning?"

"I'll have it back in an hour," I said.

The concierge put a little placard on his stand letting anyone else who came down at three A.M. know that he was busy helping a resident because that was what he lived for. Marci and I followed him down a long hallway to the back entrance.

"Button up your shirt," I said.

"Oh, you liked it."

We went out past the infinity pool, stylish jazz playing softly even at this hour. We went down the long walkway to the marina. The concierge punched in a code at the marina office and turned to us with a smile.

"I'll have to ask you to wait here for a moment, sir."

"No problem," I said.

"We can find something to do." Marci grabbed my crotch

and laughed, and the concierge grimaced and went into the office.

"Christ, you're really getting into this," I said.

"You have no idea." She leaned up and pulled my earlobe with her teeth. "Maybe we should give up this stupid idea of yours and find something better to do on the boat."

"This is important."

"An important way to get killed," said Marci.

"Trust me."

"Last chance." Marci rubbed her chest against my arm.

"No."

"Then it's not the last chance. This is stupid, and I'm not going to give up."

"You just want a chapter to spice up your book."

"Good reporters never put themselves in the book. This chapter will never see the light of day. I just don't want to write that chapter where I die."

"I can see the problem."

The concierge came out and smiled at me without looking at Marci. He led us down to a couple of small boats painted in the colors of the building. I started to get in the one with the open cockpit.

"This one, sir." The concierge motioned to the boat with a closed cabin with leather benches and enough room to hold a dozen friendly souls. "I thought you could use a little more . . . discretion."

The concierge took Marci's hand and helped her down to the boat. I noticed he wiped his hand on his jacket after he let go of Marci. I stepped aboard. The concierge came past and led us to the small pilot station in the bow of the boat.

"Let me point out the controls to you, sir."

I pointed at the panel. "Bilge pump, engine tachs, GPS, radio." I smiled and looked up.

The concierge smiled. "It is good to see that you know your way around a boat, sir."

"Do you want me to call you on the radio once we're out safely?"

"That won't be necessary, sir. In fact, I'd suggest that you not use the radio at all."

"Suit yourself." I put the key in, blew out the bilges, and started the engines.

The concierge looked concerned. "Perhaps I'd better come along and help."

Marci started unbuttoning her shirt.

"Suit yourself." I looked at Marci and back at the concierge. The concierge hopped up onto the pier, pulled the lines off of the pier cleats, and threw them onto the boat.

"I'll be at my station."

I was already backing out.

"Hey," said Marci, buttoning back up. "You haven't hit anything. Yet."

"I grew up on boats. Fished on a workboat bigger than this when I was twelve. Open those windows, will you? I want to get a sense of the wind."

The dark water slid by us as we cleared the motor sailors and the pleasure yachts of the marina, and then we had the bay to ourselves.

"God, it's cold out here." Marci snuggled up to me.

"San Francisco autumn. Hey, I told you that won't work. We need to make the call."

"No, I'm cold. Only thing I want from you out here is body heat."

I pointed at the bench.

"Check there. Should have a life jacket, keep you a little warmer. Not a bad idea anyway."

She pulled up the seat and looked in the locker below it.

"Hey, even better." She held up an orange rain slicker. She put it on.

"You don't mind," I said. "Put on a life jacket, too. Get me one while you're in there."

She put one on and buckled it and handed me another.

"Josh the Goody Two-Shoes. Yet another side to the man of mystery."

"You bet. When it comes to the water, you can't be too careful. My old man raised us to have everything buttoned down and double-checked on the boat. All the old watermen were like that. That's how they got to be old watermen. He'd fry my butt for having those lines loose like that." I pointed to the lines the concierge had tossed aboard. "He'd want them coiled and ready."

"So you grew up on the water?"

This wasn't a road I wanted to go down. "So you think I'm grown up?"

"Good point."

She snuggled next to me, not for warmth or distraction but just because she wanted to.

"It's beautiful out here. Do you believe this is the first time I've ever been out on the water?"

"I couldn't live like that." I thought about it. "Or, at least, there used to be a time I believed I couldn't live like that. The ocean was life to me. You pull up a handful of water from anywhere and it's all connected. Whether you're on a beach in the south of France or rinsing off a snapper you've caught in the Gulf of Mexico or cleaning up an oil spill in Alaska, it's all connected.

"And every handful has already got everything imaginable in it: the basics of life, of course, salt and water. But there's a little bit of everything else: whale shit, blood from the men who've died at sea, gold, silver, by-products from a million creatures of every shape and form living and loving."

"Sounds kind of icky."

"Not to me. What's icky to me is all the bullshit we pile on to try to convince ourselves we're better than all that."

I pulled out Marci's cell phone and looked at the bars on it.

"This'll work. If the gray shirts trace this back to see where the call came from, they'll be lost. We could have come out here from anywhere in San Francisco."

Marci squeezed my arm.

"I told you, that won't work."

"No, I'm not trying. I think you're right. We need the Batman. We need to know what he knows. We may need that more than the gear. I just hope this works."

"Me too." I cut the engines and we drifted in the darkness and silence on the cold water. I dialed the number. Yuri answered with a grunt.

"You know who this is?" I said.

There was a pause.

"Is man who wants to die."

"Yeah, maybe. Is Kiev back home?"

Another pause.

"Not yet."

"Then don't kill me until we get her back home."

Yuri snorted.

"Besides, I know where your SL65 is. I need to trade it to you for some stuff."

"You got nothing to trade. SL65 gone. Probably in chop shop by now. I've said goodbye to my baby. But not to you."

I didn't say anything for a minute.

"Have the gray shirts made any progress?"

"Whose side are you on? They say you part of kidnappers."

"You know that makes no sense. I had the money in my hand, Yuri. I knew the plan. I could have arranged for something—a boat maybe—to come pick me and the money up. And if I had Kiev, she'd be home now. You know that."

"Everybody mad now. They say you do this."

"What do *you* say, Yuri?"

There was an exhalation of breath.

"You not kidnap Kiev. But you rob Batman."

"Yuri, the Batman set us free. You know we could never have taken your car without you letting us. The Batman in you knew that we were Kiev's only chance, and you let us go."

"Is true." Yuri's voice brightened. "You could not possibly have robbed me unless I let you. You not seem like very good chance for Kiev, though. Mother cry all time now, start to believe Kiev not come back."

I looked out over the black water, scanning for lights or the sound of boats coming.

"Yuri, we need your help."

"You had my help. I already give you car. Next time I see you, I give you bullets."

"What are you getting from the gray shirts?"

"Briefings. Hourly briefings. Reports. I think they trying to make us not see they do nothing useful. They think they're pros, but uniforms and organization doesn't make you a pro."

"We don't have any reports, but we think we know where the guys who made the phone call are. Maybe."

"Then we all go get them. We find Kiev, let me kill them, I forgive car."

"Not 'all' Yuri. We don't need the gray shirts or any of you. My partner and I will go. We just need some things from you."

Yuri grunted. "All right. What you need?"

"We're going into the woods. We don't have the gear for that. The gray shirts do. Can you get into their stores, get us stuff?"

"Sure. They have big room with equipment in packs, ready to

go. I grab couple of packs. This time of night, they have nobody there."

"OK. Look, you know the Safeway on Sixteenth Street? Can you bring the stuff there by six in the morning?"

"Sure."

"I'll be in the middle of the lot on the northwest corner, standing by myself."

"You trust awful much."

"I know I can trust Batman. And besides, I'm awful desperate. All of us are."

CHAPTER 40

I stood in the darkened parking lot in a small puddle of light, turning around slowly, scanning for a car and listening. So far, all I heard was an occasional car up on Highway 101. I looked at my watch. Six-ten. No Yuri. But at least no black Escalades or men in gray.

I kept turning and looking. I stopped for a minute, facing the highway, watching for anyone taking the exit. Nothing. Maybe it was time to give up. Signal Marci to come get me in the SS 396 and head west, hoping we could find a sporting goods store and fake it with the rest of the stuff and hoping we could buy what we needed without the gray shirts knowing. Maybe we could—

Something hard knocked me down from behind. I jumped up to see a sleek, silent black car. Yuri jumped out of the driver's side, took two quick steps with the coat flapping behind him like a cape, and he was on me before I could get to my knees.

Yuri put his boot on my neck and hissed, "Stay down. Maybe I let you live a little longer."

I tried to say, but Yuri pushed down harder. "I talk. I give orders." He stood there a minute, then eased up on my neck. "OK, you talk little."

"I can tell you where your car is. You can get your SL65 back."

"Who want SL65? Is in pieces. Besides, was so last century. Gasoline cost money, make whole world dirty for little bunny rabbits. And make noise. Batman now swoop through the night, silent as the darkness itself." He pointed at the car. It was so black, so dark that it looked like a hole in the night. "Tesla. Electric car. Fast like lightning. And silent. Loudest noise when Yuri fart." Yuri laughed at himself. I would have laughed along to be polite, but I had this boot on my neck. Yuri seemed not to notice.

"See how fast world change. Men who made real Batman movies, not so long ago, they make Batmobile noisy monster belching smoke and fire. Got it all wrong. Now, few years later, the real Batman can fly through the night silent and almost invisible. Progress. You got to love this country."

I would have agreed but, again, there was that boot thing. I grunted and Yuri noticed and took his foot away. He reached down and pulled me up with a jolt.

"See, Batman help people up when down." I didn't want to mention that, if you wanted to be technical, it was Yuri who put me down to begin with. "I forgive you because I have big heart. Because I know you love my sister you have not even met."

"You've got the stuff?"

"Got wonderful stuff. Got two big bags of stuff. Gray shirts not know. By the time they realize the stuff is missing, we'll be home with Kiev."

"Yeah, well, it may not happen that fast."

"It happen. We have Batman. We have disappearing Josh. We have great stuff. You won't believe the stuff the gray shirts have. You got to love this country."

"The one the gray shirts run, or the one the Romanovs run?"

Yuri gritted his teeth. "They think they run country and we front for them. We know we run country and we use them. Or used to. Lately, my father and uncle do whatever the gray shirts say. Don't know why. Know one thing about country: you sure as hell don't run it anymore."

"No. You've got the reports, too?"

Yuri snorted. "Of course. Papa have all the reports from gray shirts on kidnapping, and a lot of other reports on gray shirts. I bring them all, but they good only for wiping backside."

"Where we're going, we may need them."

"You say bring gear for woods, I think you mean park or something."

"No. Woods woods. Mountains even. Probably some snow, even this time of year. That jacket won't keep you warm enough. You stay here. We'll bring Kiev back to you."

"You need the Batman. Yuri Russian. Cold no problem."

"Batman's great, but we need to travel light."

"Batman come. Not like last time. Batman come."

"The guys who took Kiev. Or have Kiev. Or might have Kiev. I don't know. Any case, they know Kiev, and they know Russians. Any chance we have of pulling any kind of scam won't work with you along."

"By the time they know I am there, it is too late for them. Are these same guys you had pictures of?"

"Yeah. Turns out they're low-level hoods. Kiev knows them. Kiev may even have gone with them. Is possible?"

Yuri shrugged. "Is possible. Evie like to play tricks, sometimes get in over her head. I don't know about the money, though. But I know this: Evie always playing like party girl, everything fun. Underneath, she not happy. Pretends to love money, but hates it."

"Still, three million would buy a lot of freedom and therapy."

"She has had a lot of both." Yuri paused. "So you think she is just play hide and seek, will come home when she is good and ready?"

I looked at Yuri and wondered what to say. He was Kiev's brother, and just a big kid himself. He was also the closest thing Marci and I had to a partner in all this.

"There's more, Yuri. These guys have a bad side. They like to hurt things. No matter how this started, Kiev might be in danger."

Yuri looked at me. He had been smiling, thinking now that this was just a fun game his little sister was playing, that she would be home soon and their parents would be mad, but he and Kiev would go out for drinks and laugh about it.

"Maybe they have already hurt her," Yuri said.

"Maybe. But I'm hoping that the fact that they haven't come home means they haven't hurt her."

"Maybe they are afraid to come home. Maybe they are running."

"Maybe, but I don't think so. Their family has power. Not like you guys, but they don't know that there are people like you and the gray shirts out there that can hurt them. No offense, Yuri, but my experience is that you people with power think nothing can hurt you."

"But I can hurt them when we catch them."

I watched Yuri while he digested this. Finally, Yuri said, "Don't tell Mother about this."

"I won't."

"No. I mean don't tell Mother part about Kiev being in danger." Yuri walked over to the passenger door and motioned for me to follow. He opened the door. Mother glared out at me with the same Glock she had back at the house.

"My husband wants to kill you. Tell me why not I shoot you. Let police find you and wonder who you were like we all wonder who you are."

"You know why, Mother. In your heart, you know why. If you thought your husband or the gray shirts were going to bring your daughter back, you'd be with them."

"Maybe she come back on her own." She gave Yuri a look. "You think your old mother not know how to roll down a window? Think a car that can fly through the city at a hundred miles an hour can't roll down a window without you hearing it?"

She waved the gun at Yuri like a ruler. "Don't you ever keep secrets from your mother again. I have one child, break Mother's heart, keep secret and run away maybe. Maybe worse. Don't you be two."

"Yes, Mother." It felt like a conversation they had had before.

"OK," said Mother. "You right. Sergei and Rudi in charge of all-important gray men. Or maybe other way around. They run around like big shots, order women to wait on them. But my Evie still not home, maybe even still not safe. So I in charge of this operation. You understand?"

I looked at Mother and nodded.

"No," she said. "Do you really understand?"

I looked at her.

"You no have children or mother or father or sister or brother?"

"No."

"Who are you close to?"

I thought about it. A bartender who tolerated me. A girlfriend I had known for three days. A skinny girl who had only recently returned to consciousness.

I looked at Mother. "You."

She sighed. "Then you do not know life. Without people in your life, the people you care for, life is empty. Everything seems wrong. What is the word you young people like so much, comes from the big animal? Bullshit. That's it. Life is either people you care about, or life is bullshit.

"I am lucky. I have many people to care for. Imperfect people." She looked at Yuri. "Very, very imperfect people. But many people I care for.

"One more is always good. You I care for, now." She waved

the Glock at me. "I keep gun to your head, make you do your job, but I care about you.

"I your mother. Take Yuri: brothers go rescue their sister. Bring your sister home to your mother.

"Give me Christmas with all my children. All around big table, pretending they have better places to go, but me knowing, this is their life.

"Give me my children for Christmas. All your mother ask."

CHAPTER 41

Yuri and I watched as Mother drove away, the car fishtailing silently through the night in the general direction of the mall exit.

"I maybe buy another car soon," said Yuri.

"I take it Mother doesn't usually drive fast cars."

"Don't know if Mother ever drive any car before. She yell at nav system, 'Go home,' until I tell her to step on the pedal."

"We may have to rescue more than one Romanov."

We stood and watched as the car slid into the road, straightened out, and accelerated past a hundred.

"Looks like she's already learned to drive like you."

"Makes a son proud."

I waved in the direction of a Dumpster on the edge of the parking lot. There was a low rumble and the SS 396 rolled toward us.

"Wow," said Yuri when the car stopped in front of him. "Chevelle SS 396." Marci got out of the car. "Classy," said Yuri.

"Thank you," Marci said.

"I meant car."

"Oh."

"I drive," said Yuri.

"Like hell," said Marci.

Yuri ran his hand over the hood.

"This is what your SL65 turned into," I said.

Yuri looked at me. "Somebody got good deal."

217

"Well, we didn't exactly have the pink slip on the Mercedes."

"You got the pink slip on this?"

"No."

"Somebody got a good deal."

"Yeah, well, let's see what kind of a deal we got with this." I started to open one of the backpacks.

"In the car." Marci motioned at the backseat. "You boys can play with your toys while I'm driving."

I nodded.

Yuri said, "You bring Sheila?"

"Yeah. Except Sheila sometimes likes to be called 'Marci.' "

"Like I'm Yuri and I'm Batman."

"Kind of like that, yeah."

I picked up a bag and tossed it in the back. "I'll ride back here with the stuff."

"Ought to make both of you children ride in the back," said Marci.

I loaded the last bag and climbed in after.

Yuri climbed in the front and said "Shotgun!" as Marci put the car in gear and popped the clutch.

"Shotgun?" She turned to Yuri as the car picked up speed across the dark parking lot. "That's the dumbest thing I've ever heard. 'Shotgun.' You don't call shotgun when you're already sitting in the front seat."

Yuri grinned. "Shotgun," he said again.

He pointed back at me.

"We need secret identity for this one."

"You have no idea," said Marci.

I opened one of the two packs and started taking things out.

"Morphine packs? What do we need morphine packs for?"

Yuri shrugged in the front seat, looking ahead.

"What I know? I grab one pack from shelf labeled 'Survival,' one from Surveillance shelf. We got what we got."

"Yeah, well, maybe we can inject the kidnappers, get them hooked, trade Kiev for drugs."

"Sounds like a plan," said Marci.

We were on the Bay Bridge crossing to Oakland. The sun was coming up, glinting on the bay all around them.

"We need to pick up some coffee," said Marci.

I opened the pack labeled "Surveillance" and pulled out another box. "Sound telescope." I passed it up to Yuri. "See what you can make of this."

Yuri took out a small piece of electronics with an earbud. He put the earbud in one ear and turned it on.

"What do you hear?" I said from the back seat. Yuri pulled the earbud out and glared at me.

"No yell. You think is funny joke, yell to blast Yuri's ears, but not funny to me."

"I didn't yell."

"Sure. Be quiet this time."

He put the earbud back and pointed at Marci.

"You. Not funny one. Whisper something. Very quiet."

"I can be funny," whispered Marci.

"Yeah. I think is one of those jokes Americans like, where you say something that everybody know is not true and everybody laugh."

"We don't make jokes like that," said Marci.

"You watch American TV?"

I wanted to change the subject and stop the kids in front from bickering.

"So what else did you hear?"

"Mostly rumble-rumble-rumble. Is a 396 you know, plodding along at barely seventy. Engine need to breathe, little girl, let those horses run."

"I need to breathe, too," said Marci. "Cops pull us over and put our IDs and descriptions out on the radio, the gray shirts will be on us before the next exit. Specially now that we got you with us." She turned her head a little toward me in the back. "Why did we pick him up? Thought we wanted the equipment. Thought we said no way, no how, to the comic book character."

"Mother said take him."

"What Momma want, Momma get." Marci was joking but the two boys nodded solemnly. She glanced at us.

"God, you men are so easy. 'Momma said.' You get a little older, it's 'What my girlfriend said' or 'What my wife said' or even 'What the cute girl at the mall who might smile at me said.' Is there ever a time when you pathetic creatures aren't wrapped around some woman's little finger?"

"No," we both said in unison.

She motioned at the sound telescope. "See that tube on the front. I think it's some kind of focusing device."

Yuri pulled, and the tube extended out a foot. He put the device in his lap, wiggled the tube around at Marci, and leered at her.

"Boys. Good thing that thing comes with instructions so you know what to do with it."

"Has no instructions."

"My point exactly."

Yuri rolled down the window and pointed the tube at a couple of guys fishing from a pier on the shore.

"Wow."

"Wow what?" said Marci.

"Can hear them talk. Can't hear you. Only hear what you point at." He pointed the tube at the car ahead of them.

"What are they saying?" said Marci.

"They say girls drive too slow."

She glared at him.

"You can't hear what they're saying. That thing won't work through the windshield."

"Maybe they just being quiet."

"Maybe you should just be quiet."

"Children, children," I said. "Ok, so we got a bunch of survival stuff here. Couple of pair of fatigues. A heavy jacket packed in some kind of cool vacuum pack to not take up too much room. Rations, compass, a couple of tiny radios, that kind of thing."

"No makeup?" said Marci.

"Jesus Christ," said Yuri.

"I'm kidding. Told you I was funny."

"You bring the reports?" I said.

"Yeah. They're in the shopping bag.

I shifted the two packs onto the floor and pulled up the shopping bag.

"Jesus, this thing is bigger than the packs."

"When Mother shops, she want everything in one bag. Besides, she always have one of us boys carrying that thing for her."

"Not servants?"

"Mother say, 'Why I need servants when I have children?' We say things, too, but she no listen."

"I bet." I pulled out a stack of papers. "Good God, you've got a damned library in here."

"I take all papers out of Father's desk."

I felt something crunching in the bag. "Hey, what's the rest of this. No wonder this thing is so heavy. Marci, this thing's full of beer and potato chips."

"Oh yeah," said Yuri. "Hand me one of those."

I passed a can forward but Marci pushed it back. "No way. We've got things to do."

"Oh come on," said Yuri.

Marci patted him on the cheek. "Leetle boy," she said in her best Russian accent, which still wasn't very good. "Clean up your room, rescue your sister, then you have beer."

"Aw," said Yuri, but he accepted it.

"I can't believe you brought this," I said. I took the beer back from Yuri. "We're going into the mountains. We're facing guys with hunting rifles who'd like to strap antlers on us and use us for practice. Your sister may be in real danger. And the thing that you think is important to bring is beer and potato chips?"

"Road trip," said Yuri.

CHAPTER 42

"Do we have any idea what we're going to do when we get there?" I said and got no reply from either of them. I drove while Marci went through the reports and typed in her laptop. Yuri was in the back, cleaning his guns. The smell of gun oil filled the car.

"I wish you wouldn't do that here," I said.

"A man takes care of his equipment."

"I just don't want you to shoot me in my equipment."

"Don't worry. That won't be an accident."

We were through Sacramento now, the land turning to brown hills and bigger gaps between the towns. The car was littered with takeout bags and coffee cups.

"Anything in those reports?" I said to Marci.

"Oh yeah. 'On day three of the operation, fourteen thirty-two hours PDT, operative three seven one two took a five-minute break for hygiene needs. Operative three eight four five relieved him.' " She lowered the report and looked at me. "It really says that."

Yuri laughed. "Maybe they really meant it. Maybe they have sense of humor."

"Yeah, these boys are funny."

"See, American sense of humor like you."

Marci glared.

"These things are scary, though. These guys have their hooks into every operation of the US and foreign governments. Most of these papers don't have anything to do with the kidnapping, just different things the gray shirts and Romanovs have been into. Listen to some of this." She rifled through the papers, then put them down. "Never going to find anything in all this crap." She picked up the laptop she had been writing notes in, tangled herself in the cord plugged into the cigarette lighter, got untangled.

"I've got almost seventy pages already and all I've done is organize the gray shirt stuff into a readable narrative. I may have a better book on the gray shirts than I do on Kiev."

"Except that you said you couldn't publish that book."

"Yeah, at least not if I want to stay alive. People need to know this stuff. I need to win the Pulitzer for writing it. But it's not worth getting killed for. I'm going to have to leave most of this out."

"OK. Enough conspiracy paranoia. What about Kiev?"

"Yeah. Here. Listen to this. 'Task force status meeting was joined by Agents Rodriques and Martin of the FBI. They will be on loan to the task force until the end of this operation. The FBI will not be informed of the nature of this investigation.' "

I glanced over for just a second. I was the careful, almost compulsive, driver of the group, with both hands on the wheel and both eyes on the road. But I looked over now, sure that Marci was joking. She wasn't.

"These guys have enough juice to get the FBI to work a case without even telling the FBI what the case is?"

"Looks that way. There's more. They've got Army units they work with. They've got all kinds of access. They even had . . ." She tapped on the keyboard to find something. "Yeah, here, look at this." She held the laptop up in my face. I pushed it away.

"Just tell me. Now would not be a good time to wrap this car around a tree."

"You ain't going to believe me till you see this item for yourself. They've got some kind of helicopter coming over from the Dutch army, something that's got some kind of one-in-the-world sensing capability."

"The Dutch government?"

"Told you," said Yuri from the back. He put his gun back in the holster. "We run the world."

"The gray shirts may run the world. You can't even run the Bat Cave," said Marci.

"We run them. Why you think they work so hard on this?"

Marci turned around toward Yuri. "Batman, I got to tell you, reading this, it looks like they run you."

Yuri glared out the window and muttered something harsh in Russian. "We used to run them. Last year my father and uncle start letting gray shirts push them around. They lose their balls when they get old."

"Yeah, maybe. From what I see, a lack of balls isn't your family's problem. The gray shirts got files on damned near everybody in your family, and there's some scary stuff there. I got some of the same files earlier from my friend in the district attorney's office. The district attorney has the same files but doesn't do shit with it. One funny thing—Kiev's file is different between the gray shirts and the DA."

"Maybe we should work on our immediate problem," I said. "Sooner we get Kiev back, the sooner they're out of our hair and we can go back to our real lives."

"You mean your Buddhist professor–detective life?"

"Yeah, that one," I said. The Western World looked better than the endless road ahead of me.

"You no get rid of us now. Mother make you Romanov for life. She might even give you room next to mine."

"Oh yeah, that's what I need."

"Is nice house."

"Is nice palace. If there were a bigger word than palace, like Taj Mahal Plus, it would be that. No, it's just that I've got my own life and I like it." As soon as I said that, I thought, no, that's bullshit. No, it's the truth. It's the truth, and it's bullshit. Now that did seem to sum up my life.

"Besides," said Marci. "He's got a girlfriend now." She gave my arm a squeeze. "He's going to have to go on book tours with me." She focused on me. "I've decided to make you the hero of the book. We both know I'm doing most of the work on this case, but I think people are a little put off by a book where the author is a hero. So I combine you and me, let you take credit for everything I do. That way, on the book tour, they can interview both the author and the quirky Buddhist detective. You get to be a celebrity, too."

"What I've always wanted." I tried to imagine my old life at the Western World, except with Marci there. I couldn't. I tried to imagine a celebrity life with Marci, and couldn't. My head hurt again.

"Well, there's not going to be any book or any room at the Romanov Inn if we don't get Kiev back. We got a plan, other than riding around in an automobile?"

"No particular place to go," said Marci.

"That's the problem."

Yuri munched on a handful of chips. He leaned forward, talking and chewing at the same time.

"I know plan."

Marci waved him away. "Nothing like the smell of gun oil, grease, and bad breath in the morning."

Yuri looked at the bag. "These things taste like crap. I hate American food."

"Then tell your minions in the worldwide conspiracy to replace all potato chips with borscht chips."

"You not even know what borscht is. Mother make for you sometime, you see."

"Yeah, sometime. Anyway, put down the chips and talk."

"Taste like crap anyway."

"Why do you eat them if they taste like crap?"

"Is road trip."

As much fun as this was, I felt the need to interrupt.

"So you think you've got a plan."

"Better than plan. I see future." Yuri reached up and patted Marci's shoulder. "Turn computer back on. You want to write this. I give it to you for free."

"I'll just try to remember it all."

Yuri raised one finger for silence.

"I see a run-down cabin in the woods."

Marci said, "The tax records say it's a trailer."

"Don't interrupt. I see a run-down cabin in the woods. Two men of evil sit at a table made of logs, playing cards and laughing. Across the room sits a beautiful young girl with long blonde hair. She is tied up in a rustic chair. She is helpless and crying."

"Kiev has long hair? I thought she had that weird Mohawk thing these days," I said.

"I don't think you should make your own sister cry," said Marci. "I don't like this story."

"Shoosh. Is no story. Girl sit in chair helpless. Who will save her? Bad men stop playing cards and rub their hands together, cackling with evil. They going to do bad things to girl if no one stop them. But who can stop? World filled with bad men while good men cower and police can do nothing. Justice a faded American dream, nothing but power and greed and shady figures who govern from the shadows while telling you that your family is in charge.

"Girl just another victim. Soon, her mother will cry. Mother will cry for a long time, and no one can help.

"Our camera pull back. Just two evil men and a helpless girl, then we pull back to a dirty cabin, then to woods, then more woods with nothing for miles around. Girl is doomed, world is doomed.

"Then out of the night sky comes a figure all in black swooping through the air. Is giant beast? Is god? No, is ordinary man, dedicated to becoming something more, dedicated to righting the wrongs of the world. He fly through the air, face set in a determined grimace.

"Fire spurts from his two pistols and the bad men die. He unties the girl. She look up at him with real admiration. They kiss, big, romantic movie kiss."

Marci said, "This is your sister we're talking about here."

"Yeah, maybe we change that part."

"Yeah, maybe," said Marci. "Where are Josh and I while all this is going on?"

"You sitting in car eating potato chips."

Chapter 43

"No, really," I said. "We need a plan."

"I gave you plan. Batman save day."

"Good. Then let's work on a backup plan."

Marci put her laptop in her bag. "OK, they're somewhere out in the woods, isolated."

"Maybe," I said.

"Maybe. But we've got to start somewhere. So we assume what? Two bozos are holed up in the woods with Kiev. If they aren't there, or if they are just hunting, then we're wasting our time, right?"

"Right."

"So they're out in the woods, engaged in some kind of a crime, so they aren't going to be friendly to visitors, so we can't just go up, say we're from the census bureau and ask how many kidnap victims are staying in the trailer."

"Wouldn't have the right forms for that, either."

"Yeah. Bunch of things wrong with that approach."

Yuri leaned up into the front and pointed to a small metal building. "Look, pizza."

"Jesus Christ, Yuri, do you ever think about anything but food?" Marci said.

"Cars. And guns. Hey, I am renaissance man."

"Yeah, just what I was thinking."

I interrupted. "He might be right, Marci. Not many towns left. Better get something while we can."

I pulled into Branson Pizza. The pizzeria shared a metal building with a small dollar store.

"OK," said Marci. "But we get it to go. No point in giving the locals any more of a look at us than necessary."

"You do know that just because the people in here wear uniforms doesn't mean they work for the gray shirts?"

"I'm not so sure, after what I've been reading."

We walked up to the counter. A teenage boy and girl sat at a table and pretended to ignore us as we walked by. A young black guy behind the counter wore a uniform that said "Branson Pizza," but that could have been a secret uniform for the gray shirts. In any case, he did ignore us.

"I'll order," said Marci. "You two sit down over there in that booth."

Marci ordered and brought three Michelobs to the booth.

"Long day. You boys deserve a reward."

"If the reward's for the boys," I said, "which one of us gets the third beer?"

"Funny," she answered by draining half of her beer.

"Here's the plan," she said.

"You got a plan?" I said.

"I got a plan for a plan, which is more than we've had so far. We take the pizza up the road, find someplace quiet, sit and plan what we do tonight."

"Sounds like a plan for a plan."

I took a long swallow of the beer and felt the alcohol hit me immediately. Felt good. It gave me an excuse not to think about all the things out there that I had to think about. I looked around and wondered if Branson Pizza had a back closet they would be willing to rent out.

A big guy with a curly dyed-blond mullet sat across from us. He wasn't ignoring us.

"You folks don't look like you're from around here," he said at a level somewhere between loud talk and shouting. The other people in the place pretended not to hear him. The way they looked at the floor said they were used to not hearing him.

Marci and Yuri and I sat silent for a minute.

"We here to hunt," said Yuri.

"You look like you're dressed to hunt." He pointed at Yuri's black silk suit. The guy slurred his speech a little. He stood up. Yuri stood up too.

"What are you hunting?"

"Fools." Yuri stepped toward him.

"Care to repeat that?" The guy stepped toward Yuri.

"Bulls," said Marci, standing up herself. "He said he's hunting bulls."

"Bulls?" Yuri and the big guy both turned to Marci and said it in unison.

"You can't hunt bulls," I said, as quiet as I could for Marci to hear. Marci shrugged.

"Only animal I could think of. I had to do something."

"Only 'bull' here is you and your friends." Mullet man poked Yuri in the chest. Yuri pulled the jacket back so the two automatics gleamed against the black fabric.

"So maybe Yuri a bull fighter, got cape and long sword and everything."

Mullet man should have backed down but it didn't look like he would. The guy behind the counter grabbed the wooden paddle hanging on the wall beside the oven. With one quick motion, he slid it in the oven, pulled out the pizza and dropped it into a cardboard box.

"Order's ready," he said.

Marci jumped up and grabbed the pizza. I grabbed Yuri by the back of his coat. "Time to go," he said. "We've got to get back to Sacramento."

Yuri let himself be led toward the door.

Behind him, the mullet man said, "You better run, bull man."
Yuri turned to the man with a smile. "I'm Batman."

I pulled Yuri harder. "Yeah, well, we've got things to do. Remember?"

Yuri let himself be pulled out the door, still smiling and locking eyes with mullet man. Marci had the car running. The car was throwing gravel out of the parking lot before Yuri and I had our doors closed.

"Jesus Christ, Yuri. What do you want to do, get us killed or thrown in jail?" Marci said without turning around.

"Not going to jail. My father come get me out."

"Have you forgotten? Your father and his friends are looking for us. This is not something we want, Yuri."

Yuri shrugged. I had been looking back. I turned around now.

"I don't think anybody's coming after us."

"What a relief," said Marci. "The whole goddamned world is chasing us. We get away from one dumb redneck and you want to say, 'Think everything's OK now.' "

"Look, he's not going to call the gray shirts. And I don't think he's part of the Romanov family."

Marci said, "Yeah, but he might call the local police. What do you think the gray shirts will do when they hear about a tall Russian dressed in black wearing two pistols threatening people out here?"

"Yeah, maybe." I was tired and a little buzzed and wanted the other half a beer I left on the table.

We drove in silence. Marci found a dirt road that went into a thicket of oak trees. She took it until it came to a clearing.

"OK," she said. "It's going to be dark in a few hours. We need to figure out what we're going to do and get somewhere for the night."

We got out and spread the pizza on the hood. Marci opened

her laptop and brought up a map of the area.

I took a slice of pizza and bit into it. "Pizza's half-baked."

"Whose fault is that?" Marci was panning the map.

Yuri mumbled something.

"What's that?" Marci said.

"I said I'm sorry," said Yuri.

"It's OK." Marci didn't look up from the screen.

"No. Tired of always screw things up. Strut around like some big peacock, but all I do is screw up. Mother and Father always have to fix what I do. No want you and Josh to have to fix my screw-ups. I am sorry, and I am tired of being sorry."

Marci looked up from the laptop at Yuri. She reached up and put her hand on his cheek like a mother with a small child.

"You're not a screw-up. You're Batman."

He started to say something, but she held her hand up and motioned back to the screen.

"Look, we're on this road here." She picked up a slice of pizza with her other hand and took a bite. "God, this is"—she looked at Yuri—"fine. This is just fine. OK, see, we're on this road. Somewhere up here is Bozoland. I don't think they're on the road itself. So it looks like we need to go about thirteen miles more into the mountains, and then start looking for a dirt road or a jeep track off to the left."

"OK, what then?" I said. "You want me to make an aluminum foil junior sheriff's star, walk up to the trailer, and arrest them?"

"Not unless we want them to die laughing." She paused. "No. Let's drive up as quiet as we can until we see lights, then figure it out from there."

"They might be watching that path. We can't count on the trailer being far enough back for them not to see us. Plus I don't know how far this car will go up a dirt road."

"OK." Marci threw up her hands. "I'm planned out. Your

turn." She pulled the laptop onto her lap. "I'm going back to my book."

"OK," I said. "How about this? We look for the path. Then we go up a little farther and find a place to get off the road and set up a base camp for the night. From there, we can do a recon to their trailer and see where we go from there."

"Base camp? Recon? You sure you're not a plant from the gray shirts?"

"I used to be in an outfit that did that sort of thing."

"Buddhist paramilitary operations. Seriously, we get out of this, we've got to have a long talk about your past."

"*If* we get out of this."

Marci looked up from her laptop.

"Hey, how about this for a title? 'The Girl Who Wanted to Live.' "

CHAPTER 44

The road up the mountain was theoretically two lanes and theoretically graveled, but that was optimistic in both cases. I drove, picking my way around rocks and potholes.

"How far now?" said Marci, looking at the laptop.

I looked at the odometer to see how far we'd come. "Eleven point four miles."

"Could be anytime."

We were inching downhill into a small cut in the mountain between this and the next uphill, coming up on a dry creek at the bottom of the cut.

"Look at that." Marci pointed at tracks off to the left.

"Got it. Yuri, hang your head out the window and check out that path as we go past."

Yuri rolled down the window and leaned out.

"It looks like—"

"Shush," said Marci as they went past. "Roll up the window and we'll talk."

Yuri rolled up the window. "Yeah, like I'm louder than engine on this thing."

"Do what we can do. We don't want to give them any more help than we have to."

"Yes, ma."

She turned back to Yuri. "What'd you see?"

"Big tire tracks, like maybe truck or van."

"Probably don't have a Smart car up here," said Marci.

"Wouldn't be Smart," I said. "Yeah. I looked down as far as I could, too. There was a wet spot a little farther down. Looked like they spun the tires there, and looked recent."

"OK," said Marci. "That's it. We go up another half mile or so. We don't see anything else, we set up there."

The road went uphill after the turnoff, and we saw nothing more before the top of the rise. Just past the top, out of sight from the dry creek, I found a spot in a small thicket I could pull into and get turned around.

"Home, sweet home," I said. "OK. Whispers only from now on. Yuri, open up that survival pack and get out the camo fatigues. Let's see how close we can come to making us all invisible."

Yuri dug through the pack. "Only two pair of pants."

"You two take them. Hand me two of the t-shirts and a roll of the black tape. And a knife."

I cut the shirts and wrapped them around my legs. Marci pulled one pair of pants over her jeans and looked back to see what else was available.

"Yuri," she said. "Put your pants back on."

"You say change to fatigues."

"No. Put them on top of your pants."

"Yuri never do anything right."

"They'll keep you warmer, too, with two layers," I said. "Going to get cold here soon."

Yuri grumbled. Marci reached back for one of the shirts.

"No," I said. "Let Yuri and me take the shirts. You take the jacket. You'll need it to stay warm."

"I'll be OK."

"It will also make you look bigger."

"Women don't want to look bigger."

"They do if they want to scare two men with guns. Yuri's big enough already. If they see you, I want them to be as intimidated as possible."

"What about you?"

"I don't intend for them to see me."

I pulled on my shirt. "Any caps in there?"

Yuri pulled out two knit caps.

"OK. Let me have one of these. Marci, take that bandana for your head. Now everybody be quiet for a second."

I cracked the door a few inches and listened. When I heard nothing, I stepped out, picking my spots on the ground so that I made no noise.

"Josh," Marci hissed. "Where do you think you're going?"

"Recon." I eased the door closed and moved silently from tree to tree until I couldn't see the SS 396 anymore.

I came back a half hour later, eased the door open, and crawled back in.

"What you recon?" said Yuri.

"No, you don't say it like that. Never mind. Marci can fix that in the book. I think this is the place. I smelled smoke, and I thought I saw a plume in the sky."

"Let's go look."

"No. Let's stay put. Early evening is the worst time to go stomping around in the woods. You can't see where you're stepping. You make noise and you get lost. We need to rest. Just before dawn, we'll move down. Based on what we know about the bozos, I'm betting that they're not early risers."

I turned back to Yuri. "What do you have on your menu of gourmet emergency rations?"

We each got a box and ate silently. While we ate I said, "Pass me that surveillance pack up here."

Yuri passed the pack up, and I went through it. I pulled out a nightscope and the sound telescope and set them on the floorboards at my feet.

"Don't step on those," said Marci.

"I won't. I just want them handy." I took Dread's automatic from the Clampett house and set it beside them.

"OK. Let's try to get some sleep," I said when we were done eating. Marci unplugged her laptop from the lighter socket, turned, and backed into my arms. I slid my legs down until we were spooned together on the front seat.

"Hey, none of that up there," said Yuri.

"Shared body heat," I said.

"Keep body heat to yourselves. Don't embarrass Yuri."

"Right."

Soon Yuri was snoring.

I whispered to Marci, "You're going to make a great mother someday."

"I hope my baby's a little smaller than that one back there."

We were quiet for a few minutes. Then Marci said, "I kind of gave up on that a while back."

"What's that?"

"You know. Babies, house with a picket fence, all that."

"Yeah. I kind of gave up on some things, too."

We were quiet again for a while.

"Maybe after the book's out we could go somewhere, start over," she said.

"Once the book's out a lot of things will change for you. Being a big shot changes everything."

"Yeah, maybe. But I really do want the book."

"Then you should have it."

"And I want something for us, too."

I thought about that for a while.

"Yeah," I said. "Maybe we could have that, too."

Marci turned back and kissed me. I kissed back and put my hand around her breast.

"No," she said, giggling. "Not with our baby in the back."

We were both quiet for a long time. I wondered how it might

work, if I could go back to all the things I made fun of now. I fell asleep for a while. Not drunk this time, just asleep.

CHAPTER 45

I woke up and looked at Marci's watch. Almost midnight. I slipped away from Marci and cracked the door open, stepped back until my feet were both on the ground and my body still in the SS 396. I picked up the nightscope, the sound scope, and the gun and backed out into the darkness.

I stood there a minute and thought about how much I was over my head. It had been a long time since I had carried a gun into the woods trying to avoid being shot by other men with guns. Even then, mostly, I did what I was told. I looked around for the captain. No captain. No lieutenant, no sergeant either.

There was a fundamental rule in the Army: never volunteer. Damned good rule but here I was, volunteering. For a minute, I thought about getting back in the car.

But I remembered I wasn't exactly volunteering. It's not volunteering if the Romanovs have a gun in your back.

So I took one step into the darkness, watching the ground to make sure I didn't fall or make a sound. Then another step. More steps to the first tree.

It took me almost an hour of wrong moves and long pauses before I saw the trailer. There was a light on.

The trailer was an old Airstream, the shiny aluminum skin covered now in moss and slime. There was a slab outhouse twenty yards behind the trailer, and kind of a lean-to made from pine logs that had a truck and a van parked in it. The place looked abandoned except for a little garden area just beyond the trailer. A flat rock there had been swept clean. The dirt around the rock was cleared and raked in some kind of swirling pattern. On the rock was a small altar.

On the altar sat a girl.

I pulled the night sight out of my pocket and focused it. The figure was half-turned away from me, sitting motionless in a full lotus with both feet on top of her thighs. It was Kiev. The top patch of her Mohawk had been cut, and her hair was grown out to about the length of a boy's buzz cut. But even in the green glow of the nightscope, there was no mistaking the high Slavic cheekbones and full mouth that helped make her a darling of the paparazzi.

I watched her for a minute. She seemed calm and serene. At home. That was the phrase that came to mind. She seemed at home, not in danger. I relaxed. Tomorrow was going to be easier than I thought. Tomorrow we would talk to her. She would come home, and I could go back to being Josh Nobody and Nothing.

There were voices in the trailer. I moved the nightscope to the window, adjusted it to be able to see in the light of the trailer. I saw a man's back, maybe Roscoe's. I picked up the sound telescope and put the earbud in. It took me a minute to figure it out, but then I heard Roscoe.

"I've had it. Tomorrow we clean up this mess and go home."

Then Dread. "Still not sure about this. I don't think she's ever going to tell anybody."

"You can take that chance. I can't. She goes home to Momma. Momma says, 'Good to see you, what about that ransom call?' What's she going to say? They tell the cops, the cops come looking for us. Ain't kidnapping, but it sure as hell could be extortion. I ain't going back inside."

"She's not that bad."

"You only say that because she lets you hump her. Or used too, before she got spiritual."

I heard a laugh. Dread said, "You only say that because she doesn't let *you* hump her."

"Well, I let the big head do the thinking. And it says, 'Don't go back to jail.' Kill the bitch tomorrow; put the body in the woods on the way out. Nobody will ever find her, and they won't find us. We'll go home and folks will be like, 'Did you hear that the Russian chick disappeared?' and we'll say, 'Sorry, we were in the woods the whole time.' Only way, man," said Roscoe.

"I don't think we'll get into any trouble we can't get out of if we just take her back with us."

"You mean that your daddy can't get you out of. I ain't got no daddy to save my bacon."

There was a pause.

Roscoe said, "If your daddy would save you. You think your daddy would save you after you embarrass him by getting arrested and making him look bad?"

"Maybe."

"I bet he's celebrating right now being rid of you. What was that old phrase about something or other in the woodpile?"

"Shut up."

"Face it, son. Your daddy would be pissed if you came back in town with a white girl claiming you molested her. He'd lead the lynch mob hisself."

"Shut up."

"Face it, bro. I'm the only friend you got. We got to stick together on this."

I put the sound telescope back in my pocket and looked at the woods around the trailer. I needed to work my way around and get to Kiev before she went back inside, be the hero and get her out of there while the getting was good. I moved around behind a rock where I could see Kiev while staying out of sight of the trailer.

I was planning my next move when Kiev stood up, uncoiling from the ground in a single graceful movement. She was too far away for me to call to her. I hissed but she either didn't hear or didn't care.

She was walking toward the trailer. I whispered her name, and she paused but then went on. Any louder and the boys in the trailer would hear.

I picked up a rock and threw it at her. She jumped when it hit her in the leg and scowled in my direction. I stuck out my head and an arm, just a little, and whispered, "Evie." She thought about it, tossed her head, and walked on. I leaned out farther, whispered, "Please." She looked at me and then marched over.

"My father send you?"

"Quiet. Please. Don't get us both killed."

"My father kill people. My friends don't. You go away, tell Father that I find peace in wilderness. Not go home. No more guns. No more photographers. Or drugs or money or fame. Just peace."

"Look, your father didn't send me. Well, sort of, but sort of not. But you can't go back in there. Those men will kill you. They'll kill me, too, if they find me out here."

She snorted. "My father think anyone without money is a criminal. Rest of world think that, too. They all treat me like goddess, long as I do what they want. I done with that. These men are common men, men of the earth. Not perfect, but more good in men without money than all the real criminals with money."

"Can't argue with that. But these guys are going to kill you."

"You listen to my father too much. I the one tell men to demand my father pay money. I think then I need money to get away. Then I see I no need money. Just peace and karma and friends."

"Your friends will kill you if you don't leave now."

She snorted again. "Don't believe everything my father tell you. And you tell him, I not come back. These are my friends."

She turned and walked toward the trailer, then turned and came back.

"Tell my father and mother I love them. They do some bad things on their own, but I know they not have a choice about many other bad things. With me gone, they be free."

She turned and walked into the trailer without looking back. I heard her say something inside. Then I heard Dread, loud and drunk, talking to Kiev. "Leave me alone. Just leave me alone. I'm not your friend."

Chapter 46

"What you mean?" said Yuri. "You talk to my sister and then let her go back in trailer with men who going to kill her?"

"I had to get back to you guys," I said.

Yuri and Marci were still rubbing their eyes in the dark after I shook them awake and told them what was in the trailer. In truth, I wasn't sure I'd done the right thing. Maybe if I had tried to grab her. Maybe if I had brought Yuri with me. Clobbered her, knocked her out somehow. Maybe, maybe, maybe.

"Besides, I told you, she wouldn't come."

"Never listen to woman," said Yuri.

Marci was sleepy and let it pass.

"OK, now what?" she said.

"It took me about twenty minutes to get back, now that I know the way. We want to give them a couple of hours to get to sleep. So we've got about an hour here to plan and get ready. Then we go get Kiev and the boys. And go home."

"Think the boys will be packed up and ready to go with us?" Marci stretched. "God I stink. And my mouth tastes like crap. Hope they have a shower."

"It ain't the Holiday Inn. You got a better place up here than they got there."

"Oh good. But back to my question: what about the boys?"

"They don't expect anything. We may just catch them sleeping."

"We may not."

I nodded.

Yuri said, "Then we swoop in and blast the shit out of everything."

Marci said, "Including Kiev."

Yuri swore under his breath. "Even in own head, Yuri a screw-up. Wish I had vodka."

I wondered if a lack of beer—or vodka—explained Yuri's fading confidence. Maybe mine, too. "Let's get some food in our systems." I handed out a couple of boxes to Marci. "Oh, look. A hygiene kit. Probably got a razor so you can shave that stubble." I rubbed her cheek and she glared. "And some kind of little toothbrush." She yelped and I covered her mouth.

We didn't realize how hungry we were. We ate in silence for a few minutes.

Marci broke a cracker in half and held it up. "So, we just go up to the front door, after all this?"

"Looks that way. There's just one door in the trailer. Three windows, but they're all too small to get in. If we're lucky, the door's unlocked," I said.

"So you want to take the empty pizza box up to the door, yell 'pizza man!' and ask them for a girl for a tip? Hope she comes with you."

It sounded good to me. Put together a disguise and an identity. I was rehearsing lines when I shook myself back.

"Nah, too early in the morning for that."

"Yeah, that's what's wrong with that idea."

I thought, yeah, but it still might help.

"What if the door's locked?"

"Then we'll have to break it down. And move fast after that. Look, there's a big rock down there, just in front and off to the side of the trailer. We set up behind that and see what we do from there."

Marci pulled out the toothbrush and a small tube and started brushing.

"Oh God, this is good." Foam came out of her mouth.

"Bet she never say that to you," said Yuri.

I said, "Or looked so good saying it." Marci made a face at me. She cracked open her door, leaned out, and spat on the ground.

"You don't have to do that. It's made for you to swallow."

Yuri started to say something, but Marci pointed a finger at him in a way that let him know that the finger was loaded and ready to fire, and he kept quiet. Snickered, but didn't say anything.

"How do you know that? What makes you an expert in military toothpaste?"

I said nothing.

"Just more bullshit from you."

I said nothing again.

"So what if they don't listen to reason and let her go? What if one of them has a gun or something?" she said.

"This is a question?" said Yuri. "We kill them. We kill them anyway." He looked at us. "After we get Kiev. I got it. Get Kiev first, then kill."

"We don't kill them," said Marci.

"If we don't kill them, how they learn?"

I shook my head. "We take them with us. We get back, we let the Romanovs have them."

Marci said, "How's that different from what Yuri said? Whose side are you on here?"

"On the side of getting done with this and washing my hands clean and going back to a normal life. Going forward to a normal life. Hell, who knows, I just want to be going some-where."

We sorted out the guns and stuff and eased out of the car. I

247

reached back in and took the empty pizza box.

"What the hell is that for?" hissed Marci in the darkness.

"You'll see. Now look. We've got to be careful and invisible. We don't want one of these guys to go out to take a leak, see us, and turn this into a firefight. Follow behind me. Marci next. Yuri, you cover the rear. Try to step in my footprints. But whatever you do, look before you put your foot down. Don't step on a branch, don't step on a rock. Don't talk unless you have to. Got it?"

Marci nodded. Yuri said, "Sure, I got it." Marci put her finger on his lips, then took Yuri's head in her hands and nodded it up and down. She looked at him and arched her eyebrows into a question. He nodded up and down.

We filed out, me in the lead, Marci imitating me, and Yuri following with one hand on one of the guns in his belt holster. It took forever, it seemed. We got to the rock and crouched behind it. I set the pizza box on the ground. I pointed at the ground to indicate that they should stay there, pointed at my chest and then the trailer to indicate that I was going to scout the trailer, and then pointed two fingers at my eyes to indicate they should stay alert.

Marci just shrugged and held her hands palm up to indicate that she didn't know what the hell that meant. Yuri grinned and put his hand on top of his head and fluttered his fingers at me like a Three Stooges movie. Marci smiled back at Yuri and shuffled her hands back and forth like she was walking like an Egyptian. Yuri circled one hand over his head and said, "You do the hokey-pokey and—" before I covered his mouth.

I whispered, "Jesus. I meant I'm going to check out the trailer. You stay here. If I do this"—I made a gesture—"you come running. I do this"—different gesture—"you stay put."

I took one step, then turned back, and whispered, "I requisition commandos, I get comedians."

"Which are you?"

"OK, Marci, you got the last word. Now be quiet." I turned and disappeared. After a long stretch I came back behind the rock.

"OK, here's what we got. Everybody's sleeping, or at least everybody's in bed and not moving. The trailer's basically two rooms. The door opens into a room that's about two-thirds the length of the trailer. It's like a kitchen-dinette-whatever. Looks like one person sleeping on a bunk in there, all the way to the right.

"To the left is a little room with just a double bed. I'm guessing Dread and Kiev are in there, but I couldn't be sure. Marci, I want you to move quietly around those bushes to the right side window. Watch for us. When you see us coming to the door, peek in the window and cover us." I looked at her. "Don't shoot unless you have to."

"I won't."

I looked at her again.

"But do shoot if you do have to."

She nodded.

I picked up the pizza box and pulled out the KA-BAR knife strapped to my leg. I cut the bottom of the box.

"What the hell are you doing?"

I took out my gun and held it inside the box. It looked like I was just holding a pizza box from the bottom.

"And what is that supposed to accomplish?"

"May buy me a second. If one of them wakes up, sees a friendly pizza guy, he may hesitate before he shoots."

Marci rolled her eyes. "You just like to play dress up. Sometimes I worry about our marriage."

She was gone before I could say anything.

CHAPTER 47

I was still thinking about the marriage comment as I walked up to the trailer door. My lips were pulled back into a forced smile, and I hoped that was armor enough if one of the boys with guns was awake.

Yuri was coming up from the right, as stealthy as Yuri could be. He reached the corner of the trailer as I reached the door.

I took a breath and forced myself to keep moving slowly and consciously. I raised my left hand to the cheap doorknob and twisted. The handle turned and the door cracked open. No turning back now. I stepped through and turned to the figure in the bunk on the right. Yuri pushed in behind me with both guns drawn and went to the room on the left.

The noise woke the man in the bunk in front of me. I heard the man grunt, and then Roscoe sat up and looked at me with more of a question than surprise.

"Delivery," I said.

There was a gunshot behind me.

"Yuri," I yelled. There was no need for quiet anymore. Roscoe started to get out of the bunk. I took the pizza box off and waved him back down with the gun.

"Yuri, you OK?"

Yuri stepped back into the main room.

"Much better." He pointed the gun in his right hand at Roscoe. "Better still when this one tell us where Kiev so I can kill him, too."

"I thought she was there."

"No Kiev. Just one dead black man."

I looked at Roscoe. "Where's the girl?"

Roscoe smiled. "What girl?"

"You want to talk to me or talk to him like Dread did?"

Roscoe shrugged. "Not my friend. Never cared for the spade much." He looked at Yuri. "Or Russians."

Yuri shoved the gun in Roscoe's mouth and broke a tooth. I said, "Hey, Yuri," behind him but it didn't matter.

"Either you tell us where Kiev is or you don't," said Yuri, his face in Roscoe's. "If I have to go play hide and go seek to find my sister, you be dead first. Make up mind."

I pulled Yuri back, but only a little. "Look," I said. "Give us Kiev and we'll take you back alive. I promise. Don't, and I guarantee this guy will blow your head off right now."

Roscoe tried to say something. Yuri pulled the gun out and held it an inch in front of Roscoe's mouth while Roscoe talked.

"She's here, somewhere." Yuri started to shove the gun back.

"No, really. She got tired of sleeping with Dread a while back. She sleeps out in the van mostly." Yuri stepped back.

"Go find Kiev. We'll take this guy back." I turned back to Roscoe. "If she's in the van like he says."

"She may not be there," said Roscoe. He spat out a piece of tooth. "She goes out walking a lot. Says she likes to see the spirit of the dawn. I tell her, don't get eaten by a bear until we get our money. Bitch won't listen. Bitch only listens to nature now. That's why we missed the drop. At the last minute, she walked off into the woods and we couldn't find her. Came back that evening and said the spirit of the sun told her it wasn't time for her to leave."

Roscoe looked at Yuri.

"Really, man, we never kidnapped your sister. We're her friends. She'll tell you. It was just a gag, just a way to get a little tiny bit of your old man's money so she could run away. Dread wanted to take his share back home to impress his old man."

"We see what Kiev say," said Yuri, stepping back.

I kept watching Roscoe but I handed a cell phone out of my pocket to Yuri. "I checked. We've got a cell phone signal here. Take Marci's phone and call your family. They can get the location from the phone. We're ready for them and the gray shirts now."

Roscoe brightened. "You think we can get our money anyway, kind of like a reward. Really, man, we never hurt her."

"You get what you deserve." Yuri backed into Marci coming into the door. For a moment, I thought Roscoe was going to make a move while the two of them were tangled up. I waved my gun side to side and Roscoe lay back.

"Keep your hands out of the covers where I can see them," I said.

I could hear Marci exhale behind me. "You're both OK."

"Dread's not so lucky."

Marci could smell the blood over the stale air of the trailer.

"Yeah," she said.

Yuri moved around her. "I go find Kiev."

I kept my eyes on Roscoe but said to Yuri, "No more shooting. You might shoot Marci or me or even Kiev."

"No more shoot." Yuri looked at Roscoe. "For now."

He went out.

"Better hope he finds her." I moved over to make room for Marci.

"Come on, man. This was just a gag. We didn't hurt anybody." Roscoe brightened as he realized something. "But you sure as hell did. Your buddy came up here and killed an innocent hunter. You're in more trouble than we are." He grinned. "Yeah. That's right. Why don't we just call this even? You get the girl, go on back home, make up some story. I'll take care of Dread.

You go your way and I'll go mine."

"You were going to kill Kiev."

Roscoe looked startled, then hurt.

"No man, we wouldn't do that. Who told you that?"

"A little birdy heard you."

"Oh, so the bitch overheard us. That's why she took off."

"No."

"Well, she got it all wrong. Don't listen to her, man."

"We don't have her."

"Whatever. Let's just work this out, man. You got as much skin in this game as I have. Let's all just disappear."

That much sounded good. I was starting to come down from the adrenaline rush now and just wanted to go home.

"Yeah," I said. "Let's all just disappear and go home. Only I'm going to drop you and whatever's left of your buddy and Yuri and Kiev off at the Romanovs. There's a very nice lady there waiting to see Yuri and Kiev and some Romanov men who want to talk to you."

Roscoe just sat there.

"Marci, can you go get the car and bring it down here? I got this guy."

"Sure." She turned back at the door and smiled at me.

"Bye, bye, birdie."

CHAPTER 48

"Very funny." I felt a gun in my back. I had been watching Roscoe for a few minutes, listening to Roscoe's pleading and motioning at Roscoe's hands every time they moved to reach under the covers.

The gun in my back didn't move. "Enough, Marci."

"My father send this Marci up here, too?" I recognized the Russian accent and knew it wasn't Marci.

Roscoe smiled.

"Put your gun down on the table," he said.

"Kiev, we're here to rescue you from these guys."

"You here to take me back home. No need to be rescued."

I looked at Roscoe. "Still think she was the one who told us you were planning on killing her?"

Roscoe reached over and took the gun out of my hand and pointed it back at me. He reached under the covers and pulled out his own gun.

"Dread's got a gun just like this at home."

I smiled.

"What was the shot?" said Kiev behind him.

"I've got bad news for you," said Roscoe. "Look in the bedroom."

She stepped into the room and made a small yelp. She was back in a second and waved the hunting rifle at me.

"You did this?"

Roscoe said, "No, it was that crazy brother of yours. I think

254

these guys told him Dread and I kidnapped you."

"Where you get that idea? Oh. You mean that silly ransom call. Is a game. We not even go pick up the money. I am more spiritual than that. No need money. Mother know it a joke."

"Mother is heartbroken. Your whole family is torn apart by this."

Kiev's face fell and she muttered something in Russian. "I wish I could explain to her."

"So go explain it. Then go away and be a wood spirit, if that's what you want."

"Is not possible. Would break her heart more if she knew truth."

"They care about you."

Kiev made a gesture. "All of us Romanovs care about each other. We family, and we protect each other against the rest of the world. Is why I'm here." She paused. "Which brother?"

"Yuri."

She rolled her eyes. "Oh, the Batman. Always threatening to kill my boyfriends. Mother will be mad about that." She turned to Roscoe and smiled. "You'll like Yuri."

Roscoe seemed to be used to playing along with Kiev. "Yeah. We met. He seems like a fine Christian boy."

She laughed. "That Yuri. He so much fun."

I said, "You do know your boyfriend is dead?"

She shrugged. "Boyfriends come, boyfriends go. I spiritual— see beyond the illusion of life and death. Besides, father clean up. Is what he does."

"I thought you weren't ready to go back?"

"I not." She seemed to think about the contradiction for a moment, but it was only a short moment. "No matter. My karma will make it all right." She looked at me. "I can see you no understand about karma. I tell you." She paused a second, trying to remember the words just the way she had learned them. "I am a good person and a child of God. Because I am a good person, I have good karma. My good karma will protect me from all harm and shower my life with blessings."

"No matter what you do?"

"No matter. The universe sees my goodness." She paused and added, "I hope."

I looked at Roscoe. Roscoe smiled and said, "Maybe you should give me the gun before you hurt someone, honey."

She handed the rifle to him barrel first. Roscoe set it on the bed beside him next to the other guns.

"Oh, don't worry," she said. "Is not loaded."

There was a noise at the door, and Yuri stepped in.

"She's not out"—Yuri said, then he saw Kiev—"there." He smiled until he saw Roscoe had the guns.

"You supposed to have the gun," he said to me. I shrugged.

Kiev opened her arms to hug Yuri. Roscoe said, "Get those two guns of his first."

"Oh, this is Yuri. He no hurt nobody."

"Dread begs to differ. Get his guns, honey, then say hello."

She took his guns. All of them. Yuri stood there as his face went from joy to rage then finally just to tears. Kiev threw the guns on the bed and hugged Yuri. Yuri hugged her back hard and kissed the top of her head.

"See? I told you, we're a very close family."

"Don't you love heartwarming family drama?" Roscoe said to me. Roscoe turned to Kiev. "We're all going into town soon so you can have a real family reunion, just you and Yuri. Then he can go home, Yuri can tell your mother how happy you are, and you can go back to the mountain."

They heard the car pull up. Roscoe motioned to Yuri and me. "You two, in that corner. Kiev, go look after Dread for a minute."

Marci opened the door, looking down at the floor and not

paying attention. She looked up at Yuri and me, and paid attention.

"What are you two doing in the corner?" she said. She stepped into the room and saw Roscoe pointing one of the guns at her. "Oh."

"Where's your gun?" I said.

"In the car." She looked at me for a minute, trying to figure out what had gone wrong and who was to blame. She figured something out and put her hands on her hips and glared at me.

"You're supposed to have the gun."

Chapter 49

"I still don't know why we need to tie everybody up," said Kiev.

"It's for their own safety," said Roscoe. "If they try to take you back to your daddy, I'll have to shoot them."

She beamed at him. "You such a good person. Dread always said you were mean, but I could tell you had real good karma."

"The best."

Marci and I were tied up near the front of the van, sitting on the dirty metal floor facing each other with our hands tied to some kind of brackets on the walls. Kiev tied Yuri to a brace at the back.

"Brother, is good to see you," said Kiev.

"Sister, is good to see you alive. Everybody worried about you."

"Well, that's silly. I would have called if I were hurt."

"Mother worried."

Kiev bit her lip. "She know my karma looks out for me."

"Yeah, well, she not such a big believer in your karma after Father bail you out so many times."

"Father has done much for me. Now I must do for him." She straightened up now that Yuri was tied to a bracket. "Besides, karma put Father there when I need him. Karma brought you to me."

"They not see it that way. Not after this guy call Mother and threaten to kill you."

"Roscoe wouldn't kill me."

"Yeah, well, he no explain to Mother that he was only kidding."

She gave Roscoe a look.

"Hey, you got to say that part," Roscoe said to Kiev, "threaten to kill the hostage. It's kind of like it's something you have to say in a kidnapping call."

"So you just trying to do the right thing?"

"Yeah."

She gave Yuri a look. "See?" she said. He didn't bother arguing.

"Come sit up here by me, honey," said Roscoe.

"I sit beside my brother." She plopped down on the floor beside him, beaming. Roscoe started the van and we bounced down the trail to the gravel road.

"So now what?" I said to Roscoe.

Roscoe smiled. "Told you, we're going to a reunion."

"Yeah, I heard you say that. Really, though, you think you're going to get us someplace quiet, kill us all, and bury us. You got a busy day ahead of you."

"I might ask you to help with the digging." Roscoe grinned.

"What digging?" said Kiev. "Why do we need to dig at a reunion?"

Roscoe glared back at me. "You just shut up."

"Oh yeah. I promise. Look, if you're going to do this, you need to do this right. Not saying that you need to do this at all. Look, think about this: just let us go. We can't make it out of these mountains alive without help. Instead of one grave site, they'll find four random bodies. Nothing to point to you."

"Yeah." He said back to Kiev. "Be like a big reunion game of hide and seek."

"See?" said Kiev. "He planning stuff for us already."

"Nice try," Roscoe said to me after a while. We were bouncing from pothole to pothole. "Think I'll stick with the sure approach."

"Need to think more. There are four of us back here and just one of you."

Kiev interrupted. "No, I'm on his side, remember. So any games we have, it's really three to two." She squeezed Yuri's arm. "And Yuri's on my team. So it's three of us to two of you."

"Honey, remember that Yuri shot Dread," said Roscoe. "Yuri's not on our side."

"Oh, Yuri's always shooting people. That just Yuri."

"Roscoe likes to shoot people, too." I looked at Kiev. "He's going to shoot us all. He has to."

"You don't shoot family. Everybody knows that. You get mad at each other, you fight, but you don't shoot family. Yuri is family. You two, on the other hand . . ." She smiled. Maybe it was an apology.

"You still got a problem," I said back to Roscoe alone in the front. "Four people, one with her hands untied, against one. Still too much chance of something going wrong. One mistake, one guy head butts you and knocks you out, and you lose the game."

"Why don't you shut the hell up?"

"Why? I'm a dead man. We're all dead back here. Even she's dead."

Kiev looked at Yuri, and he nodded and looked sad. Her smile faded just a little.

"So let's just enjoy the game, like Miss Romanov says," I said. "This is like one of those puzzles, the one where a farmer has a rowboat and he has to get the fox and a chicken and some chicken feed to the other side without losing any. You ever play any of those games, Roscoe?"

"I don't play games. And I said for you to shut up."

"Yeah, I get that. You don't play games. You're kind of like the opposite of Little Miss Sunshine here, all good karma. The only thing you like to do is hurt things and take things." I turned to Kiev. "You've seen him hurt things, haven't you?"

Kiev brightened. She had another story to tell, and an audience to teach. "Yeah. Was this one time, he shot rabbit and brought it back to trailer. No big deal, they always killing stuff and bringing it back to eat. I told them that it was wrong to kill things but they wouldn't listen. I don't eat meat myself. Not unless it's already dead. Then it's OK and won't affect my karma.

"Anyway, Roscoe got rabbit and rabbit still alive and making this squealing sound: you know, kind of 'eek-eek' every few seconds. Roscoe decide to skin poor bunny alive. He grinning and having more fun than we ever see Roscoe have, and bunny's squealing. I told him, that's not good for your karma."

"I bet he's got so much bad karma inside him it could make him do a bad thing. A really bad thing."

Kiev said, "I told him." Her smile was fading now.

"Wonder if he's going to make us squeal like bunny rabbits?"

"I told you to shut the hell up back there."

"Still trying to solve the problem. Do you shoot the girl first? Let her brother watch. Shoot the guys first? Lot of possibilities here."

"Shut up. Shut up, or I'm going to come back there and shoot you all now and get some peace and quiet." He half turned to smile at Kiev. "Except for you, honey."

But he had left someone else out. Kiev was looking at Yuri.

I leaned over and whispered to her, "You know, it might make the game more fun if you untied your brother, let him get away just for the fun of it."

She brightened. I saw her back up to Yuri, her hands with his, working on the ropes. I needed to keep Roscoe busy.

"You know, Roscoe, this old van's pretty rusty. I think I feel the metal I'm tied to starting to give. You better come back and re-tie me. Better stop and re-tie everybody."

"Yeah, right. Maybe I'll bring you a complimentary in-flight beverage while I'm back there."

"Jack Daniel's," I said, and I meant it. "I used to love Jack when I could afford the good stuff. Southern Comfort was nice, too, but too sweet to drink much of it." I realized that I was having too much fun with this kind of reminiscing.

"Sorry, pal, we're all out."

I looked over. Yuri flexed his hands behind his back and nodded.

"Still say, if this were my operation, I'd come back and make sure everybody's still tied up."

"Ain't happening." Roscoe smiled. "One stop only on this flight."

"You going to shoot the girl first?"

Roscoe turned around. "Told you to shut up about that."

I saw what I was watching for: a wide pothole appeared at the edge of the headlights. I looked back at Yuri and got his attention, extended all five fingers of my right hand and counted them down as I watched us approach the pothole. When we were about to hit, I counted to zero and clenched my fist and shook it at Yuri.

The van bounced as we hit the pothole, and Roscoe fought with the wheel. Yuri jumped and kicked the rear door open, and then he was gone into the predawn darkness.

Roscoe grabbed his gun from the seat and fired three quick shots out the back after Yuri. He stopped the van with a slide and jumped out cursing.

"Go," I hissed at Kiev. She shook her head and smiled.

"Yuri make game more fun. Roscoe no hurt me. I think you wrong about him."

Roscoe slammed the doors shut and came around to the driver's seat.

"Don't matter none. I got him. No sign of him, but there's a lot of blood on the ground. He won't get far in this country."

Kiev's smile was gone.

I looked at her. "Kiev, the Batman's tough."

She smiled back a little weakly. "And he has good karma."

Roscoe said to Kiev, "Well, bring your karma up here to the passenger seat. Now." When she was there he told her to put her seat belt on. "Now slide your hands under the belt and keep them there. I'm not so sure you didn't help your brother escape."

"Of course I did. My karma make me do good things. Now we have more fun."

Roscoe swore and cranked up the car. I leaned as far as I could toward the front.

"You could have gotten out, too, Kiev. You had a chance. He shot Yuri. You could be there helping him."

Roscoe leaned over and smiled at Kiev. "Kiev, I just said that for their benefit, to make the game seem better. There was no blood there. I wouldn't shoot your brother."

"See? My karma not let us be hurt." Her smile was back now.

Chapter 50

Roscoe drove down the mountain for another ten minutes, then pulled off and followed a dirt trail to a rockslide. He tied Kiev's hands behind her back and told her it was part of the game. He turned to Marci and tied her arms at the elbow, then untied the rope holding her to the bracket in the van.

"Not bad," I said. "Never leave anybody untied. You've done this before."

Roscoe smiled.

"I do like my fun," Roscoe said. He winked at Kiev. "Makes a great game."

I looked at Kiev's reaction. She was smiling again, playing. A child.

I thought about sliding down a little and trying to trip Roscoe with my legs but Roscoe stayed out of range. Roscoe looped a long rope through the girls' arms and tethered them to the bumper like a pair of horses. He added me to the long rope and led the string of us to a dusty spot at the base of the rockslide.

Marci bumped up against me and said, "Hey, I don't mind being tied up with you, Josh, but I always imagined at least one of us would keep his hands free."

I smiled but it was a little weak. "Lot of things we never did. Sorry."

"We'll get out of this and do them all. You'll see. Keep a positive attitude."

Kiev smiled back at us. "A positive attitude will get you through anything."

Marci scowled at Kiev. "Not what I meant."

Roscoe waved the gun back at us. "A loaded gun trumps positive thinking, every time."

Trees closed in on the small dusty circle on both sides. A small beam of light fell through the trees onto the dirt and was snuffed into darkness in the surrounding forest. Roscoe sat me down on a pile of rocks by the dirt and untied my hands. Stepped back and pointed the gun at me.

"Stand up."

I stood up.

"Losing the big guy means more work for you." Roscoe tossed a small shovel at me. I stood there passively and the shovel hit me in the chest and clattered onto the rocks.

"Not going to get very deep here," I said. "You need to think this thing through."

"Don't have to be deep. Just enough dirt to cover up a little bit. See that?" Roscoe gestured behind me to the rockslide. The side of the mountain here was just a pile of big rocks, a remnant of a rockslide that had made it part way down and then stopped. "Once you guys are resting good and proper, half a stick of dynamite will bring the rest of those rocks down. It would take a week of digging to find you, if anybody knew where to look. Winter's coming. Nobody can get up this mountain once the snow comes. By spring, nobody will even remember you."

I looked and couldn't see anything wrong with the plan. Roscoe was a pro, at least at this.

I shook my head. I needed to come up with my own plan and not just stand here admiring Roscoe's. I looked around. If we could get to the trees and keep moving downhill, maybe we could get to a farm or a road or something. Maybe. Maybe if even one of us could get away we could tell someone eventually.

Wouldn't keep the other two alive, but at least Roscoe wouldn't get away with it.

I studied the geometry. Roscoe was facing me. The girls were off to Roscoe's right, tied to a rock with the long rope. Nothing really useful came to mind immediately.

Marci was jerking her head trying to get my attention. The trouble was, I didn't know what her idea was. While Roscoe was looking at me, Marci kept jerking her head and making a face that meant absolutely nothing to me. Roscoe turned to the girls. I looked at Marci and shrugged my shoulders and arched my eyebrows, trying to say "what you talking about" as clearly as I could. Roscoe turned back to me. As soon as he did, Marci went back to jerking her head and gave me a look that clearly said, "You never listen to me anyway." Ah, the joys of couple-hood.

Kiev picked up on the signals and said, "Charades."

Roscoe looked at Kiev and realized that, as usual, he had no idea what she meant. Neither did I. Maybe men were never meant to understand women.

"Dig." Roscoe turned back to me.

I just stood there, dragging things out as much as I could. "Die sweaty or die without working. Easy choice."

"Give you another choice. I don't care who goes when. You pick up the shovel and start digging. Long as you dig, everybody's happy. The game," he looked over at Kiev and winked, "is this: soon as you pause, or stop, or get tired, the girl with the big mouth dies."

"Which one?" said Kiev. "Must have clear rules for enjoyment of game."

"His broad."

I wanted to say to Marci, "Aw, now you're officially my broad," but I picked up the shovel and went to work. Roscoe was focused on me. After a few minutes Roscoe said, "Move back a little. That one's good enough." I stepped back and looked over at Marci. She was working her hands down behind her back trying to get the rope to the front. They were under her knees now. She motioned to me with her head again and this time I got it.

I stepped back, but stepped to my right so Roscoe had to turn his back a little more on Marci to keep an eye on me. I hit the shovel on a small rock and let it bounce off with a loud clang.

"Too rocky here." I took another step to my right.

"Just dig. Unless you're getting too tired."

"Ain't no ways tired." I looked up at Roscoe and smiled, trying to keep our eyes locked while I pushed dirt around randomly. "What's that line come from anyway? You're an educated man, Roscoe. Was that like a movie or something? That just came to me, but I know I've heard it somewhere else."

"Don't know. Sounds like something from one of those stupid rap songs Dread was always listening to."

"Yeah, that's it." I snuck a quick peek at Marci. Apparently, getting tied-up hands from the back to the front was harder than one would have thought. Marci had lost her balance and was rolling on her back, legs up in the air as she struggled to get her hands past her feet. Kiev was watching with a big grin. What a great game.

"Not a rap song," I said. "Gospel, I think. One of the old time slaves-working-in-the-fields songs." I grinned at Roscoe like we were buddies. "Kind of fits, don't you think?"

"Think you're getting tired. About ready to take a break? Tell you what, I'll make the game more interesting. You stop now, I'll let you have a ten-minute break. Water, too. Course, I shoot the girl and you go back to digging after that. You'll find it's not so bad watching a woman die. Particularly your own woman."

Roscoe paused and then grinned. "I think you're a lot like me. I don't think either one of us like people very much."

I paused, startled, and thought about it.

Roscoe grinned. "You ready to take a break, watch somebody crash and burn like you want the whole world to do?"

I dug furiously. "That ain't it."

"Sure it is."

"That ain't it." I glared at Roscoe. Marci had her hands in the front now. She stood up quiet and slow.

I had had enough of the conversation with Roscoe. I dug furiously for a couple of shovelfuls and glanced up. Marci had picked up a big rock and gathered up all the slack in the rope. She was coming up behind Roscoe.

Roscoe was done with the conversation, too. He started to turn back to the girls. I had to say something.

"That ain't it." I was loud, almost shouting. "That ain't it. The world is crashing and burning, and there's not a damned thing I can do but dig graves."

"Then let it burn."

Marci was behind Roscoe, raising the rock up. I locked eyes with Roscoe and just said, "No" as she started to bring the rock down.

Kiev jerked the rope. Like a puppet on a string, Marci dropped the rock and flew back.

"Hey," she said. "This a game. Can't actually hurt people in a game."

Roscoe turned and saw what was going on. He kicked Marci.

"Hey," said Kiev, pouting at Roscoe now. "Can't hurt people in a game."

"It's not a game, Kiev," I said. "Someone's going to die here. Maybe Yuri already has."

"Is too a game." Kiev tried to smile and sound sure but it

came out more like a plea. "Our karma will protect us. Protect Yuri, too."

Roscoe looked at me and smiled. "You've got karma," he said, "and I've got a gun."

CHAPTER 51

"That qualifies as a break," said Roscoe. The sun was high now, and I was sweating. Roscoe had moved into the shade of a big pine and he was ready to get on the road. He pointed the gun at Marci.

"No," I said, "I'm still digging." I attacked the ground in short furious strokes and threw up as much dirt as I could.

Roscoe looked over. Marci got to her feet.

"Stay down," he said.

Marci refused.

"When we hide?" said Kiev. "This game get old."

"Yeah. It is." Roscoe looked over at me. "That looks good enough."

"No," I said, louder than I meant. "We need more."

"I'm done," said Roscoe. He turned and pointed the gun at Marci. Just as he fired, Kiev jerked the rope again. Marci fell toward Kiev, and Roscoe missed her.

"Hey," said Kiev. "This no game no more. I am Kiev Romanov. I demand you release us all. You no do that, I tell my father, and the Romanov family will kill you."

"Sorry." Roscoe pointed the gun at Kiev.

There was a rustling in the dark branches over Roscoe's head and a black shape dropped down out of the tree. Yuri had a sharp stick in one hand and blood dripping down his side. His cape flared around him, and he screamed as he flew at Roscoe. Roscoe turned and fired. Yuri hit Roscoe, and the stick drove into Roscoe's chest as the gun went off. Yuri stood up for a second but blood was running down both sides now. Roscoe wasn't moving, and Yuri fell on top of him. I went over to Yuri and rolled him over.

"Come on," I yelled. "Hang in Batman." I pressed my hands on both of Yuri's wounds, but blood still came through my fingers.

"Forgot my magic body armor." Yuri smiled.

Kiev strained to get to Yuri but the rope was too short.

"Yuri." She started to cry. Marci backed up to her and started untying Kiev's hands.

Yuri looked at the blood coming through my hands. "I no think matter."

"You ever read the Batman comic where Batman dies?"

"No."

"That's my point. We're going to get you down the hill to a hospital."

"Need SL65 for that. Van not make it."

"We won't tie you up this time."

Kiev was untied now. She ran over.

"Yuri, Yuri. How could he shoot you?"

"Bang, bang. Always easy when I do it."

"Not the same. You my brother. Family don't get shot."

There was nothing either of us could say to that.

The bleeding was slowing, but Yuri was getting pale. I looked around for a medic and remembered that there were no medics here in this field. I looked at Yuri and knew he would never make the trip. Kiev stroked his face. "You saved me, Batman."

Yuri tried to smile. "Told you. I save day."

"You saved the day."

"Is good."

He closed his eyes.

Kiev rubbed his cheek and knew immediately.

"Oh, Yuri," she said. She started to cry. She smoothed his hair like the little boy he had once been to her.

"Oh, Yuri," she kept saying. I stood up. My hands were covered in Yuri's blood. Marci leaned against me. I looked down, saw that her hands were still tied, and absently untied her. She bent down after her hands were free and touched Yuri's neck.

"He's gone."

Kiev cried softly. "How could he die?" She turned to me with pleading in her eyes. "Real people not die. People who matter not die. What it mean when even your karma won't protect you?"

I had no answer.

We heard choppers. We looked up as the first black helicopter came over the trees, kicking up dust from the field around us. Then a second and a third. We watched as two of the choppers landed at a clearing somewhere down the mountain, while the third hovered over our heads.

I finally looked back at Roscoe.

"He's dead, too," Marci said.

I stood there breathing hard for a minute. "Good." I reached down and put my hand on Kiev's shoulder. As if that will help. I stood up and turned to Marci.

"You saved Yuri's sister. If you hadn't been a bullshit detective, she wouldn't be standing here with helicopters waiting to take her home."

"Maybe."

I went to the van and took out an old blanket. Brought it out and covered Yuri.

Kiev looked at me. "What about Roscoe?"

"Roscoe can rot in hell."

"You're supposed to treat all men with respect."

"I do. I respect what Yuri did, and I respect what Roscoe did. Roscoe can rot in hell."

Kiev stood up. "What have I done?"

Marci went over and put her arm around Kiev.

"You didn't kill Yuri."

"No. I never do anything bad. Not really bad. But Yuri be alive if I not do one more silly thing. This not add up in my head.

"I see my brothers kill men. Every time, they explain that the dead man deserve it, the world better without this guy. I thought they heroes. This first time for me, even good guys with good karma get killed."

Marci started to answer some of that and decided to let it alone. "You'll be home soon. Momma and Poppa will make you feel better. Look at the leaves changing. Soon it will be Christmas. You'll all be sad without Yuri, but you'll come together as a family. They'll get you through it."

Kiev just said, "No." She pulled away from Marci and knelt by Yuri. She bent down and kissed Yuri on his forehead. She made the sign of the cross and muttered something sing-song in Russian. She slapped him gently on one cheek, laughed, and said one last thing, then stood up and looked away.

Kiev looked at the helicopter overhead for a long time.

"I not go home."

"We can't let you get away," said Marci.

Kiev put her hand on Marci's cheek.

"That's sweet. I know these woods; you don't. Once I three steps into trees, you never find me."

Marci started to argue. Kiev put her finger on Marci's lips.

"And you don't want to. I go home, men with gray shirts will own my family. Like they have for one year."

Kiev took a deep breath.

"Somebody die at a party I was at. I didn't kill them, but it look like I did. The men with gray shirts know. I don't know how, but they know somehow. They tell father and uncle, 'Do what we want, or baby Kiev go to jail.' Romanov men go to jail all the time. They tough, can handle. They no laugh at their baby girl going to jail." She looked at Marci. "If I go home, they own my family. If I go away forever, my family free. I do one thing right finally and set family free." She smiled. "Maybe is my karma."

She turned and stepped into the woods and disappeared. Marci looked at me.

I stared at the spot where Kiev had stepped out of the world.

"Hope she finds a good bar."

"What the hell's that supposed to mean? Come on, we've got to catch her."

"Let her go."

"The Romanovs aren't going to like you."

We sat on the ground by the bodies. One chopper still circled overhead. I waved at it every now and then, but nobody waved back.

Gray figures came out of the woods with rifles pointed at us.

"On the ground, now," someone yelled.

"Guys, this is silly," Marci yelled back.

"Now, now, now," one of them yelled, running toward us waving his rifle.

"Ground looks good." I pulled Marci down on the ground with me.

"This is stupid." Marci's mouth was in the dirt.

The first guy put his boot on my neck a little too hard.

"Oh yeah," said Marci. "Like he's the bigger threat. I am sick and tired of this macho bullshit."

Another boot came down on Marci's neck, and she stopped complaining. I would have laughed, but I was having trouble breathing.

Somebody yelled, "Gun." More men came running now. Several of them stood in a ring around Marci and I with their guns pointed at our heads. Two more stood at attention over Roscoe's automatic where it lay on the ground. Nobody paid much attention to the bodies that weren't moving.

I could see the trees out of my one open eye. Jackson and the two Romanov brothers came toward us with more men.

"Let them up," said Jackson when they got close. "But keep a gun on them."

I looked around and saw snipers up on the rocks. "Looks like you've got enough guns on us."

"Yeah. And they've got orders to shoot if you run or do anything stupid."

Jackson motioned for one of the men to pull the blanket off the body.

"Kiev?" he asked me.

I was sitting up and brushing dirt off. "No. Yuri."

As I said it the blanket came off and Rudi Romanov saw his son's body. His face went from fear to relief to anger as he went from bracing himself for the death of one child to blaming me for the loss of another.

"Kiev ran off," I said.

Jackson looked at me. "Yeah, that's convenient."

"Not for me. She hit those trees after she heard your choppers."

Jackson motioned two men toward the woods. They took off at a run.

Rudi had gone back inside of himself, cold and all-business. He looked at me.

"Usually my rule is, you kill one of mine, I kill ten of yours. This time, I think I settle for two."

"We didn't kill him. That guy did. Yuri saved Kiev."

"My daughter who is not here?"

I sighed. "The daughter who is not here."

"Yuri shot dead. You here with gun and two dead bodies and no daughter. You think I stupid."

"No."

"Then you come up with better explanation now."

I locked eyes with Rudi. "She said she was protecting you by running away."

Rudi's face softened, but he said nothing.

"Madness, madness," said Marci. She stood up. She put her face in Jackson's. "You remember that movie *The Bridge on the River Kwai*? Bunch of man-child soldiers just like you, standing around after a heroic battle with everybody dead. One guy looks at it all and says, 'Madness, madness.' That's all you've got here."

Jackson stood his ground but said nothing.

"Well, I'm done with it." Marci was almost spitting in his face. "Done with it. This is over, and I'm making it over."

Jackson still wasn't giving her the fight she wanted. She stepped back.

"This is over. You know what? I'm going to step into those woods, right there, and take a pee. Not 'relieve myself at fourteen-twenty hours' like some bullshit hero. Take a pee. Then you're going to take us home."

She brushed past one gray shirt and almost knocked him down. She took a step and stubbed her toe on Roscoe's gun lying in the dirt.

"Guns!" she screamed. "I am sick of all of your goddamned guns."

She picked up the gun, waved it at Jackson, and started to throw it at him. In mid-throw, with her arm back and her face fierce, she collapsed like a rag doll. I heard the shot from the sniper as she fell.

"Stand down! Stand down!" Jackson yelled into a radio.

I ran to Marci and turned her over. There was a small hole in her chest and a big hole in her back with blood everywhere. I picked her up and knew she was dead. I buried my head in her hair and started to cry.

Behind me I heard Rudi.

"We kill man who do this."

Jackson nodded and spoke into the radio. "Bring him down here."

I stood in the dusty field surrounded by uniforms and guns like I had years ago in that faraway country. I looked down at Marci and knew that the best thing I had ever known was gone and, like the boy in the village years ago with his dead mother, knew there was nothing I could ever do about it. I spun around to Jackson and Rudi.

"No," I screamed. "No more blaming soldiers for following orders. Marci was right. It ends here."

I turned and walked into the woods with Marci in my arms.

Chapter 52

I had been at the monastery for a week before Kiev came to my room one morning.

"How you know where to find me?" she said. She was dressed in a long brown robe of rough wool with her head shaved. She looked like any of the other Buddhist monks here.

I looked at her and smiled a tired smile. "The kids at the coffee shop mentioned this place. It seemed like a perfect place for you to go hide."

"Not hiding. This where I live, now. I told you, I can't go home."

"Read this." I turned Marci's laptop toward Kiev. "I've got to go plow the potato field. My deal with the monks has me plowing the fields in the mornings. For that, I get food and I get this small cell to sleep in and write. I'll be back after lunch."

I came back in the afternoon. Kiev looked up from the laptop. Her face had tear streaks, but she was calm.

"Is true," she said, "that Marci lived and wrote this?"

"No," I said. "But the gray shirts won't know that. The book will go out in Marci's name."

I looked out the small window for a few seconds.

"Marci had already written all the important parts about the gray shirts and how they operate. I just added the beginning and end, the part about how Marci fought to survive after they left her for dead and now lives in hiding while she battles the gray shirts."

"Is that where the title comes from, *The Girl Who Wanted to Live?* Marci come up with that?"

I started to explain what the title originally meant but just said, "Yeah."

Kiev said, "But no one will ever see this. They will stop you from publishing."

"They're too late. I put a short version on the Internet last week. It's been picked up by most of the national press. They'll have a hard time threatening Marci, or stopping this now." I looked out the window. "I emailed the last chapter of the book to Marci's agent in her name today. He thinks it'll be a best seller. It's the hottest story in the press now." I smiled. "Outside of the monastery. Here, the hot story is the potato crop."

"That's why I like it here."

"Me, too," I said. "Kind of reminds me of a bar."

Kiev started to ask me about that but said nothing. After a minute she said, "Did she write the part about me?"

"Yeah. She found the stuff about the killing in your father's papers, the version the gray shirts had told him. She also found the real story from the DA. With this out there, no one can prosecute you."

Kiev stared out the window.

"It's not over," I said. "You and your family still have a lot to deal with. The gray shirts won't protect them from the police anymore."

Kiev looked out at the sky and said, "I may have to earn some of my own karma."

I nodded.

Kiev turned and looked at me with the imperial Romanov stare. "We go home now."

There were no men in gray uniforms at the guardhouse for the Romanov compound. I parked the SS 396 in the drive and Kiev and I walked up to the door. Kiev put her hand on the doorknob, hesitated, then pushed her way in.

The living room was dark. A large Christmas tree stood in the center, decorated but unlit. Mother sat in a massive chair in front of the tree, her head drooped and staring at the floor. She turned to see who was at the door. Her mouth dropped open and her eyes lit up. She jumped up.

"Evie!"

Kiev ran to her. A step before she reached Mother's arms, Mother drew back her right hand and slapped Kiev so hard Kiev stopped dead and just stood there, rocking back and forth. I thought she was going to go down but she stood her ground. Then Kiev was crying. Then Mother was crying. Mother threw her arms around her and they were one organism again, mother and daughter and tears flowing together. Mother dragged Kiev to a couch and they sat down, crying and making incomprehensible Russian sounds for a long time.

Sergei walked in to see what the commotion was. He looked at Mother and then smiled and walked over to me.

"Somehow, I always expected to see Kiev again," he said. "You were another matter."

I shrugged. "I promised Mother to bring her daughter home for Christmas. I didn't know it would cost her a son."

"It's been hard on her. Hard on all of us, but most hard on Mother. My brother put up the Christmas tree, but she wouldn't let him turn on the lights. I think I turn on the lights now."

Sergei walked over to a table and picked up a remote control and punched a button. The dark room slowly lit up as strings of lights and decorations on the walls came on one by one. The last one to come on was a big white star on top of the tree. I looked at the star and thought of Marci.

"We've all lost a lot," I said.

Sergei just nodded.

"Gray shirts?"

"Gone. Course they're replaced by policemen and district attorney lawyers and TV reporters and Hollywood guys who want to turn us into a reality TV show."

I said, "A lot to sort out."

"We got lawyers, too. You think justice triumphs over money?"

I thought a minute. "No."

I was sitting by the pool sipping Russian tea when Mother came to me. Her makeup was streaked from crying but her smile made her beautiful. She sat down next to me with her own tea.

"You brought my daughter home to me for Christmas."

"I cost you your son."

She sipped her tea. "No. Yuri had the life he wanted. Is true he died bravely?"

"The Batman saved us all."

She swore in Russian. "Men and their silly games. Dying bravely is still dying. Mothers still cry. But it is what he wanted."

She sipped some more and said, "So what you want, Josh with no real name?"

"I don't know."

"Let me tell you what you need, not what you want. You need home. I make home here. My family do much wrong. I know. I not blind like they think. But I make home for them here. No matter what they do, they come here and find people who know their heart and accept it even if they don't. Boys no like to hear word, but word for such a place is love.

"You have home here, my son Josh. For always, this your home."

"Thank you, Mother. Maybe this is what I need." The two of us sat side by side and looked out at the grass in silence and sipped our tea together, and it felt good. After a while, I turned to Mother. "Thank you, Mother, but no. I have a home and I need to go there." I stood up and kissed her on the top of her head. "I do have a Mother here, though. For always."

I pulled the SS 396 behind Terri's broken-down Toyota. Terri's son was playing on the sidewalk with a broken toy soldier. Terri was in the car changing the baby. She looked up at me and smiled.

"The man who finds money."

I smiled. "This time I found a car."

Terri's eyes opened, but then she said, "I can't take no car."

"It's not from me. A woman named Marci wanted you to have it. It's in good shape. It will get you home."

Terri looked at it for a long time. "For the kids' sake," she said.

"For the kids' sake," I said. I started to walk away. When I was too far for Terri to argue, I turned back.

"Marci left some money in the glove box, too."

I walked into the Western World and my eyes slowly adjusted back to the darkness I knew here. I laid my shopping bag and Marci's laptop down on the bar. Mayor countered by setting my tumbler on the bar in front of me and filling it. I looked at it a long time, and poured it into the sink. I set the tumbler back on the bar and moved it out of the way to make room for the laptop.

The skinny girl closed her book, looked up at me, and smiled. She picked up the tumbler and stuck it behind the bar. Mayor smiled, just for a moment. When Mayor realized that the skinny girl and I had seen him smiling out of character, he wiped his face to its expected look of perpetual doubt and went back to polishing the bar.

ABOUT THE AUTHOR

Michael Guillebeau lives in Huntsville, Alabama, and Panama City Beach, Florida. He has written software for a variety of NASA and DoD programs, including the International Space Station. *Josh Whoever* is his first book. Visit michaelguillebeau .com for more of Mike's books, stories, and characters.